A REAL COWBOY ALWAYS TRUSTS HIS HEART

A Wyoming Rebels Novel

STEPHANIE ROWE

Authenticity Playground, LLC

For Kasey Richardson. You go girl! I couldn't do this without you! Never forget how awesome you are! I admire you so much!

ACKNOWLEDGMENTS

Special thanks to my beta readers and the Rockstars. You guys are the best! There are so many to thank by name, more than I could count, but here are those who I want to called out specially for all they did to help this book come to life: Alencia Bates Salters, Alyssa Bird, Jean Bowden, Shell Bryce, Denise Fluhr, Heidi Hoffman, Jeanne Stone, Dottie Jones, Deb Julienne, Bridget Koan, Helen Loyal, Felicia Low Mikoll, Suzanne Mayer, Jodi Moore, Ashlee Murphy Beck, Judi Pflughoeft, Carol Pretorius, Kasey Richardson, Caryn Santee, Amber Ellison Shriver, Summer Steelman, Regina Thomas, and Linda Watson. Special thanks to my family, who I love with every fiber of my heart and soul. And to AER, who is my world. Love you so much, baby girl! And to Joe, who teaches me every day what romance and true love really is. I love you, babe!

COPYRIGHT

CHAPTER ONE

IT WAS the yellow daisies on the "help wanted" sign that got Zoey Wilson's attention.

She turned her head as she jogged down the sidewalk opposite the little café, checking out the sign in the window. It looked hand painted, maybe by a kid. Bright colors.

Handmade art. It had been so long since she'd thought of painting, of poster boards calling for decoration, even though she'd spent a lot of time with a brush in her hand when she was a kid.

On a whim, she jogged across the street to the café, so she could see it better. She stopped in front of the sign, smiling when she saw it up close. Daisies. A few hearts. A shooting star.

Definitely the work of a child who had no problems with stars being purple polka-dotted, and hearts being filled with butterflies. Smiling, she touched the glass, remembering a time when she hadn't cared about how things were supposed to be, or what the rules told her to do.

How long ago that had been. How much she had changed. How much life had changed.

1

Movement from inside caught her attention, and she looked up as a woman walked in through the swinging doors that led from the kitchen. The woman was about her age, singing and dancing as she wiped down the counter.

God. When was the last time Zoey had felt like dancing? Or singing?

Weight settled on her shoulders, and the joy she'd felt at the sign faded.

The woman looked up, saw her, and waved at her to come in. Zoey waved back, but shook her head.

Yes, she'd moved back to her hometown of Rogue Valley, Wyoming, to try to get herself back on track, but she wasn't ready to talk to anyone. She'd arrived late last night, woken up at four in the morning after a restless sleep, and had decided to go for a run instead of sitting in her depressing rented apartment, wondering how she'd gotten to this place.

She had originally planned to go over to her brother Dane's house later in the morning to tell him that she'd arrived in town last night, two weeks ahead of schedule. Right now, however, in the pre-dawn light, she needed time to process the fact that she was back in this small town of her youth that looked the same, and yet so different at the same time.

She wasn't sure how to fit in here, and she certainly couldn't figure out why she'd decided this was the answer to the darkness that haunted her at every moment.

She turned away—

"Hey, come on in. I just opened." The woman from the café poked her head out the front door. "Coffee will be ready in a minute."

"I'm all set, thanks." Even as she said it, Zoey caught the scent of fresh coffee, a rich, dark roast that smelled amazing. "What is that?"

"A local brand. It's fantastic." The woman held the door open wider. "Come on in. You'll love it."

"I didn't bring any money on my run—"

The woman winked. "Free coffee to all first-timers. It's so good you'll be back every morning. I've created many addicts that way." She grinned. "I look sweet, but I'm really a ruthless mercenary with an entire town of minions."

Zoey laughed, unable to resist the woman's warmth. "How do I say no to that?"

"Perfect." The woman stepped back to let Zoey pass her. "My name's Lissa. You?"

"Zoey."

Lissa's eyebrows went up, and she got a thoughtful look on her face. "Not Dane's sister?"

"Yes." Zoey tensed, not prepared to have to identify herself so soon. She wanted to be anonymous, which was kind of stupid, given that she'd moved back to her hometown, but that didn't change the fact that Lissa's identification felt like pressure she wasn't ready for. "You know Dane?"

"Of course." Lissa grinned. "Everyone knows Dane."

Everyone knows Dane. She supposed it made sense. When she'd left town, Dane had been just starting out as a cop, but now he was the sheriff. Of course Lissa would know him. While she'd been gone, Dane had made the town his own.

"Come on." Lissa waved her in. "Grab a seat at the counter. Want an omelet?"

"No, thanks. Coffee is good." The door jangled as she stepped inside, and she was greeted with the charming sound of country music from the ceiling speakers. She recognized the music of country superstar Travis Turner, the stage name for the youngest Stockton brother. She'd known him when he used to sit on the fence at Ol' Skip's ranch and sing, and now he'd gone platinum.

He'd made his dreams come true, and she was happy for

him. He was such a nice guy. All the Stocktons were, despite their rough childhood.

The tables in the café were old and quaint. Mismatched wooden chairs, some painted, some not, gave the café a homey feeling. On each table was a mason jar filled with daisies and a paper mâché heart on a stick.

It was so small town. So different than the life she'd lived in Boston for the last decade. That was why she'd come back, to get away from the life she'd trapped herself in. She wasn't going to stay forever. Just until she found her footing again. Until she found the courage to keep going. A day. A week. A month. A year. She didn't know for sure how long it would take, or what she needed to figure out. She just knew she couldn't keep going the way she had been, and she hadn't been able to think of any other place to go.

Except this place was so different than she'd remembered. There were new stores, new developments, and at the same time, so much had stayed the same. But *she* was different, and that made everything look different than it had once appeared to a desperate hometown girl trying to run away from who she was.

She sighed as she looked around. The café was so warm. So inviting. As if it were a giant hug that she could never quite get. She hadn't fit in here as a kid. What had made her think she'd fit in now that she'd been away for so long? Suddenly, she felt so weary. Exhausted. "I'll take the coffee to go."

"No problem. It'll be ready in a couple minutes." Lissa patted the counter. "Have a seat."

Zoey shifted restlessly, staying close to the front window. "I'm fine. I'll just wait here."

"By the door?" Lissa raised her brows. "I don't bite, you know. I'm quite friendly, really."

Yeah, okay, that sounded weird, right? A café full of empty

seats, and she wanted to stand awkwardly by the door? "Yeah, okay, thanks." She made her way around the tables set with paper placements and charmingly mismatched salt and pepper shakers, and then slid onto the nearest stool.

Lissa bustled around, getting items ready for opening. "So, you're back in town for good, eh?"

"No." She shook her head quickly. "Just for a bit. Maybe six months, or so." Yeah, that sounded good. Long enough to get a break, but not so long that she'd be trapped here.

Lissa raised her brows. "That's it? I thought you were moving back?"

Zoey frowned. How much had Dane been telling people about her? Why did Lissa know so much? What did it matter what she did? "Just for a while."

"You got a job while you're here?" Lissa pulled a tray of coffee mugs out from under the counter and set them next to the three percolating coffee machines.

"No. I'm taking some time off—"

"Want to work here? I saw you looking at the sign."

Zoey frowned. "Here? I don't know anything about working in a café." In Boston, she'd been a partner at her own law firm. Her life had been late nights, paperwork, betrayal, and broken dreams. "I don't want to work right now. I'm burned out." Not just burned out. Lost. Broken. Exhausted. Crushed all the way to her soul? Yeah, those worked.

"It's not work. It's a chance to socialize and chat with people." Lissa leaned on the counter, propping her chin up on her hands. "You'll catch on quick. It might be the best way to get reconnected with the community. Pretty much everyone in town comes through here over the course of the week. It's been how long since you lived here? A decade?"

"Yeah, about." How had ten years gone by? It had been so fast, and so slow at the same time.

Lissa set a carafe of cream on the counter, along with a

dish of sweeteners. "Dane's been so excited for you to come back. And Ryder—"

"Ryder?" Zoey sucked in her breath, her heart stuttering at the mention of the one man she hadn't been able to stop thinking about since the moment she'd decided to come home. "I thought he didn't live in town."

"He doesn't. But he comes through from time to time." Lissa raised her brows. "He's complicated, isn't he?"

"I don't know. I haven't talked to him since I left." She hadn't talked to him in ten years, but she'd thought of him. Constantly at first. Then less often. But as time to come home had neared, he'd been consuming her thoughts again.

Ryder, the guy who'd been her big brother's best friend, her protector...until her senior prom, when a pity date by Ryder had turned into a night of firsts...her first kiss, her first slow dance, her first lover.

God, how that night had haunted her.

Lissa peered at her. "Are you okay?"

"Yeah, sure." Zoey cleared her throat. "Is that coffee almost ready?"

"Yep." Lissa didn't move. "Ryder's antsy for you to come back. I can see it in him."

Her heart leapt. "Really?" At Lissa's curious look, Zoey quickly backpedaled, not wanting anything to get back to Ryder about her reaction. She knew how small towns worked. "Not that it matters, though. I mean, whatever, right? He's always been one of Dane's best friends." She quickly changed the subject. "How do you know Dane and Ryder so well?"

Lissa gave her a knowing look, but went along. "Dane married my husband's sister, so we're all family now."

"Your husband's sister?" Although Zoey hadn't come back for her brother's wedding, she knew he had married a Stockton. Jaimi was the only girl in a family of nine boys, one of which was Ryder.

If Lissa was married to one of Jaimi's brothers, it meant she was Ryder's sister-in-law. Unless...Ryder was the Stockton she'd married! The thought made Zoey's stomach lurch. "Who's your husband? Ryder?" If Lissa said yes, Zoey felt like she would throw up. She hadn't heard that Ryder had gotten married, so she'd assumed he hadn't, but what if he had? What if he had some woman he adored who he'd pledged his life to? What if Lissa knew so much about Ryder because *she'd married him?* Nausea churned in Zoey's stomach, and she gripped the edge of the counter.

"Ryder?" Lissa laughed and waved her hand. "No, of course not. Not that he's not a great guy, of course, but hell, no."

The surge of relief was so profound that Zoey slumped, almost gasping as she tried to catch her breath. Not Ryder. Her hands started shaking, and she hid them in her lap as she tried to cover up her reaction. "No? Which Stockton, then?"

"Travis." Lissa's face softened with pure happiness. "You remember him, right?"

The musician whose music was being piped in through the speakers. That made sense. "Yes, of course." Zoey remembered them all. Her brother had been best friends with the twins Ryder and Maddox Stockton, which meant that he knew the rest of the Stocktons as well. As Dane's little sister, she'd hung out with them a lot, and knew them all.

They'd been a rough group from a tough home situation. They scared most of the other kids in school, but not Zoey, because she'd seen the side of them they didn't show anyone else. The rest of the world saw aggressive, dangerous boys. She'd seen the loyal protectors who'd taken her into their circle.

She was the one who would wake up in the middle of the night to find one or more of the brothers sleeping on her floor...and it was usually Ryder. Her throat tightened, remembering how safe she'd feel when she'd wake up and see Ryder asleep in her room, knowing that no one, especially her uncle, could get to her when he was there. "Yes," she said softly. "I remember Travis. I remember all of them."

Lissa laughed. "How could anyone forget a Stockton, right? Those men are a force unto themselves." She winked. "Ryder's not married. He's never even had a date in all the years I've known him. Completely single."

Zoey tried unsuccessfully to not care about that awesome piece of news. "Ryder's social life isn't my business."

Lissa raised her brows. "No?"

"Not at all." Zoey felt her cheeks flush even as relief settled deep in her gut. *Ryder was still single.* She knew she shouldn't care, but she couldn't help it. She cared.

Dammit. What was wrong with her? Ryder was her past, a gritty, ugly past that had left her heart so broken that it still hadn't completely healed from him. She didn't want to open that door again, not today, not ever.

"Of course it's not." Lissa grinned. The coffee machine beeped, and she turned away. "Large?"

"Sure—" The door jangled, and Zoey instinctively looked over her shoulder.

Four Stocktons walked in.

The oldest, Chase, entered first, tall and muscular. Then, behind him, was Travis. After him, Maddox, Ryder's twin, then, behind him, last in line...*Ryder.*

She froze, her heart thundering. There was nowhere for her to hide. Nowhere for her to go.

He wasn't supposed to be in town. He wasn't supposed to be *here*.

But he was.

He was in deep conversation with Maddox, and didn't look over as they walked in. His cowboy hat was tipped back, letting her see his blue eyes, his whiskered jaw, and the way his lips curved in a smile. God, that smile had melted her heart so many times as a teenager.

He was taller now. Broader. Just bigger. More man. His jeans were faded, splattered with mud, and his boots were heavy work boots instead of cowboy boots. His gray tee shirt had paint on it, ragged and worn, just like he'd always been.

But there was a presence to him that hadn't been there before. He held himself like he belonged. Back when she'd known him, he had a swagger designed to tell the world to fuck off. He didn't have it anymore, but there was a harder edge to him, a rough, untamed edge that made her belly tighten.

"Good morning, gentlemen," Lissa called out. "Did none of you notice we have a visitor?"

Zoey winced. "No, don't—"

But it was too late. All four men looked over, but it was Ryder who she watched.

His gaze darted around the café, and then it landed on her.

He stopped, his face going utterly still.

Neither of them moved.

She couldn't breathe. She couldn't think. All she could do was stare at him, at those blue eyes she'd dreamed of so many times, at the man who'd broken her heart more than she'd thought was possible.

The man she'd never been able to forget.

CHAPTER TWO

RYDER STOCKTON CAUGHT his breath when he saw Zoey's face for the first time in over a decade. *She was back.*

Her eyes. God, those eyes he'd dreamed of so many times. That mouth, the one he could still remember kissing. The last time he'd seen her, those green eyes had been full of tears and accusation, of hate that he'd completely deserved.

He'd let her go that day. He'd *made* her go. He'd sacrificed everything to give her what she needed, to free her to live the life she deserved.

And now, she was back.

Here.

Twenty feet away from him.

She stared at him, her face pale, her lips pressed together in silence.

He remembered the curve of her jaw, the slant of her nose, the flush of her cheeks. She was the same, but there was a wisdom and strength to her that hadn't been there before. She seemed taller now, stronger, a woman, not a girl. But at the same time, she looked exactly as she had so long ago. It was his Zoey, the one he'd promised to protect forever, the one he'd failed.

The need to go to her was so strong, so visceral, that it took all his strength to stay still, but he didn't go over to her. How could he? She hadn't needed him back then, and she didn't need him now.

"Zoey!" Chase walked over to her and pulled her into a hug.

She dragged her gaze off Ryder and hugged his brother. "Hi, Chase."

Ryder inhaled at the sound of her voice, and something deep inside him vibrated, almost violently. *He'd missed her.* Hell, he'd missed her so much that his chest actually hurt.

Travis pushed Chase aside to embrace her. Then Maddox. His brothers encircled her, welcoming her, asking her about her trip, when she'd arrived, where she was staying.

He didn't move.

His feet were stuck to the floor, his legs frozen as he listened to her talk, letting the sound of her voice wash over him. He'd forgotten what her voice felt like, how deeply it touched him, how much he'd yearned to hear it.

She looked over at him as she chatted with his brothers, her face pinched and tense. Because he was there? Was it his presence that was causing such pain and discomfort on her face?

Shit. He should leave. Give her space.

But he couldn't make himself do it.

He watched Lissa hand her a cup of coffee. Zoey grabbed it and then slid off the stool, waving off his brothers as she ducked past them. She hurried toward the door, her gaze sliding toward Ryder as she neared.

Jesus.

She was so close.

They met gazes, and for a moment, he thought she would

say something, anything, to break the ice, to let him know he was forgiven.

But her gaze dropped, and she turned away, hurrying out the door.

The bell jangled, as he watched her scurry past the front window, heading down the sidewalk, away from him.

He let her go. He had to let her go, just like before. She deserved it—

"Was she always that sad?" Lissa asked softly.

Ryder looked back over his shoulder at Lissa, who had moved up behind him. "She looked sad?"

She nodded. "Broken, even. From the moment she walked in."

Shit. He glanced back at his brothers, who all nodded. "She didn't even make eye contact," Chase said. "She's not the Zoey who left here."

Son of a bitch.

Protectiveness surged through Ryder. No one messed with Zoey. Ever. With a muttered oath, he sprinted for the door, yanked it open, and ran outside. "Zoey!"

Zoey closed her eyes when she heard Ryder shout her name. His voice was deep and strong, deeper than it had once been, but instantly familiar, sliding under her skin like a caress she'd been longing for. *Ryder.*

God, how long she'd yearned to hear his voice. To hear him say her name. To have him chase her down, demand she not leave him, beg her to stay. For years, she'd dreamed of walking down the street in Boston, only to find him racing after her, having tracked her down after all that time.

He'd never been there.

He'd never come after her.

He'd never shouted her name...until now.

She swallowed, steeling herself as she turned to face him. Her fingers tightened around the coffee as he jogged toward her, in that same, athletic stride he'd had so long ago.

After years of being in his constant presence, she hadn't seen him, talked to him, or even texted him since the day after her prom, a gaping loss that had carved indelible scars into her heart. And now, he was walking toward her, his tan cowboy hat pulled low over his forehead, almost shielding his face from her.

She could barely even recognize him as the youth who had hid her innocently in his bed many nights when she'd been hiding from her uncle and his lecherous tendencies, swearing he'd protect her with his life if her uncle ever came for her.

Approaching her was a hard, weathered cowboy, with dust on his boots, and weariness in his strong shoulders, nothing like the boy she'd hung around with.

He came to a stop in front of her, and tipped his hat back, revealing his blue eyes, the eyes she knew so well. "Hey, ZoeyBear."

ZoeyBear. His nickname for her, his reminder that deep inside her was the strength of a grizzly that could handle whatever life threw at her. It was him. *It was really him.* She didn't know what to say. It had been so long. So awkward. So silent. There were a million things to say...and nothing at all to say.

Honestly. What was she supposed to say to the guy who, prior to taking her virginity on prom night, had been her protector, her best friend, her defense against the world? The guy who had shattered her heart into a million pieces and hadn't stayed to help her fix it.

Nothing. She could think of absolutely nothing to say.

Regret flickered across his face. "No response?"

"Ryder." His name slipped out, an aching whisper.

"I'm so sorry," he said softly, his voice almost breaking with emotion. "I'm so sorry for what I did."

It was the apology she'd always wanted, and yet, now that she had it, she realized that it didn't change anything. It didn't change what had happened, and how completely she'd been shattered. She'd trusted him with more than her heart, more than her soul. She shook her head, fighting against the sudden tears. "It was ten years ago. It doesn't matter."

"It matters." He took her hand, his fingers rough and callused. "I should never have made love to you that night. It was wrong."

She stared at their entwined fingers. That was what he regretted? Making love to her? He didn't regret losing her? "It was a mutual decision. It was fine."

"Zoey." He gently touched her jaw, forcing her to look up at him. "Where's the sparkle that once danced in those green eyes?" he asked softly.

"It died a long time ago," she whispered.

Regret filled his face. "Because of me? Did I break you?"

He looked so sad, so regretful that her heart ached for him. "No," she admitted truthfully. "It has been so much more than you." He was but one factor in the life that had become more than she could handle. "I'll be fine, though. That's why I'm here. A little R&R, and I'll be back at work in a few months." Maybe. She hoped. She prayed. But she feared she was wrong.

His eyes darkened. "I thought you were moving home for good."

"No. Just six months." The timeframe rolled more easily off her lips this time, but with Ryder standing in front of her, suddenly six months felt both agonizingly short and unbearably long to be around him.

His fingers tightened around her hand for a split second,

then he released her. The loss of contact with him made her want to cry, but she pulled back, standing straighter.

"You're going to leave again," he said. It wasn't a statement, really. More of an acknowledgment of a truth he had to process.

She nodded. "I have to. You know I don't fit in here. I never did."

He said nothing. He just looked at her, his gaze searching for the truth she could never hide from him.

I missed you. She wanted to say it, to beg him to hug her, to fold her into that embrace that always made her world better. But there was a wall between them now, a wall that she didn't know how to take down.

"You need help unpacking?" he asked.

She hesitated. "No—"

"I'd like to help you."

She thought of all the boxes lined up in her living room.

She thought of how achingly lonely it had been waking up in that apartment a few hours ago.

She thought of how long it had been since she had felt okay.

"You need a friend," he said quietly. "I'm that friend."

She wanted to say yes. She wanted to beg him to fill her little apartment with his warmth, his humor, and his kindness. But she'd made that mistake before, thinking that he could fill the emptiness inside her, thinking any man could fill the emptiness inside her.

She knew she had to do it herself this time. "Thanks, but I'm all set. I'll see you around."

Then, before she could change her mind, she turned and walked away.

She almost managed not to look back to see if he was watching her, but when she reached the corner, she took a quick peek.

He was standing exactly where she'd left him, waiting for her to turn around.

Her heart leapt, and she hesitated. She didn't need romance. She didn't want romance. But a friend? A friend who knew all her secrets, all her fears, all her weaknesses? A friend who always knew how to make her feel stronger than she was?

There was only one person in the world who was that kind of a friend, and he was standing right there.

Damn him.

With a muttered curse, she turned around and stalked back over to him. "Here's the deal," she said, poking him in the chest. "You're right. I need my friend Ryder. Not the asshole who took my virginity and then dumped my ass the next day for reasons he refused to explain. If my friend Ryder can show up at my apartment, then he's welcome. If he brings the jerk who broke my heart, then he can't. Got it?"

He grinned. "Got it."

"Fine. 321 Maple Grove Apartments, number 3D. Bring groceries. I have no food."

"I'm on it. Give me two hours, and I'll be there."

She nodded. "Okay, then." She handed him the cup of coffee. "I can't run with this. It's yours."

He took it, his fingers brushing against hers. "Hey, Zoey?"

She started to jog away from him. "What?"

"Welcome home."

CHAPTER THREE

RYDER HADN'T BEEN to the Maple Grove Apartments before. He'd figured they were some new condo development perfect for Zoey and her high-class Boston life.

He wasn't prepared for them to be shitty, rundown buildings with rickety stairs, peeling paint, and missing gutters.

Swearing under his breath, he pulled in between a decent rental car he assumed was Zoey's, and a rusted pickup truck with two kegs in the back. There were old, faded lawn chairs strewn around an old barbeque grill in the browned-out grass to the side of the building, along with an overflowing trash can that had a couple empty cases of beer tossed beside it. There were burned spots on the grass, as if the residents were more interested in drinking than making sure the coals stayed in the grill.

How could she be living here? This wasn't supposed to be how her life turned out.

Scowling, he parked his truck, slung six grocery bags over his shoulders, and then carried the other four in his arms as he strode across the parking lot, narrowing his eyes at a twenty-something kid smoking a joint on the bottom step. "You live here?"

The dude gazed at him with bleary eyes. "What's it to you?"

"The woman in 3D is under my protection. Make sure everyone knows it."

He raised his brows. "The pretty one?"

Ryder narrowed his eyes. "The one you don't get to talk to."

The youth stood up, tall and lean in his black leather jacket and nose ring. "You don't get to tell me who to talk to."

Ryder tensed. "Did I mention my name?"

"Who gives a shit?"

"My name's Ryder Stockton. You may have heard of me or my brothers?"

Fear flickered in the youth's eyes for a split second, then he shrugged. "Maybe."

"Stay away from her. Got it?"

"Whatever." He tossed his butt aside and stood up. "Get a life, old man." Then he walked off, sneering at Ryder once he figured he was out of range.

"You think I can't reach you from here?" Ryder asked conversationally.

The kid paled and took off in a dead sprint, disappearing around the corner.

Ryder sighed and looked around, but he didn't see anyone else loitering. The curtain in one window fluttered, as if someone had been watching him. *Shit.* He didn't want Zoey living here. He'd sacrificed everything so this wouldn't be her life. What had gone wrong?

With a rising sense of anger, Ryder took the steps two at a time, following the signs to the third floor. Zoey's apartment was the second to last on the left, the door opening off an exterior landing that anyone could access. The apartment at the end, next to Zoey's, had more empty cases of beer stacked up outside, another rusted barbeque grill that had to be against fire code, and cigarette butts scattered on the ground.

Damn.

He let out a grim sigh as he reached Zoey's. Her front door was open, and he could see cardboard boxes stacked everywhere.

No security whatsoever.

Shit.

"Hey, Ryder!"

He turned to see Zoey walking toward him along the landing. The moment he saw her, the tension inside him eased. It was just so damn good to be near her again, after all that time. She was in sweatpants and a tee shirt, her hair in a ponytail, wearing what looked like a pair of decades-old sneakers. The clothes were baggy, and she looked adorable in them. He'd always loved her in sweats. Her body had filled out since she'd left, giving her more curves that were tempting as all hell. He cleared his throat, dragging his gaze off her body. "Hey, ZoeyBear."

She smiled, a big-ass smile that made him grin. "You came." She sounded pleased, which made him a little less cranky.

"Of course I did." He shifted the bags. "You left your door open?" he asked, trying not to sound as pissed as he was.

"I was just dropping a few boxes off in the recycling." She smiled. "Come on in." As she spoke, she slipped past him, her shoulder brushing against his chest.

His reaction to her touch was sudden, instant, and visceral, a cruel stab of desire so fierce that he had to close his eyes to fight it off. *Jesus.*

He stepped back, gripping the grocery bags tighter. He hadn't expected to react this way when he'd headed over here this morning to help her unpack. Seeing her at Lissa's café had been emotional, but he'd been in protector mode, determined to do whatever he needed to keep her safe. In that moment, she'd been his Zoey, the one he took care of.

But when she'd touched him just now, everything had changed.

He hadn't expected his heart to start hammering, or for his fists to clench, or for such need to crash over him. The need to hear her voice, to see the way her eyes sparkled when she laughed, to run his fingers through her hair, to fall asleep under the stars with her in his arms...like the old days...only with deep, intimate kissing and so much more.

Shit.

He could *not* do that to her.

He was there as her friend, as the only person she'd ever been able to lean on during her hellacious childhood, someone with whom she'd shared the secrets that she hadn't even been able to tell her own brother. He was not there as a man who wanted to taste her lips, trail his kisses down her neck, and bury his hands in her hair.

Ryder had promised he wouldn't show up as her accidental, one-night-of-hellacious-decision-making ex-lover. He needed to be the man who wanted nothing from her, other than to be the friend she so desperately needed. He needed to be there as a comrade she could trust and lean on while she rebuilt her life. But as he stood on that crappy landing, watching her cross the threadbare carpet of her new home, he realized that as much as he'd wanted her when they were teenagers, it was a thousand times more now.

He wanted her now. He wanted her thoroughly kissed, naked, and his.

Fuck.

He knew from Dane how much she'd been through, and

there was *no way* he was going to betray her by crossing that line that he'd torn through so long ago.

But he knew there was no way he could walk into her apartment right now, not with the way he was reacting to her. There was no fucking way he could shut down the need thundering through him right now. He hadn't prepared for this response to her. It was time to bail, and regroup—

She paused in the middle of her living room, looking back at him. "You're not coming in?" There was an edge to her voice, a tightness, as if she was already preparing for him to disappoint her again.

If he had any sense of decency, he'd drop the groceries, get back in his truck, and leave. He'd walk away now, and she'd never have to deal with him again, and he wouldn't have to fight off the intense need pounding through him. He could do that.

But if he did...if he walked away...wouldn't that be a second betrayal?

She needed him now. He knew that. His job was to be there for her, not to let his own need for her drive the wedge more firmly between them. *Shit.*

Her expression cooled and became distant. "Never mind. It's fine." She turned away, walking back into her kitchen. "You can leave the groceries by the door."

The moment she gave up on him, he knew he had no choice. He stepped forward, out of the sunlight, and into the darkness of her apartment.

CHAPTER FOUR

"I THINK I'M OFFICIALLY OLD." Zoey set her hands on her hips and bent over, trying to work out the cramps in her lower back. "Twelve hours of unpacking is too much."

"It's been a hell of a day." Ryder set another box on her kitchen counter. "We're making good progress, though."

She eyed him as he ripped it open, his biceps flexing. He'd been working like a man on a mission all day, barely pausing to eat or talk. She would have quit hours ago, but how could she pass out on her couch while he was still working on her stuff?

There was still so much to unpack, despite the twelve-hour day, mostly because the majority of the day hadn't been spent unpacking. Ryder had taken one look at the outlets in the kitchen, declared them unsafe, and that had been it. He'd spent half the morning rewiring the outlets so they were all grounded. Then he'd put a new deadbolt on the front door, and special locks on the windows that opened onto the landing.

After that? He'd reinforced the frame on the front door so no one would be able to break in, and then he'd fixed the drain in the bathroom so it would actually drain. The whole time, he'd been muttering about her being in an unsafe situation.

His help had made her feel better, because who wouldn't feel better with Ryder Stockton in protector mode? But at the same time, his deep concern about her safety had gotten in her head and started to freak her out that an axe murderer was going to hack his way into her apartment and chop her up as soon as she fell asleep tonight.

While Ryder was stalking around the apartment with a hammer, the idea of an axe murderer didn't seem so scary, but she knew that once she was lying in bed alone, being hunted by a rusted blade wouldn't feel quite so special.

And in truth, despite the fact that she felt safer having him there, it had been uncomfortably awkward working with him. They were like polite strangers, careful not to bump into each other, or say the wrong thing, and she hated it. She'd needed her friend tonight, not this guy that was practically a stranger. A decade apart had put a rift between them that she hadn't expected, and she was exhausted trying to deal with it.

They'd ordered pizza over an hour ago, and she was nearly in tears waiting for it to show up and give her an excuse to sit down, take a break, and then kick him out. She was exhausted, cranky, and at the end of her ability to cope.

She glanced at him, then grimaced when she saw him lift a stack of plates, making his damned biceps flex again.

And she couldn't lie to herself. Half the tension gripping her so tightly was because she couldn't stop noticing the thickness of his whiskers, the beautiful richness of his voice as he muttered to himself, or the way the muscles rippled in his back as he hammered on the front door. She couldn't help but notice the strength of his forearms, or the blue of his eyes, or the way he watched her when he thought she wasn't looking.

She didn't want to notice. Damn him for being so incredibly sexy and mouth-wateringly *male*.

Ryder paused suddenly, a stack of plates in his hands. "Are you okay?"

She cleared her throat and stood up a little taller. "Fine. Just tired." And sexually frustrated, but who was going to admit that? Not her. She pulled a picture of her parents out of a box, and bit her lip, because looking at a picture of her long-dead parents was exactly the uplifting kick-in-the-ass she so desperately needed right now.

He studied her for another minute, then set down the plates. "Sit."

She lifted her chin and looked around, trying to find an open surface to set the picture on. "No, I'm fine."

"Sit. I got this."

She slanted an irritated glance at him. "I'm not going to sit while you work on my stuff—"

"You're tired." He pointed at the couch. "Sit, or I'll make you."

Her heart jumped at the thought of him tackling her to the couch, like he'd done plenty of times when they were younger, before the night when everything had changed for them. What would it be like if he did it now? His body would be hard and strong against hers, and the way his fingers would wrap around her wrists—

His eyes darkened. "Don't look at me like that, Zoey. I'm not made of steel."

She sucked in her breath. "Like what?" Dear God. Had she been that obvious?

"You're looking at me like—" A knock at the door interrupted him. "Food's here. I'll get that. You take a seat." He headed toward the door, leaving his sentence unfinished.

What had he meant by that? Was he having as much trouble as she was, being so close to each other? She'd meant it when she said he could help her only as friends, but she'd been so aware of him all day as a man, as an incredibly sexy, tempting man who had once held every piece of her heart in his hands. But what if he still remembered what it was like to kiss her? What if he still thought about how it had felt to be in each other's arms? *What if he hadn't forgotten either?*

Her heart started to hammer, and she clenched the photograph more tightly, watching as he opened the door and pulled out his wallet, acting like he lived there. He paid the delivery guy, then walked back across the room with the pizza and drinks. He raised his brows as he neared. "You going to eat standing up?"

"No." She quickly set the photo back into an open box and sank down onto the couch. The kitchen table was piled high with items that hadn't found a home yet, so the only available flat surface for the pizza was the couch.

She'd tried to put most of her things in storage, but she'd brought with her everything that really mattered to her, the things that she didn't want left in some storage unit two thousand miles away. But as disciplined as she'd tried to be about what she'd brought with her, there was still way more than her tiny apartment could accommodate. She was overwhelmed with the sheer amount of stuff, and the lack of places for all of it to go.

It was clutter, disarray, and chaos.

And possibly axe murderers.

And definitely a man who was too damn sexy for anyone's good.

Ryder set the pizza and drinks on the table, and then sat down next to her.

The couch shifted under his weight, tilting her toward him.

She made herself lean away from him as she grabbed a

paper plate and slid a piece of pizza onto it. "Thanks for buying dinner."

"No problem." He tossed several slices onto his plate, then bent over the coffee table, eating silently.

The silence was heavy between them, growing in tension as they ate. The only sound was the thud of music from the apartment next door, along with the steady rumble of male voices as they partied, just like they had the night before.

Maybe the axe murderer would come from there. That would be fun. He'd be all hopped up on cheap keg beer, nicotine, and frat-boy mentality. That was definitely the best kind of axe murderer to be killed by, right?

She glanced at Ryder, but his face was stoic. He appeared to be completely focused on the pizza, entirely unaffected by how close they were sitting.

She couldn't think of anything to say to break the silence. How did she pretend to care about the weather or some other mundane topic when there was so much tension between them?

Ryder suddenly put down his pizza and turned to face her. "I don't like it."

She blinked. "The pizza?"

"You living here."

Something inside her shrank. "In town? You're mad that I'm back?"

"No. Shit, no. I don't like you living *here*." He gestured at the living room. "This apartment complex isn't safe. The guys next door are trouble. They've been playing poker and drinking all night."

Oh. That. Yeah, she'd been pretty crushed when she'd driven up last night. Moving from a beautiful condo to here had not been the uplifting homecoming she'd been hoping for. "The pictures were much nicer online."

"They couldn't have been that nice." He cocked his head,

studying her. "What happened to your money? You're a lawyer back in Boston, right? Why don't you have the money for something better than this?"

She stiffened. "My financial situation isn't your concern."

He ran his hand through his hair. "I know, but this wasn't how it was supposed to be."

She narrowed her eyes. "How what was supposed to be?"

"Your life. You were so smart. So talented. So alive. You were supposed to get out of this town and have a life worthy of you." He searched her face. "What happened, ZoeyBear? How did you wind up here?"

She pressed her lips together, suddenly not hungry. There was so much to say, so much that it left nothing that she wanted to talk about. "Life happens."

"It shouldn't happen to you."

Anger suddenly flared inside her. "Well, it did."

He studied her. "Tell me about it. Tell me what happened after you left here."

She hesitated, surprised by his question. "Didn't Dane tell you?"

"A few things. Not much. Not enough to fill a decade." Something inscrutable flickered in his eyes. "I know you got married."

Her throat tightened. "And divorced," she said quickly, somehow needing to make that clear to him.

"Why'd you get divorced?"

She looked down at her pizza. "I don't want to talk about it. Let it go, Ryder."

He was silent for a moment, then he set his hand on the back of her neck, his fingers rubbing gently. "ZoeyBear," he said softly. "Talk to me."

Tears threatened at the feel of his hand on her. It felt so good that she wanted to cry. It had been so long since a man had touched her that way, out of kindness, out of affection, out of comfort. "We met in college," she said quietly, "and decided early on not to have kids so we could focus on our careers." She closed her eyes so she could concentrate on Ryder's touch grounding her. "I worked my ass off, and I thought he was doing the same. As it turned out, he was the stereotype. Long nights at the office were actually being spent with another woman."

Ryder's fingers tightened on her neck. "Bastard."

"He got her pregnant, and they were both so delighted that he divorced me as fast as he could so he could marry her before the baby was born." She'd never forget that moment when he'd walked into their condo late that night. He'd looked so happy, happier than she'd ever seen him. "He was glowing with joy when he told me he was leaving me and why. He said his only regret was that he'd married me in the first place and wasted as many years of his life on me as he had."

God, those words had hurt.

They still hurt.

The fact that he was a bastard pig was surprisingly unhelpful in disempowering those words from biting deep.

And then what had happened after that? God, she'd been so stupid to trust him.

"Oh, babe." Ryder wrapped his arms around her and pulled her against him.

She didn't resist, burying her face in his neck, fighting back the waves of loneliness and grief from that night. Ryder's body was hard and warm against hers, and she could smell that same amazing scent he'd always had, that one that made something inside her breathe deeply and relax.

He kissed the top of her head, just as he'd done so many times before, and it felt just as good. "I missed you," she whispered. "I needed you."

"I'm sorry I wasn't there for you," he said, brushing a kiss over her forehead. "I had no idea you were going through that. I would have beat the shit out of him if I'd known."

She laughed softly against his chest at the thought of Ryder storming into their law firm and knocking the shit out of Nathan, in his fancy suit and polished shoes. "He would've had you arrested."

"That's fine. Totally worth it." He kissed her forehead again. "When did this happen?"

"About a year ago. I tried to stay there, to keep going, but then I found out that he..." She cut herself off, not wanting to admit how stupid she'd been. "It just made sense to get away from everything for a bit," she said instead. But even as she said it, her voice started to tremble, and she squeezed her eyes shut. "I don't have anything left," she whispered. "I feel like there's just this big, empty darkness inside me that I can't shake, and it scares me."

Ryder's arms tightened around her. "You got this."

The words couldn't reach her heart. "Not this time."

"Yeah, you do." He pulled back, cupping her jaw with his fingers as he studied her face. "So beautiful," he whispered.

Her heart started to hammer as she stared at him. He was so close to her, his lips only inches from hers. She wanted him to kiss her so badly. To envelop her in his strength, like he had so long ago. To be her magical fairytale hero and sweep her away.

His gaze dropped to her mouth, and his eyes darkened.

She didn't move, afraid to breathe.

He looked back into her eyes, the blue depths of his gaze stormy and turbulent.

It was the same as that moment on her prom night, when all the tension that had been mounting between them came to a head, hovering on a precipice, waiting for them to retreat or grab each other's hands and jump.

They'd jumped.

And they'd crashed.

She couldn't survive another crash, especially not with him. "Don't," she whispered. "Don't kiss me."

He swore under his breath and closed his eyes. "I'm not going to." He gently set her back to her side of the couch. "Let's call it a night. We're both beat."

She nodded, biting her lip against the need to protest. "That's probably a good plan. My back is killing me."

His gaze flicked to her back, as if he wanted to offer to rub it for her.

"I'll take some ibuprofen," she said quickly. "We unpacked that, at least."

"Yeah." He hesitated another moment, then stood up. "I have meetings in the morning, but I'll come by tomorrow afternoon to help you finish. Around two?"

"You'll still be in town?" Lissa had said he didn't live in town anymore. "When do you leave?" Fear gripped her. She'd just found him again. She wasn't ready to let him go yet. At the same time, she needed him to leave before she got too dependent on him and forgot that she'd come here to find her own strength, not to lean on anyone else's anymore.

He grabbed his cowboy hat from the back of a kitchen chair. "Chase coerced me into being the general contractor for a new barn he wants to build on the ranch. I'll be in town a lot over the next six months."

Her heart thudded, and she wasn't sure if she was happy about that, or super upset. "Where are you staying?"

"A house down by the river. I'm away this weekend, then back a couple days next week, and then away. I have a few other projects I'm managing in addition to this one, so I'll be in and out."

"Oh." She didn't know what she thought of that. A part of her was so glad to have him around, but a deeper part of her wanted him as far away as possible. God, it was so complicated with him. So many mixed-up emotions.

He set his hat on his head. "It's a ten-bedroom house. Plenty of room if you get tired of this place."

Her belly fluttered. "You think sleeping in the same building is a good idea?"

He studied her for a long moment. "Maybe."

"It's not." She stood up, grimacing at the protests from her muscles. She so needed him out of there before he tempted her enough that she had to get angry at him to keep the distance between them. "Good night, Ryder. Thank you for your help."

"Yeah, sure." He walked to the door. "Zoey?"

"What?"

He hesitated. "Lock the door after I leave and stay in for the rest of the night," he finally said. "I don't trust those guys next door."

"That's it?" He wanted her to lock herself up? Nothing about the missing ten years between them, or that night, that morning, when all they'd had fell apart?

"That's it." But as he stepped outside and shut the door behind him, she knew that wasn't all he'd wanted to say.

There had been more.

But, like always, he hadn't said it.

He knew all her secrets, but she knew so few of his.

CHAPTER FIVE

RYDER SAT in his truck after he walked out of Zoey's.

He sat there and watched more and more people heading into the apartment next to hers. Most of them were male and carrying cases of alcohol.

He looked around at the parking lot.

A couple guys were sitting on the back of a pickup truck with beer.

Trash was piled up around the dumpster.

An old swing set in the side yard was rusted and falling down, as if once this had been a place for children and families. Not anymore. It was a place that had once had hope and now had nothing but dead ends and lost futures.

What the hell was she doing here? How had this happened?

He'd met Zoey through Dane, because he'd been friends with her big brother. She'd been five or six, maybe, at best. Funny. Irreverent. Sassy. All the things he'd never been. She'd been this symbol of all that could be good in this world, and from that first moment when he'd met her, he'd gravitated to her innocence and her irrepressible spirit. His home life had been so shitty that he hadn't known that someone like Zoey could even exist, until he'd met her.

As a teenager, she'd been the one in his life with the sparkle in her eye. She'd been the only one who'd been able to get him to laugh. She was the one who'd taught him there were people in this world besides his brothers that he could trust. That was why he'd fought so damn hard to protect her. With his own home life such a war zone, he knew damn well how bad it could be, so once her parents had died when she was seven, he'd made it his job to make certain that she never had to face the kind of shit that had rained down upon him and his brothers.

He'd kept an eye on her when she and Dane had been placed with their aunt and uncle as guardians.

He'd noticed the moment that her uncle had started looking at her in ways that no man should look at a young girl.

After that, he'd made sure that she never slept alone. Either he, Dane, or one of his brothers was always sleeping on her floor after that, every single night that her uncle was in town. If his own dad was out of town, he'd sometimes have her sleep in his room.

No one ever got to her because he'd made sure she was safe.

He'd made her laugh when kids at school had bullied her for her love of art.

He'd taken her to her prom when no one would go with her.

And then he'd stood back and let her leave this shitty little town so she could get the life she'd deserved.

She'd left Rogue Valley on a full scholarship to Harvard. She'd gone to law school. She'd had it all.

But something had happened while she'd been gone. She'd lost it all, including the parts of her soul that had been so precious before she'd left. *What the hell had happened to her for the last ten years?*

He had to find out.

And there was one man who would have the answers.

WHEN RYDER TURNED into Dane's driveway a short while later, the living room light was still on, which almost pissed him off. He was so annoyed at Dane right now that he would actually have gotten a little satisfaction dragging him out of the first sound sleep he'd gotten in months.

He parked by the front door and jogged up the steps, knocking lightly on the front door in case the baby was asleep. He was fine to wake up Dane, but the baby? Not so much.

The door opened after a few minutes to reveal Dane in sweats, a tee shirt, and bare feet, a crying baby over his shoulder. He looked tired, stressed, and surprised to see Ryder. "What's up?" The baby looked over at Ryder and immediately held out his arms, still screaming.

Some of Ryder's anger dissipated at the sight of his nephew. "Hey, shortcake." He instinctively took little Justin, tucking him against his chest as he stepped inside. "You driving your dad nuts tonight, I hope?"

Justin took a shuddering breath, the sobs easing as he snuggled against Ryder.

"I'll take that as a yes." Ryder glanced around and saw that neither Jaimi nor their daughter Emily appeared to be up. "The girls asleep?"

"Yeah." Dane ran a weary hand through his tousled hair as he shut the door behind Ryder. "You're the only one he'll calm down for. You're like the baby whisperer."

"Don't tell anyone. It's bad for my reputation." Ryder

grinned as little Justin sighed again, snuggling deeper against him. He wasn't going to lie. It was extremely satisfying to be able to get the baby to calm down when his own dad couldn't. "You realize I'm better at this baby thing than you are, right?"

"I'm a great dad. My kids are lucky as hell to have me." There was no mistaking the pride in Dane's voice, which irked Ryder.

How could Dane be patting himself on the back about being a great dad when his own sister was in such rough shape? Maybe he didn't know. Maybe she'd lied to Dane about her life. More of Ryder's anger dissipated. Zoey had always been stubborn as hell. Maybe she'd hidden everything from her brother as well. "Hey, have you seen Zoey since she's been back?"

Dane retreated to the kitchen and poured himself a cup of coffee. "Not yet. She was supposed to come by today, but she decided to unpack instead. She's coming by tomorrow." He held up a mug. "Want some?"

"No." Ryder rubbed little Justin's back. "She's in rough shape," he said, watching Dane's reaction. "She's out of money. She's...she seems broken." Just saying those words made all his anger flood back. His Zoey. Broken. While he'd been sitting on his ass doing nothing for her.

Dane sighed. "Yeah. I know."

Ryder tensed. "You know? You knew before today? And you didn't tell me?"

"Ah...." Dane grimaced and turned away to put the coffee pot back on the burner. Instead of answering, Dane held up a plate with banana bread on it. "Emily and I made it fresh tonight. That kid is turning me into a domestic softie. Try it. It's impressive."

"No, thanks." Ryder narrowed his eyes as he bounced Justin. Dane's delight at being a stepdad to Emily was great and all, but Ryder wasn't buying the distraction. He'd been best friends with the guy for enough decades that he knew evasive tactics when he saw them. "I had dinner at Zoey's tonight. She's living in a hellhole. Her asshole ex treated her like shit. She's closed off. There's nothing left of the Zoey who left here. Why didn't you tell me how rough she's had it?"

Dane put the plate back down. "You had dinner with her? Tonight?"

"Yeah, I helped her unpack all day, and we ordered in."

"So, you're the reason she didn't come over here? Because she was with you?"

Ryder frowned at the edge in his friend's voice. "You're pissed I helped her?"

Dane held out his hands for his son, and Ryder handed him back, scowling as Dane rocked the now-sleeping baby gently. "No, of course not. I'm glad you were there for her."

Ryder blinked at the way Dane avoided his gaze. Son of a bitch. Dane was straight-out lying to him. "Why would you be mad I helped her unpack?"

Dane looked at him, and there was no mistaking the fury in his eyes. "Stay the hell away from her."

Anger swelled hard and fast inside Ryder at the command. "What does that mean? I'm not—"

"Ryder?" Jaimi walked into the living room, wearing flannel pajama bottoms and a tee shirt. She looked like she'd just woken up. "What are you doing here?"

He took a breath, reining in his anger. "Just stopping by to talk about Zoey. You doing okay?" He didn't know much about babies, but with his brothers acquiring kids left and right, he was picking up some trivia, like the fact that newborn babies didn't appear to sleep at all during the night.

"Tired, but wonderful." Jaimi took Justin from Dane's arms, kissing both of her boys as she did so. "I am so looking forward to meeting Zoey. Hopefully tomorrow."

"Unless Ryder distracts her again," Dane muttered.

Jaimi's gaze sharpened as she looked at Dane, and then at Ryder. "Oh, babe," she said to Dane. "Don't do this. She doesn't need you to be like that right now."

Ryder looked back and forth between them. "Like what? What's going on with Zoey?"

"Nothing." Dane answered too quickly.

Jaimi rolled her eyes. "Dane is in protector mode with her. I'm sure that's why she hasn't come by. He gets all papa bear on her every time he speaks to her." She looked at Dane. "Let her be, baby. She'll find her way."

Ryder focused his gaze on Jaimi. "So, you knew, too?"

"Knew what?"

"How shitty things were going for her?"

Jaimi glanced at Dane, then nodded. "Yes, Dane told me."

Aggravation rushed through Ryder as he turned back to his friend. "You made it sound like her life was great out there. Was it all a lie?"

Dane hesitated, and glanced at Jaimi again. "Yeah, I guess."

"You guess?" Ryder swore under his breath. He felt like such an ass. He'd been Zoey's protector for years when they were kids. He'd promised to always be there for her. That was why he'd had to let her go the day after the prom. Because he had her back. But all this time, when he'd given her space, she'd been suffering? "I let her go because I wanted her to have a better life. She didn't, did she? All this time, and she didn't. And you knew? And you didn't tell me?"

"She will." Dane kept his voice low, so as not to wake his son. "She just needs to regroup. Don't go and try to talk her into staying here. This isn't where she belongs."

Ryder's jaw dropped in astonishment. "Me? Talk her into staying in Rogue Valley? Why would I do that?"

"Because you—" Dane stopped himself suddenly, glancing

helplessly at his wife, who was shaking her head at him. "Nothing."

"I what?"

Dane sighed. "Zoey always looked at you like you were her hero, Ryder. You're the only one she has ever listened to. You have to make her go back."

"And back to where? Boston? The life that sucked the joy out of her?" That didn't feel right. He'd seen the shadows in her eyes, and he knew damn well he wasn't responsible for all of them.

"It's where she belongs. She deserves better than this. We both know it."

Ryder closed his eyes and took a deep breath. He knew the conversation he and Dane had had that night so long ago. Ten years ago, actually. "Maybe going back to Boston isn't right for her."

"Staying here damn sure isn't," Dane snapped. "I gave up everything to give her a better life. You don't get to trap her here."

"Trap her?" Ryder stared at his friend. "I'd never trap her."

"Then leave her alone. Don't let her use you as an excuse to stay here. She's vulnerable, Ryder. You're her safe zone. If you let her hide behind you, she'll never go back to where she belongs." Dane's voice was low. "Do what you did before, Ryder."

What he did before had haunted him for ten years. "Maybe it's time for her to decide what she wants."

Dane's face was weary. "This town isn't it, Ryder. Even you won't live here. It's a dead end."

Yeah, he had a point there. "You live here. You let your wife and kids live here."

Dane's face softened, and he looked over at Jaimi. "It's right for us," he said softly. "For us, it's beautiful."

Jaimi smiled, her eyes filled with warmth and love. "I love

this town," she said. "I love everything about living here, including being around all my brothers and their families. It's the home I've always wanted." She stood on her tiptoes and pressed a kiss to Dane's cheek. "But maybe, just maybe, you don't know everything that's right for your sister."

His arm slid around her waist, pulling her and the sleeping baby against him. "I know ugly memories can trap you forever. This place became okay for me only when you came into it." He looked at Ryder. "You hide from the memories of this place, too. For people like us, like Zoey, this place is a quicksand that will suck you back into the hell that will destroy you."

Jaimi sighed and rested her head on his chest, tears glistening in her eyes.

Ryder hesitated. He knew the truth to Dane's words. The reason he had consistently refused his brother Chase's request to move back to town was because he couldn't take the memories when he was here. That was why all the Stockton brothers except Chase had left town as soon as they'd been old enough, and it was why he and Dane had worked so hard to get Zoey liberated from it. Their childhood had been hell, and the darkness was too strong, at least for Ryder. Five of his brothers had moved back to town and started families, but that wasn't for him.

He'd never move back to Rogue Valley. He couldn't. So, yeah, he agreed Zoey didn't need this hell either, including the shadows he brought with him, but at the same time, it was clear to him that what she'd been doing for the last ten years hadn't been good for her either.

Suddenly weary, he rubbed his forehead. "Maybe I can help her—"

"You can't," Dane said. "I love you, bro, but you're so fucked up. You're like this walking volcano of anger, and there's a darkness in you that's pure hell. You're not good for her, and this place isn't either. The only way this place could be okay for her is if she found someone like Jaimi, someone from the outside who can chase away the shadows. Someone who can shine light on her." He met Ryder's gaze. "That's not you."

Ryder pressed his lips together. "Yeah, I'm not all sunshine and strawberries." He studied Dane. "Is that why you didn't tell me what she was going through? Because you thought I'd run out to Boston and drag her back here?"

"The thought crossed my mind," Dane admitted.

"Really?" Ryder's eyes narrowed as he had a sudden thought. "Ten years ago, when you talked to me about making sure Zoey left town after graduation, was it Rogue Valley you wanted to get her away from, or was it *me*?"

Dane hesitated, and there was silence.

Holy shit.

Ryder took a step backward, stunned. "It was me. The whole time, ten years ago, it was *me* that you wanted her to get away from? Not the town? It was *me*?"

Dane swore. "You come from hell, Ryder. All your brothers do. I love you, but Zoey is special. She needs something more. She needs kindness, gentleness, and light. She can't survive your darkness, but I saw the way she looked at you. She would have lost herself in your hell. Don't give her that chance."

Ryder was shocked by Dane's words. "I slept in her room almost every night. You had no problem with that."

"You're a hell of a friend, Ryder. As long as you were her friend, it was all good. But once she started looking at you differently...that changed the rules. I know you. I know what nightmares live inside you. I can't turn my sister over to that, to you. I just can't. I—"

Jaimi put her hand on his arm. "Enough, Dane." She looked at Ryder. "You're a good man, Ryder. I see it."

Dane scowled. "Jaimi—"

"You know what? Forget it." Emotions swirled through Ryder, dark, angry emotions that threatened to overwhelm him. "I'm going to head out."

Dane frowned. "Don't take it personally, Ryder. It's not personal."

"Fuck yeah, it is." He nodded at Jaimi, who was holding Justin against her chest. "See ya, Jaimi."

She reached for him. "Wait, Ryder—"

"Not now, Jaimi. Not now." Ryder headed for the door, not turning when Jaimi called his name again.

Dane didn't try to stop him. The man who'd been his best friend since they were kids, the one who knew him better than he knew himself, didn't make a move to stop him, or apologize, or take his words back.

Because they both knew that he'd meant them.

Ryder's soul had been damned the day he'd been born, and he knew it. Dane was right.

He was not good for Zoey. He'd been a selfish asshole to even go over to her place tonight.

First thing in the morning, he was going to tell Chase that he wasn't staying around to do the new barn.

And then he was leaving town. For good. Before he could destroy her.

CHAPTER SIX

ZOEY HAD JUST MANAGED to fall into a restless sleep when the shrill wail of the fire alarm jerked her awake. Her first thought was that it sucked to be living in an apartment building, and her second one was whether she needed to actually get up or not.

Then she smelled smoke.

"Holy crap!" She kicked the blankets off and leapt out of bed, stumbling over the pile of clothes that hadn't made it into her dresser yet. She flipped on the light, grabbed her phone, and a sweatshirt, then hurried toward the door.

Her lungs tickled as she ran into the living room. Her eyes started to sting. From the smoke? Was there actual *smoke* in her apartment?

She glanced around the living room, at her most important belongings strewn about. What did she have time to grab? Maybe the picture of her mom and dad, before they'd died. Or the—

There was a loud crash that shook her apartment, and then she heard footsteps racing past her door, as some guy started yelling for everyone to get out.

Panic shot through her, and she stopped looking for the photo. Instead, she grabbed her computer bag off the kitchen table and yanked open her front door.

A wall of smoke hit her hard, pushing her back.

She quickly looked around, and saw flames licking up the outside of the apartment next to hers. Holy shit! Her eyes started to water, and a wracking cough seized her lungs.

She held her sweatshirt to her face and ran along the landing, her heart pounding as she hurried toward the rickety steps. People streamed out of the apartments and gathered in the parking lot, pointing up at her corner of the building.

She started down the stairs, clutching her bag and her phone, the metal steps harsh on her bare feet. She had made it down only two steps when a guy lurched drunkenly up behind her. "Move!" He shoved her hard to the side as he pushed past her down the steps.

She lost her balance, and her foot slipped into a gap in the grating, plunging her off balance. "Shit!" She lurched forward, her ankle twisting as her foot caught in the grating. She grabbed for the railing, but her fingers slid off the rusty metal, and she fell forward. Her cheek slammed into the railing and her elbow ricocheted off the step as she crashed down.

She lay still, gasping for breath as pain gripped her. Her ankle was screaming with pain, her cheek was throbbing, her eyes burning.

"That lady fell," someone yelled.

"Get up!" someone else screamed.

Well, gee, ya think? She fumbled for the railing, trying to grab it. Her foot was still caught in a stair several steps above her head, and she could tell her face was bleeding. She tried to twist her foot free and then yelped at the stab of pain.

"I got you." Ryder was suddenly beside her, his hands on her shoulders. "You okay?"

"My foot," she gasped. "It's stuck."

He swore under his breath and leaned past her to check it. He touched her ankle, and she gasped at the pain. "No! Don't pull it!"

"We need to take the weight off so you can get it out." He came back down and crouched beside her, sliding his arms under her. "Hold onto me."

She nodded, gritting her teeth against the pain as she wrapped her arms around his neck. "Be careful," she ordered.

"I've got you." His arms tightened and he lifted her up, taking all her weight off her trapped foot as he gently moved her back toward the higher stair.

She gasped as the pressure eased off her ankle, and she was able to pull her foot free. "I'm out."

"Great." He shifted her weight so he was cradling her to his chest. "Let's go." He turned sideways and carried her down the stairs, moving fast. She braced herself for more pain, but not once did he accidentally bang her ankle against the railing, even when the fire fighters raced up the stairs past her.

When they reached the ground, he carried her right over to the ambulance, calling for help. As he set her down, she looked up and saw flames engulf the front of her apartment, battling with the fire hoses for victory. Anguish tore through her. "Oh, God. Look, Ryder."

Ryder followed her glance and he swore. "I'm so sorry, Zoey."

Her heart seemed to break as she watched the flames eat away at the walls of her apartment, hissing as they fought with the water for supremacy. In that apartment were the things most precious to her, the only things that had mattered enough to take them cross-country.

It didn't matter how soon the firemen got the fire out.

She knew it would be too late.

~

"STOP PACING. You're giving me a headache." Zoey closed her eyes as she rested on the hospital bed, her ankle throbbing as they waited for her to be seen. Her face had been cleaned up, her cut had been taped shut, her ankle had been x-rayed, and they were waiting to find out if it was broken.

Ryder paused. "Can I get you something? Coffee? Water? Food?"

She shook her head. "No. I'm fine. Just tired."

"I'll go get coffee."

"Stop." She opened her eyes to look at him. His face was stark, like he'd been kicked in the gut. He looked restless and uncomfortable. Did hospitals bother him? "Come here."

Alarm flashed across his face. "Why?"

Sudden tears burned in her eyes. "Because I need a hug, dammit. I almost died in a freaking fire tonight!"

He swore under his breath and came right over. He sat next to her and pulled her onto his lap, wrapping his strong arms around her. She wrapped her hands around his muscular forearms and closed her eyes, pressing her face against his chest. His body was so familiar and so reassuring, the solid warmth that had been her foundation as a teenager.

She focused on the feel of his body against hers everywhere they were touching. His hip against hers. Her breasts against his ribs. The roughness of his shirt against her cheek. The gentle thud of his heart. His arms around her shoulders and upper arms, locking her against him.

Slowly, her tension began to ease, and she took a shuddering breath. "Do you think all my stuff is burned up?"

"I don't know. Maybe they stopped it before it got inside your place." He started to release her.

"No, don't!" Panic hit her until he tightened his arms

around her again. "Why does it feel so good to have you hold me? I'm still mad at you for what happened ten years ago."

He was quiet for a moment. "Because we were friends once," he said. "Friends that stood by each other. I was your shield."

"Friends," she said softly. They'd been friends. And then they'd been lovers. And then they'd been nothing. "I missed having your friendship. I never found anyone like you in Boston."

He sucked in his breath in a hiss. "There are a lot of people like me out there. You don't need me."

She laughed softly. "There's literally no one like you, Ryder."

"Because I'm a fucked-up mess?"

"Because you're you." She relaxed into him, keeping her eyes closed. "You were the only one I ever really trusted. Until you blew it, of course."

He didn't laugh.

She poked his chest. "I was joking."

"Were you?"

"Yes—" Then she stopped. "No, I guess not. That was pretty awful." She pulled back to look at him. "What happened that day? Why did you cut me off like that? I mean, not even a single word since you dropped me off after the prom. You just disappeared from my life."

He swore under his breath and gently pushed a tendril of hair back from her face. "It's complicated."

"Tell me."

He sighed. "I—"

"Zoey!" Dane burst into the room.

Ryder swore and leapt off the bed so fast that Zoey almost fell off. He awkwardly shoved her back in place, then nearly bolted across the tiny room to the opposite wall.

Dane glared at Ryder before turning to her. "Sorry it took

so long to get here. Trying to find you in this place was a circus."

She stared at her brother, startled by his appearance. She hadn't seen him in ten years. *Ten years*, and now he was standing in her hospital room. He looked so much older than when she'd left. Bigger. He was much more muscular, with broad shoulders. His face was leaner, and he looked like he hadn't shaved in weeks. But he was her *big brother*. Sudden tears threatened. "Dane?" she whispered.

His face softened. "Zoey." He strode across the room and wrapped her up in a hug.

She closed her eyes against the swell of emotions as she hugged the only family she had left. God, it had been so long. He felt strong and solid, familiar, the big brother who'd made it possible for her to afford to go to college.

"I missed you, sis." He pulled back, searching her face.

She nodded, tears blurring her vision. "Me, too."

Dane touched her cheek. "Stitches?"

"Tape. It's not a big deal, apparently. It won't leave a scar."

"Good." He glared at Ryder again before sitting next to her. "So, when are you heading back to Boston?"

She blinked. "I just got here."

"Yeah, but you're not staying, right?"

The shield that had momentarily dissolved sprang back up around her heart. She'd forgotten about how hard Dane had pushed her away ten years ago, and how much it had grated on her that he'd tried to control her life. She deflected the question with one of her own, unable to bear arguing with him about his need to get her out of his life. "Why are you here?"

"Because I care."

"No, I mean, how did you even know I was in the hospital?"

"Ryder called me." Dane scowled at her. "A fire? What the

47

hell were you doing staying in that place? I answer calls over there all the time."

She glanced at Ryder, startled when she saw raw, stark despair in his eyes. The moment he realized she was looking at him, he looked away, masking his emotions. What was wrong with him?

"I drove by the place on the way here," Dane continued. "It's definitely shut down for at least a few days. You won't be able to stay there, so Jaimi and I want you to stay with us."

Zoey tensed. "With you guys?" With their baby, and their daughter, and their happy little world? She'd never even met Jaimi. She'd been in the midst of a crumbling marriage when Dane and Jaimi had gotten married, and she hadn't had the emotional capacity to come back for a festival of love and happiness.

"Yeah. We got space." Dane smiled. "Jaimi's super excited to meet you."

"I'm looking forward to meeting her." She felt panic closing in. Her brother was almost a stranger to her, and everyone in his home *was* a stranger. She didn't have any idea how to fit in. "But I don't want to intrude." She didn't want to be the pathetic sister living in her brother's house, interfering with his happy family.

Dammit. What had she been thinking, coming back to town? Dane had literally shoved her out of town after graduation, and he'd fought her hard every time she'd talked about coming home. He'd made it clear he didn't want her in town. And Ryder, God. Ryder. He'd pushed her away as well, and yet she'd been stupid enough to think that forcing her way back into their lives would somehow make the darkness stop swirling through her.

She'd been wrong.

She'd thought coming back home would feel better, but it didn't. She felt worse, because she was supposed to belong here, and she didn't. At least in Boston, it had never been her home, so feeling lost had been expected. Here? She'd cooked it up in her mind that this was her oasis, her last place of refuge, to save her when nothing else could help.

And yet, now that she was here, it was achingly obvious that she wasn't supposed to be here either. But where did that leave her? Nowhere. She had no idea where she could go that would feel better.

"It's not an intrusion." But even as Dane said it, she saw how tired he looked. And she knew how much he'd wanted her out of town.

He didn't want to take her on. She knew it. But he had to, because he had always looked out for her, and now she'd marched homeless, back into his life and his town.

She couldn't do that to him. To herself. To Jaimi. She managed a smile. "Thanks, but I already have somewhere to stay."

"Really? Already? Where?" Dane's eyebrows went up skeptically. "I won't let you stay in a hotel when you can stay with us, and you can't stay in another dangerous rental."

"I'm not." She looked desperately across the room at the man who had once been her best friend. "Ryder said I could stay at his place. He has ten bedrooms."

The look of shock on Ryder's face was so aghast that it was almost comical. "What?"

Her gut dropped. "Didn't you...didn't you invite me?" Dear God. Had she done it again? Somehow misread his intentions? She'd thought he'd loved her once, that they had loved each other, and that was why she'd slept with him. And then he'd cut her off. And now...Dear God. Had she been that stupid again?

Ryder's face softened as he looked at her. "Yeah," he said quietly. "I did invite you."

Relief rushed through her, and she smiled. "Okay."

Anger flashed across Dane's face, and he stood up. "No."

"No, what?" Zoey frowned at him. "What are you talking about?"

Dane glared at Ryder, who immediately stood taller, narrowing his gaze at Dane. "She needs a place to stay," Ryder said, his voice unyielding. "I have plenty of space. You don't."

"I have room—"

"I got it covered," Ryder said. "She's coming home with me."

Dane swore again. "Can I talk to you in the hall?"

"No need." Ryder didn't move. "I was able to fully grasp everything the first time." His voice was hard. "I got Zoey's back. I always do." There was an edge to his voice, an undercurrent she couldn't quite figure out. Why was there so much tension between them?

Dane studied Ryder for a moment, then nodded. "Okay."

Ryder nodded.

Then they both turned to her. "I'll be by to see you tomorrow," Dane said. "Sound good?"

"Yeah, okay." Zoey looked back and forth between the only two men in her life who'd ever really mattered to her. God, they were both so complicated. Did she really want to deal with that?

No. She didn't have enough left inside her to be around them, to deal with the emotions they both brought up, to navigate through the tension strung so tightly between them.

As soon as morning came, she was going to start looking for her next stop, the next place, the place that would somehow help her find her way back.

Ryder caught her eye, and he gave her a half-smile, the same half-smile that had completely melted her heart so long ago.

And just like that, something inside her melted again... and an ugly, terrifying truth settled on her.

She hadn't come home because she'd wanted to return to Rogue Valley. Or to Dane. Or to her past.

She'd come back for Ryder.

And *that* was the biggest mistake she could have made.

Dear God. How stupid was she? Going for the trifecta of heartbreak? First Ryder. Then Nathan. And then Ryder again?

She had to get out of there, and fast, or what little was left of her heart would be broken forever. "It won't be for long," she said quickly. "I'm not staying in town. I'll be gone in a few days."

She didn't miss the look of relief on Dane's face.

Or the way Ryder turned his head away, hiding his reaction from her.

CHAPTER SEVEN

IT WAS ALMOST four in the morning by the time Ryder got Zoey home and settled in one of the bedrooms. The house was owned by the Harts, who were the siblings of his brother Maddox's wife, Hannah. They were good people, and the bond between the Stockton clan and the Harts was already building. Only four bedrooms were furnished, and two of them had been claimed by a couple of the Harts for when they were in town. Ryder had the third one, which meant there was only one for Zoey to choose from.

It was the room next to Ryder's, which meant Zoey would be sleeping only a few yards from his bed.

So, he didn't go to bed.

He went downstairs instead.

And now, it was past five, and he still hadn't gone to sleep.

He was sitting on the screened-in-porch, overlooking the river, thinking.

He was cold. Restless. Unsettled. And wondering what the fuck he was supposed to do.

In his hand was his phone. He'd texted Chase last night after he'd left Dane's, asking him to call as soon as he got up.

Chase was always up early. He'd be calling soon, and Ryder was going to turn down the new barn project.

But as he sat there, waiting for Chase's call, he'd been thinking. Thinking, and thinking, and thinking.

That moment, when he'd driven past Zoey's apartment on the way back and seen that fire... Jesus. He'd never been so terrified in his life. He felt like he'd been in slow motion, leaping out of his truck and sprinting for the stairs, watching as she fell when that guy had pushed her. Watching her stumble. Unable to get close enough to catch her. Terrified that she would fall off the stairs to the pavement below.

Shit.

He stood up, trying to shake it off, trying to calm down.

Zoey was safe.

She was upstairs sleeping.

Trusting him to keep her safe.

It was okay. She was okay.

He hadn't been able to shake his terror until she'd finally called him over in the hospital room and climbed into his lap. Feeling her in his arms, curled up against him, had broken through the panic gripping him.

And then, that moment in the hospital, when she'd said she was staying with him, the look on her face had been so vulnerable, so lost. There had been no damn way he could have refused her, regardless of how mad Dane might have been.

He hadn't forgotten Dane's speech. He knew he was no good for Zoey romantically.

But as a friend. God, as a friend. She needed him. And, maybe more importantly, he needed to be there for her. If he could help her, maybe it would ease the restlessness that had haunted him for so long.

But she was planning to leave again, before he could help her find that sparkle again.

He sat back down and bowed his head, pressing his palms to his eyes. What the fuck was he supposed to do? She was so freaking lost. And she was determined to leave. He knew she meant it. She was a woman on the run, fleeing from the monster that was inside her.

He couldn't force her to stay. She'd never allow it, and he'd never take the freedom of choice away from her.

But if he could get her to *choose* to stay, that would be different. It would be okay, maybe. He could help her while she figured out her next steps, right?

He leaned back, clasping his hands behind his head. What was he thinking? Could he really help her? And, maybe more importantly, how could he share a house with her and stay only friends when he wanted to cross that line so fucking badly?

His phone rang, startling him. He glanced at the display. Chase already. He answered it. "Hey, bro. You're early. I figured you wouldn't be up before six."

"I'm still in bed. Just saw your text. What's up?"

Ryder hesitated.

"Ryder? What's going on?"

"I don't know."

"Hang on." There was some shuffling, and then Chase came back on the phone. "I'm out in the hallway so I don't wake Mira. What's wrong?"

"Zoey." He hadn't intended to bring her up. He'd meant to talk about the barn.

"Ah... What about her?"

"She arrived yesterday, but she wants to leave town again. She's...shit, Chase. She's fucking wrecked."

"Yeah, I saw that in the cafe. She's had a rough time of it."

Ryder rubbed his wrist over his forehead. "I want to help her."

"Good. She needs you."

Ryder said nothing. He couldn't.

Chase was quiet for a moment, then, "What's the problem?"

"Me." He didn't need to say more. Chase had grown up with the same abusive, bastard father that he had. They all had the same fucked-up darkness inside them.

Chase sighed. "Give yourself a break, bro."

"Dane says she needs light. Sunshine. A break from the past. Not me."

"What do you think?"

Ryder closed his eyes and ground his palms into his eyes. "I don't know."

"Yeah, you do. What does your gut say?"

He grimaced. "I think I can help her," he finally admitted. "I think it's gotta be me. I'm the only one she trusts." Or trusted, at least.

"Then do it." Chase sounded pleased.

"I don't know if I can," he admitted. "What if..." Jesus. There were so many ways he could screw it up, including crossing that line between them, the line he'd crossed on her prom night.

"She came home for a reason. You're that reason. You know it. You've always been the only one who could reach her."

At Chase's words, something flickered to life inside Ryder. Hope. Faith. Something. "You think she came home for me?"

"Yeah. Be the guy she needs."

Ryder stood up and walked over to the window, looking out across the river, weighing those words. The sun was just starting to rise, casting faint orange hues across the Wyoming sky. "I don't know if I can get her to stay long enough to help her."

Chase chuckled. "Zoey's part of our family, bro. She always has been. You may have been the one she really connected with, but she was in the Stockton brother circle of protection. It's a team effort. We'll get her to stay in town. You help her heal."

The tension that had been gripping Ryder so tightly began to ease. "How are you going to convince her to stay?"

"Not me. We need to send in our big guns."

A slow smile spread across Ryder's face. "Damn, bro. You don't mess around."

"Never. Not when it's people I love." A little voice yelled "Daddy" in the background. "I gotta go. Listen, can we go over some things for the barn later today? I have some ideas."

The barn. The project he'd been planning to quit this morning so he could leave town, and leave Zoey behind. The project that would keep him in town most days once it got underway. In town, and sleeping in the same house as Zoey.

"Ryder? You're still in on the barn, right?"

He took a deep breath, then grinned. "Hell, yeah, I'm in."

CHAPTER EIGHT

THE HOUSE WAS quiet when Zoey finally ventured downstairs for breakfast the next morning.

She'd awoken tense and agitated, not wanting to see Ryder or Dane or anyone, so she'd laid in bed for a while, listening to make sure Ryder was gone and no one else had arrived.

The silence had convinced her she had the place to herself, time to get online, and figure out where she was going to go next. She'd put on the sweatpants and sweatshirt that Ryder had left for her, but gave up on socks or a bra since hers were stinky with smoke. She limped downstairs on her yay-not-broken ankle to try to find something to eat.

When she got down to the kitchen, however, she was unprepared for what she saw.

The kitchen was gorgeous with granite counters and beautiful wood cabinets, but that wasn't what made her stop. The room stretched across the back of the house, with huge windows opening to a breathtaking view of a river, endless blue sky, and limitless fields. It was pure Wyoming freedom, beautiful beyond words.

Her heart stuttered, and she walked across the kitchen,

stepping out onto a screened porch. The air was fresh and clean, crisp but not cold as it filled her lungs. There were blue wildflowers dotting the fields, and a few spots of white and yellow, the first signs of spring.

God, she'd forgotten about spring in Wyoming, about how the vast expanse of nature made her feel so small, and yet so unconstrained.

There were no sounds, except the rushing water. No cars. No sirens. No machinery. Just a quiet serenity that filled her with peace. So different than Boston, with its high energy, buzzing crowds, and constant motion.

She rested her palms on the screen and pressed her face against the mesh. "So beautiful," she whispered.

"Isn't it?" Ryder said.

She jumped and spun around, her breath catching as Ryder walked onto the porch, holding a neon yellow water bottle. He was in a pair of running shorts, a tech tee shirt, and running sneakers, with sweat glistening on his forehead. His thighs were corded, and his arms were chiseled muscle. He hadn't shaved, and his whiskers were thick on his face. He looked like pure testosterone, and she felt like whimpering. Damn him for being so freaking male!

She swallowed. "I thought you were gone for the day."

"Nope. Just went out for a run. Brilliant day out there." He took a long drink from his glass. "Got almost ten miles in. Nothing like a run when you got stuff on your mind." His gaze was intense, never wavering from her face. "How are you?"

She shrugged. "Fine." What did he have on his mind? Her?

"Your ankle?"

"Not bad."

He touched his forehead. "You're getting a bruise there."

"It hurts."

He walked across the porch, and she tensed as he neared, her breath quickening as he stopped in front of her. He raised his hand, brushing her hair back from her face as he peered at her wound. "It's a little swollen, but doesn't look infected." He grinned down at her. "You look like a fierce badass."

"I feel like a train wreck," she admitted.

He let his hand slide down to her shoulder and squeezed gently. "You've been through a rough time," he said quietly. "But you're strong."

"I know I'm strong, but—" She stopped, not wanting to get into it with him. If she were going to leave, she needed to stand on her own, not start leaning on him. "Is there something I can grab for breakfast?"

He didn't move. "But what?"

She wrinkled her nose at him. "I changed the subject because I didn't want to complete my thought."

"Yeah, I know, but I want to hear what you were thinking."

"You're super annoying."

He grinned. "Yeah, I get that a lot. So, you were saying... You know you're strong, but— what?"

She sighed. "I was just going to say that sometimes being strong might keep you going, but it can leave you feeling like an empty wasteland inside."

Pain flashed across Ryder's face. "Is that what you feel like? An empty wasteland?"

God, that sounded pathetic. "No, not at all. It was just a random analogy." She forced herself to duck away from his hand and head back into the kitchen. "So, where can I find food? Cereal, maybe? And do you have Wi-Fi? I want to figure out where I'm headed to."

"When are you leaving town?" he asked as he followed her back into the kitchen.

"Today," she said firmly.

He sucked in his breath, but turned away to open the fridge, so she couldn't see his face. "Is that so?"

"Yes." She noticed a coffee machine on the counter. "Can I make some coffee?"

"Sure. I don't know how to use it. Brody bought it, but I don't drink coffee."

"Brody?" She opened a couple cabinets, looking for coffee. "Who's that?"

"Brody Hart. My brother-in-law." He peered into the fridge. "Maddox married into a huge family."

Ah...Zoey remembered hearing about how Ryder's twin had married a woman with a big family, as well as a young daughter. So much had happened with the Stocktons in the time she'd been gone. "What's his wife's name again?"

"Hannah." Ryder pulled some eggs out of the fridge, then some cheese. "She grew up homeless, living under a bridge with about ten other kids. They gave themselves the last name of Hart, and bought a big ranch in Oregon that they all work together. They're good people."

Zoey's heart tightened. "Really? They were homeless? All of them?"

"Yep. They're extremely loyal to each other. Family by bond, not blood." The admiration in his voice was apparent, and Zoey smiled.

The Stockton brothers had had such a tough childhood, and they'd been ostracized by much of the town, but they stood by each other, no matter what. Once the Stocktons brought you into their circle of protection, it never wavered, which was how she'd gotten to know them. Dane had become friends with the Stocktons, which meant Zoey, as his little sister, was part of the gang. "I can see why you'd like them."

He nodded. "They're horse people, too."

"Really?" The Stocktons had lived in a run-down shack with their alcoholic dad and his string of women, but their salvation had been the time they'd spent on Ol' Skip's ranch. Even she had gone there to hide with the horses from time to time. "That's cool."

"Yep."

She glanced at him as she pulled a bag of coffee beans out of the cabinet. "Why did Brody buy coffee for your house?"

"It's his house, actually. The Stocktons and the Harts are starting a joint venture with some of their ranching business. The barn I'm overseeing is going to be the base of the new Stockton-Hart Ranch. Once it opens, there will be a lot of Harts in and out of Rogue Valley, so Brody bought this place. Makes it easier for them to come and go."

She frowned. "Are there any staying here now?" She so didn't want to have to deal with even more strangers.

"No, not this week." Ryder put some eggs and milk on the counter. "Want some French toast?"

Her heart tightened. "You still make it? The same way as before?"

"You bet." He held up a jar of cinnamon. "I still remember how you like it."

She smiled as he began to work on the eggs. "Thank you." How did he remember how she liked her breakfast? "I haven't had French toast in years."

"Then you're overdue." He winked at her as he got to work, singing her favorite country song from high school under his breath.

Her heart lifted, and she began to sing with him as she prepared the coffee. It was like they were teenagers again, their voices melding together so naturally. He grinned at her as he sliced a loaf of fresh bread. "We still got it," he said.

"We should have teamed up with Travis and gone pro," she said. She still couldn't believe that the youngest Stockton brother had become a country music superstar. Travis had always been talented, but to become a huge celebrity was amazing.

"Yeah, he'd be much more successful if we'd joined him, though. We totally let him down."

"Right?" Mugs. Where would mugs be? She turned around to check the cabinet, just as Ryder reached for a plate, and she ran into his arm. He caught her, and her heart leapt at the feel of his hand on her lower back.

They both froze, and her heart started hammering. They were so close. All he'd have to do was lean down, and his lips would be on hers.

"Dammit." She jumped back, twisting out of his way. She would not be that stupid again. She wouldn't. "Don't."

Frustration flashed across his face. "Sorry."

"It's fine. It's doesn't matter." She bent her head and focused on the coffee. "So, I'm going to stop by my old apartment to see what I can salvage this morning, then I'll start driving west. Maybe to Colorado? I've always wanted to see that part of the country." She had to get out of there soon, or she was going to pour herself into Ryder's arms and beg him to make everything better.

She couldn't do that. She had to find her way herself. *She had to.*

"You can stay here for as long as you want." Ryder's voice was casual.

She glanced over at him, but he was too busy sautéing the bread to notice. "I think my apartment burning up was a sign from the universe that I'm not supposed to stay in Rogue Valley."

He raised his brows. "Really?"

She nodded. "I need to leave. I don't belong here."

A muscle in his cheek ticked. "Where do you belong, then?"

"I don't know."

He glanced over at her. "Why not stay here while you figure it out?"

"Because staying here will suck me back into my past, into the pathetic, lonely, lost little girl that I once was." She tensed at the thought of staying here, of forcing her way back into the lives of people she didn't fit in with anymore...people who she'd never fit in with, actually. "I can't go back to that life, Ryder. I can't. Don't push me to stay. Please."

The muscle in his cheek flexed again, but he nodded. "I understand."

Relief rushed through her. He was going to give her space. "Thanks."

He nodded as he scooped the French toast off the pan. "So, you're leaving this morning, then?"

"Yes." But as she said it, she felt even emptier. Because she didn't know where to go? Because she was running, running, running, like she'd been doing for so long?

"Hello?" A woman's voice echoed through the house just as Ryder set their plates on the kitchen table. "Is anyone here?"

Zoey's stomach sank but Ryder's face lit up. "In the kitchen," he called out. "Come on back."

"Who is it?" Zoey stood awkwardly by the counter, waiting for the coffee to finish percolating.

"Lissa. Travis's wife. She owns the Wildflower Café you were at the other morning."

"Oh...right. I remember her." Before Zoey could duck upstairs, Lissa came into the room, holding several shopping bags.

"Good morning," Lissa said, beaming at both of them as she set the two shopping bags on the kitchen table. "Zoey, I heard your clothes got a little smoky last night, so I brought a bunch of stuff for you. You look like you're a little smaller than I am, so I brought you all the clothes from before I met

Travis." She patted her hips with a wink. "Being married has rounded me out. I call it love curves."

Zoey stared in surprise at the bags. "You brought me clothes?" She was so surprised that she didn't know what to say. How had Lissa even found out about the fire? And to think of her, knowing she would need clothes? It was so kind, so unbearably thoughtful that she wanted to cry. "Thank you," she whispered.

"Of course! You're family. Can't have you running around naked while you live with Ryder. It would be much too awkward, right?" She winked at Zoey as she sat down. "Can I have some? You know your French toast is my favorite meal in the world."

"Sure." He grinned as he slid a plate across the table. "Have a seat, Zoey. It's best when it's hot."

Reluctantly, Zoey nodded. "Want some coffee?"

"Yes, definitely. Is that Brody's blend? I love that kind he brings from Oregon. I'm considering adding it to my menu. It's that good." Lissa beamed at them both as they gathered their food and coffee and sat down. As soon as Zoey sat, Lissa turned to her. "So, listen, I need a favor from you, sister to sister."

Zoey shifted awkwardly. "We're not sisters."

"Of course we are! Your brother married my husband's sister. That's close enough for me." She paused to take a bite of the French toast, then sighed. "God, this is amazing, Ryder. You're sure you won't come cook for me?"

He grinned. "It's the only thing I make, but thanks."

Lissa wrinkled her nose and turned to Zoey. "So, this favor. I'm moving into the busy season, and the gal who helps me quit last week. Can you help me out until I find someone new? It shouldn't take more than a month or so?"

Zoey's gut froze. "Work for you? For a *month*?"

Lissa nodded. "Yep. I'm desperate. I'll pay you a fair wage, and you keep all the tips."

Zoey shifted in her chair. "I'm leaving town today."

"Really?" Lissa frowned. "Where are you going?"

"I don't know yet."

Lissa smiled and nodded. "I get it. That's how I ended up here when I was seventeen. I just left town and started driving."

Zoey frowned, surprised by the story. "You left home when you were seventeen?" She had too, but she'd headed off to college, not randomly driving around Wyoming.

"Yep. I was single, broke, pregnant, and disowned by my mom. It was a fun challenge, of course."

Zoey bit her lip, guessing that the sparkle in Lissa's eyes hadn't been there when she was seventeen. "I'm sorry." Seventeen, homeless, and pregnant? She couldn't imagine how much courage it had taken for Lissa to start a new life for herself. She felt so weak and pathetic in comparison.

Lissa shrugged. "Sometimes life knows that we have to get stronger before we can get happy." She leaned forward. "I totally understand that you need to keep going, but is there any chance you can delay your departure for a week or two? I'm really desperate. Family to family?"

Ryder kept his head down, focused on his French toast, giving her no out.

Zoey bit her lip. "I'd like to, but I really need to be on my way."

"How about just today, then? One day? That would give me time to try to find someone for tomorrow. Please?"

"I don't—" Zoey looked at the bags of clothes by her feet, thought of Lissa so desperate when she was a teenager, and suddenly, she didn't want to say no. She wanted to be around this woman who had strength that she didn't have, who was so *nice* to her. One day. How much would one day hurt? She sighed. "One day, I guess would be okay."

"Yay! You're the best!" Lissa leapt up and hugged her, a strong, enthusiastic hug that made Zoey smile. "How soon can you come in? I closed for an hour to come over here since it always gets slow mid-morning, but I'm opening back up as soon as I get back."

Zoey shrugged. "Not long. All I need to do is change my clothes."

"Fantastic! Thank you so much! Since today is Friday, I'm open until ten, so it will be a long day, but I promise I'll feed you!" Lissa slid the French toast onto a napkin. "I'll see you there." She kissed Ryder's cheek. "Thanks for breakfast, Ryder. See you later."

"Bye, Liss." He gave her a quick hug, then settled back down, grinning at Zoey. "That was really nice of you to help her out. She's a great person."

Zoey nodded, but something inside her was already starting to tighten up. There was no way she could leave town today if she was working until ten. She had to sleep here again, in Ryder's house. She sighed, trying to stay positive. "It was incredibly thoughtful of her to bring clothes for me."

Ryder leaned forward, his voice low. "What's wrong?"

Tears filled her eyes. "I don't know. I just... I don't know." She looked at him. "I feel like such a wreck. I don't know why. I mean, everything is okay, right? She brought me clothes. I have a place to stay. I'm not married to an asshole anymore. It's great. My life is great." But even as she pep-talked herself, a tear slipped free and trickled down her cheek.

He sighed and pressed his lips together as he gently thumbed her tear away.

Dammit. She didn't want to be like this, all weak and pathetic. She hadn't come back here to be a burden on anyone. She pulled away. "You know what? It's fine. I'm happy to help her out. It'll be fine. Everything's fine." She stood up, gripping her coffee. "I'll just change and go."

"Wait." Ryder caught her wrist, gently pulling her to a stop.

Zoey bit her lip and glanced at him. "What?"

"Meet me here after your shift? I have an idea."

Desperate hope leapt through her. "An idea for what?" Fixing the empty void inside her? A direction? A how-to guide on slapping some sense into her stupid head and getting herself back on track? Because those would be super helpful.

"It's a surprise."

She sighed. A new set of earrings wouldn't help. She'd already tried that. "What kind of surprise?"

He grinned. "Don't you trust me?"

She hesitated. She used to. Did she now?

Sadness flashed in his eyes. "Stupid question," he said softly. "I don't deserve your trust, I know. But it's a good surprise. Meet here after your shift?"

She managed a smile. "It'll be super late. I'm sure I'll be exhausted—"

"It's agreed, then. After your shift." He grabbed the bags of clothes. "If you aren't here, I'll track you down. You know I can find you anywhere, ZoeyBear, so don't test me."

She couldn't help the small smile as she followed him up the stairs. "It's kind of fun to test you."

"I know. Drives me nuts."

Her smile faded at his words. "Is that what happened? Do I drive you nuts?"

He stopped in her doorway and turned to face her. With a sigh, he dropped the bags on the floor and walked over to her. He slid his hands down her arms and encircled her wrists with his fingers. "We need to talk, don't we?"

Did she really want to know what had happened that

night? Yes. She needed to. Maybe resolution over that night would start a healing process that she couldn't seem to accomplish on her own. A large part of her didn't want to rehash a crappy night from a decade ago, but it would be a lie to say that it didn't still haunt her. Reluctantly, she nodded. Maybe that was why she'd come home. To face Ryder. To start at the beginning and heal. "I think that would be good."

He sighed. "Tonight."

"Can we do it now?" Otherwise, she'd be stressing about it all day. Was he going to say things that would wrench the knife into her heart more deeply? She wasn't sure there was anything he could say that would erase the pain. "Get it over with?"

He hesitated. "You have to leave soon. Lissa's expecting you."

"It's been ten years, Ryder. Just talk to me, for God's sake." She searched his face. "Just tell me. Right now. It's time."

He rubbed his fingers on the inside of her wrists, then finally sighed. "You deserve more than a rush job. Tonight. I swear."

She wrinkled her nose. "You're a pain in the ass."

"Yeah. But I'll tell you everything tonight."

She searched his face. "You promise?"

He met her gaze. "I promise."

She knew he meant it, and sudden fear gripped her. She was finally going to find out why the boy she'd loved, the only person in the world she'd ever allowed to get close to her, the only guy she'd ever trusted, had made love to her and then walked away without another word.

Could she handle the truth?

He pressed a kiss to her forehead. "Tonight, ZoeyBear," he said softly. "Tonight."

She was going to find out.

CHAPTER NINE

Twelve hours later, Zoey was beyond exhausted, and happy about it. Happy because it meant she would probably be able to sleep tonight, instead of lying awake all night, haunted by emotions she couldn't shake.

She could barely keep her eyes open as she drove along Ryder's driveway, her injured ankle was aching from waitress hell, and her throat was sore from talking all night. Not one Stockton had come in. No one she knew at all, despite the fact she'd grown up here. She'd been anonymous, practically running back and forth from the kitchen with food, too busy to think about anything but what the hell the customer had just asked her for.

It had been exhausting, but at the same time, it had been a beautiful relief to be so busy she didn't have time to dwell. She'd even found herself laughing a few times, sharing a moment with customers over french fries or a cheeseburger gone wrong.

Cleaning up with Lissa had been enjoyable, too. Lissa was fun, hard-working, and had a sense of humor that Zoey appreciated. She hadn't been friends with a woman for a long time, and it had felt good to be working side-by-side with her. Travis had been home with their daughter, so it had just been them. It hadn't taken Lissa's five million "thank you's" for Zoey to know that her help had made a difference tonight.

She'd mattered, and it felt good.

So, when Lissa had begged her to come back for the rest of the week to help out...well...she'd said yes.

Four more days in town. At the time, she'd almost leapt at the chance to lose herself in the distraction of waitressing, but once she'd gotten in the car and started driving, the high of the evening had quickly begun to fade.

Staying in town for a few more days hadn't seemed like such a bad idea at the time, but as Zoey drove toward the house and Ryder, the weight began to settle on her again.

What if tonight was terrible with him? What if she couldn't take staying in the same house with him afterwards? Was she going to sleep in her car?

She parked her car in front of the house and rested her arms on the steering wheel, staring at the lights blazing from inside the house. Was Ryder in there, waiting for her?

The front door opened, and he stepped out onto the front porch.

Her breath caught as he folded his arms and leaned against a pillar, waiting for her. He was wearing jeans and cowboy boots, his dark hair was reflecting the glow from the porch light, and his biceps were so freaking muscular. He was pure male, and her stupid heart did a little leap at the sight of him.

This was it.

Time to break down the walls that had stood between them for the last decade.

She took a deep breath, and then opened her car door. "Hi."

"Hi." His voice was low and rough, sliding under her skin

like the caress she'd dreamed of so many times when she was younger. "How was the night?"

"Long. Hard. A good distraction." Her sneakers crunched on the gravel as she walked toward him. "She talked me into another four days."

He smiled, that same adorable smile that used to make her feel so safe. "She's pesky like that. Every Stockton has spent many a day in that place helping out. I think she might actually avoid hiring actual staff so she has an excuse to keep us busy. Welcome to her family."

Zoey relaxed slightly at his easy tone. "Thanks. She's really nice."

"That she is." Ryder didn't move as she walked up the steps, blocking her path.

She stopped. "Are you going to let me in?"

"Yeah." He didn't move, though. He just studied her, searching her face as if her eyes held the answers to the questions he'd been asking his entire life. "Zoey," he said softly. "You're really here."

Her heart tightened. "Don't talk to me like that, Ryder. You're not allowed."

His brow furrowed. "Like what?"

"Like you care." She pushed him out of the way. "I'm going inside." She waited for him to stop her, but he didn't.

He just followed her into the house and closed the door behind them. "Want a drink?"

"No." She headed right for the stairs. "I'm tired. I'm going to bed."

His voice stopped her. "Zoey."

She closed her eyes but didn't turn around. "What?"

"Come to the porch for a moment."

She shook her head. "I don't want to do this anymore," she whispered. "Forget it."

He said nothing, but she heard his footsteps as he walked

up behind her. She tensed as he slid his fingers through hers. The feel of his hand around hers made her suck in her breath. Why did it feel so good to touch him? "Come on, ZoeyBear. I got you something."

She held herself rigid. "Can we do it in the morning?"

"Nope." He tugged gently on her hand. "Come on. You'll like it." Still gripping her hand, he began to back toward the porch, pulling her with him.

She opened her eyes with a sigh. "You're incorrigible."

He grinned, and she realized there was a sparkle in his eye, one she hadn't seen since she'd been back. "I am. I think you'll like this. Come on."

Realizing that resistance was futile, Zoey gave in and allowed him to lead her down the hall toward the kitchen. He stopped just before the porch door. "Close your eyes."

She raised her brows. "Seriously?"

"Yep." He grinned and wiggled his eyebrows at her.

She giggled at his goofiness, a tiny spark of excitement fluttering through her. "If I close my eyes, I might fall asleep on my feet."

"No problem. I work out. I could lift you with my left pinkie." He rolled his eyes impatiently. "Close your damn eyes, Wilson. I got shit to show you."

She burst out laughing and closed her eyes. "Fine. You're so bossy."

"Damn straight I am." He set his hands on her shoulders. "Walk forward, hot stuff. I'll direct you."

She settled into the strength of his hands and started walking, limping slightly. "Don't drive me into a wall."

"Damn. You ruined the surprise. I guess I'll have to come up with something else. Watch the carpet."

She lifted her foot high enough to clear the edge of the rug. "It's kind of chilly out here."

"It's Wyoming spring. What do you expect? This ain't the

tropics of Boston, girl." He stopped her. "Okay. Hold out your hand."

"Should I be scared?" She put her hand out, palm up.

"Probably." He set something in her hand, but she couldn't tell what it was. "Okay. Go for it."

She opened her eyes and looked down. In her hand was a paintbrush, the same kind he'd bought her as a sweet sixteen birthday present. Back then, it had been the most beautiful, most expensive, most thoughtful gift she'd ever received. Her heart clenched, and she looked up at him. "I don't paint anymore," she said reluctantly. "I don't even own a canvas."

He grinned and gestured to his right.

Her gaze jumped in that direction, and then she gasped. An easel was set up by the back wall, with a large canvas on it. In front of it was a tall stool, and on a table to the left were more paint brushes, a palette, and her favorite paint. It was set up so she could look across the river and plains and paint the scene that had taken her breath away earlier that morning.

"Oh, Ryder." She breathed his name, too stunned to say anything more. His thoughtfulness was overwhelming.

His face softened. "Go check it out."

Fighting against the almost insurmountable need to cry, she silently walked over to it and spread her palm tentatively across the canvas, feeling the fabric under her fingers. She could almost feel how alive it was, begging to be brought to life with magic that had once been a part of her. "It's beautiful," she whispered.

"Painting used to make you smile," Ryder said quietly. "I was hoping it would help you find your smile again."

At his words, tears filled her eyes. "Is it that obvious?" she asked. She tried to hide it. To be strong.

"To me, yeah."

She looked over at him. "I stopped painting because the

pictures wouldn't come anymore," she admitted. "I would sit there at the easel, and nothing would happen. Eventually, I just stopped trying." She picked up a tube of paint, waiting for images to flash through her mind of what that paint wanted to be, but there was nothing. Just...nothing. She looked at him. "Still nothing." Where had her spark gone? She needed to find it so desperately.

He sighed and held out his hand. "Come sit. We need to talk."

She tensed. "About prom night?"

"Yeah." He continued to hold his hand out to her. "It's time."

For a long moment, she didn't move. Now that the chance for the truth was here, she was suddenly afraid.

"We need to do this," he said quietly. "We both do."

She met his gaze, and saw the raw pain in them, pain that surprised her. Had that night been haunting him all this time as well? God, how stupid they'd been to let one night mean so much. He was right. It was time to let it go. She put her hand in his. "Okay."

CHAPTER TEN

"I'M AN ASS."

Zoey almost laughed at the serious expression on Ryder's face as he sat across from her at the kitchen table. "That's not an excuse, Ryder."

He ran his hand through his hair, shifting restlessly. She was surprised at how tense he was. She'd thought he hadn't given her a thought since she'd left, but she was beginning to think she was wrong.

"No, it's not an excuse. It's a reason."

She frowned. "What do you mean?"

He stood up and paced across the kitchen. His shoulders were taut, and his jaw was flexing. When he reached the far side of the kitchen, as distant as he could get and still be in the same room, he turned to face her. "You were eighteen. Innocent. I stole that."

She leaned back in her chair, watching him. "Innocent? Really?"

"Yeah."

She leaned forward. "Here's how I see it. My parents died in a wreck when I was seven. I barely remember them, but I remember my uncle and how he would look at me. I know why you and your brothers and Dane slept in my room. I knew what you were protecting me from."

He looked at her sharply. "He didn't—"

"No, because you never let him." Sadness filled her heart. "I saw the rages your dad went into. I saw the cigarette burns on your arms from your dad. I saw the string of women who lived in your house after your mom died. I saw the anger and fury in your eyes, and those of your brothers. Innocence died for me when my parents died, Ryder. Hanging out with the Stocktons opened my eyes even more. I was far from innocent on the night of my prom."

Ryder rubbed his hand over his forearm, where a tattoo of an eagle now covered the marks his father had left on him. "You were a virgin."

She sighed. "Yes, this is true."

He stalked back across the room and perched on the edge of a chair. "You were this innocent, ebullient, sassy kid. You were like my little sister, and I would have gone after anyone who hurt you. When you were ten, and I was a fucked-up sixteen-year-old, you were the only thing that got me off my shit. If I hadn't had to make sure you were safe, I would have gone off drinking or turned to drugs to get away from the monster in my head, but I knew that if I was fucked up, no one would look out for you." He searched her face. "You saved me, Zoey. Without you, I would have followed my dad into hell."

Her throat tightened. She knew none of the Stockton brothers ever drank alcohol because of their dad, but she hadn't known that Ryder had abstained for her. "I didn't know I was helping you."

"You saved me."

His words were simple, but they made her eyes get a little teary. "I'm glad I was able to give you something back. You gave me safety, and I treasured that." She thought of how Ryder's fury and anger had made her feel safe. It was never directed at her. Instead, it surrounded her with a shield that no one would dare penetrate. "So, why did you walk away after prom night?"

He swore under his breath and got up, pacing away from her again.

She draped her arm across the back of her chair and turned to watch him, surprised by the level of tension radiating through him. He'd fought through a lot of tough stuff as a kid, but since she'd been back, he'd seemed more chill and relaxed, but right now, she could feel those same emotions rumbling beneath the surface.

He stood in front of the sink, his hands clasped on top of his head. "You were Dane's little sister. That's how I always thought of you. My friend's little sister. When he said that you weren't going to the prom because no one would go with you, I got pissed. What the fuck was wrong with the kids that no one could see how amazing you were?"

She smiled, remembering his prom offer. "You stormed into my room, said that all the kids in my class were stupid fucks, and you were taking me to my damn prom, and then left."

He grimaced. "Yeah, it was classy, right?"

"It was you. It was perfect."

He let out his breath. "Here's the thing, Zoey. When I made the offer, it was to my best friend's little sister. But Dane came to me the next day and he said..." He swore. "He said that you were falling in love with me, and I had to back off. He was worried you would decide to give up your scholarship to Harvard and stay in town to be with me."

Zoey blinked. "Dane said that?"

"Yeah." Ryder walked back over and sat down again at the table. "Here's the thing, Zoey. Before Dane told me that, I'd never thought about you romantically. I was six years older than you were. You were a kid. But when he said that, he put something in my head, and when you walked out the door in that dress on prom night." He shook his head. "You were a fucking goddess. In that moment, you were no longer a kid. You were the most beautiful, most amazing woman and all I wanted to do was make you mine."

She blinked, her cheeks heating up at the roughness in his voice. "Really?"

"Yeah." He leaned forward. "I seduced you that night, Zoey. I knew I was going to have you. I *had* to have you."

"You didn't seduce me," she said. "I wanted you. I chose that dress on purpose—"

"No. You were an eighteen-year-old innocent. I was a twenty-four-year-old fuck-up who had no business seducing a girl whose destiny was to become more than the salvation of some bastard pig who would never be good enough for her."

The venom in his voice was startling, both in its intensity, and how it was directed at himself. "Ryder—"

"No." He held up his hand to silence her. "I need to finish."

She bit her lip and nodded. "Okay."

"When we were lying there after we made love, you were in my arms, your head on my chest. I could feel the beat of your heart against my ribs. You were so small and vulnerable, your skin so smooth and pure compared to all the scars on mine. You smelled like lilacs. It was the best moment of my entire fucking life. I lay there, holding you, and, then this thought went through my mind."

She remembered that moment, lying there with him, feeling the strength of his body surrounding her. She'd never forget it. She'd never felt that sense of rightness again. "What thought?"

He met her gaze. "I wanted more. I wanted that moment again and again and again. I wanted you to save me. "

Her heart started to pound. "Really?"

"Yeah." His blue eyes were intense and turbulent, churning with self-hate. "I wanted you to give up college and stay in Rogue Valley with me. I wanted that so badly that I started to panic at the idea of you leaving me."

She couldn't believe what he was saying. "Why didn't you tell me?"

He met her gaze. "You had a chance to get out of the hell that we all grew up with. You had a full-ride to Harvard. I was...I was nothing more than a demon who would destroy you if I kept you." He shrugged. "My only chance to set you free was to walk away. Otherwise, I'd keep you. If I let myself decide to keep you, it wouldn't have mattered if you wanted to leave. I would have found a way to destroy your dreams and trap you in my hell."

Shock rippled through her as she stared at him. "I would have stayed for you," she whispered. "If you'd shown me *any* of that, I would have stayed."

He nodded. "I knew that."

She leaned back, stunned by his words. What if he'd told her? What if she hadn't left? "Did it ever occur to you that I could have made my own choice?"

He met her gaze. "You would have chosen me, and I couldn't let you do that."

"Why not?"

"Because you were special. I was poison."

A tear slipped out of her eyes and strayed down her cheek. "Poison? How can you say that? You were my guardian angel."

He was quiet for a moment, then he looked at her. "If your mom had still been alive when you were eighteen, what would she have wanted for you? To attend Harvard and follow your dreams? Or to give that up, get a minimum wage job at a convenience store in Rogue Valley, and marry a man who came from violence, alcoholism, and anger? What would she have wanted for you?"

Zoey sat back, her heart tightening. She didn't have to think about it. She knew. "Harvard," she whispered.

He inclined his head. "I wanted Harvard for you, too, Zoey. And so did you, even if you were too young to realize it."

She swallowed, biting back tears. Was he right? Had she used his rejection all these years as an excuse to doubt herself and hate her only friend, when he'd actually given her exactly what she would have wanted?

Ryder leaned toward her, searching her face. "I have to ask you something."

She nodded, wiping the back of her hand across her cheek. "Sure."

"Now that it's ten years later, and you saw how your life turned out, do you wish you hadn't gone to Harvard? Do you wish you'd stayed here?"

She closed her eyes at the question, reliving all the anguish over the last few years. The betrayal by Nathan on so many levels. The slow destruction of her soul. How lost she felt.

And then, she thought of the joys of learning, of growing since she'd left Rogue Valley. How empowering it had been to find a huge world opening up to her through her professors, her classmates, and the city of Boston. The wonder of becoming so much more than she ever would have been if she'd never left. Would she have traded all of that to avoid the pain? To have had a chance to stay in Rogue Valley with the boy she'd loved with all her heart?

She wanted to say yes.

She wanted to say she'd loved Ryder so much that she'd been willing to give it all up for him.

There were so many nights she'd huddled in bed, aching for a sense of belonging, one that she'd never found, except when she was hiding in the circle of Ryder's arms.

Hiding. That was the operative word, the one that scared her the most, her need to hide instead of fight.

She'd hidden behind Ryder her whole childhood, and for the last ten years she'd never forgiven him for stealing that shield from her and making her face life on her own. All she'd wanted to do was hide, and she hadn't found anyone willing to let her hide behind them except Ryder.

She wanted to tell him yes, she wished she'd stayed, because otherwise, she'd have to admit to herself that the last ten years of bitterness she'd lived with since he'd ghosted her had been nothing but an excuse to keep from living.

But as she sat there across from him, could she keep telling herself that she wished she'd had the chance to remain the scared, fragile girl who'd hidden behind him?

She let her breath out.

No. She couldn't.

She had no idea who she was supposed to be now, but the one thing she had to admit to herself, finally, was that she didn't wish she'd stayed who she once was.

Leaving Ryder and the town behind was the only way she could have changed.

The only way.

She opened her eyes and looked at him, at the deep blue of his eyes, searching hers. "For ten years, I hated you for dumping me after prom night."

He nodded.

"I didn't think there was anything you could say that could pry that hate out of me. There was no excuse you could give that could make it okay."

Regret flickered in his eyes.

She took a deep breath. "But now..." She sighed and met his gaze. "I can't blame you anymore," she said softly. "I have to let it go, because you're right."

His eyebrows went up. "About which part?"

"I would have stayed with you if you'd given me the chance." She let out her breath, a deep sigh that seemed to strip away a decade of anger and regret and blame. "And that would have been the wrong choice."

CHAPTER ELEVEN

Ryder felt like he'd been punched.

He jerked back, almost flinching at her words.

As broken as Zoey was right now, she would still have chosen the hell of the last decade over being with him.

Wow.

"Ryder?" Zoey frowned at him. "Are you okay?"

"Yeah, sure." He gripped his hands beneath the table. Her answer made it clear he'd done the right thing to let her leave. It should feel like a relief that the doubt was gone, but it didn't. It felt wrong, wrong, *wrong.* "So you don't hate me anymore?"

She smiled faintly. "No." She sighed. "It actually feels like this huge weight has been lifted off my shoulders."

"Does it?" He felt like he couldn't breathe. Remembering how intensely he'd felt about her, how it had been to hold her in his arms after lovemaking, how deeply he'd needed her...it had brought back emotions he'd forgotten. A need. A need that was still there, burning inside him.

"Yeah. It's exhausting to convince yourself to hate someone you love." Her smile became stronger. "It's like I'm finally free from the stories I told myself about that night. I used it as an excuse to feel powerless and angry, and miserable, and now..." She shrugged. "You've taken that away."

He raised his brows. "That's good?"

She nodded. "I obsessed over how stupid I had been to trust you. I thought that I'd misjudged your feelings for me. I never would have slept with you if I'd thought you didn't love me, but when you walked away like that..." She shrugged. "I thought it was because I didn't mean anything to you. I felt like an idiot. I felt betrayed."

He pressed his lips together and nodded.

"But now I know that I wasn't stupid, or used, or taken advantage of." She reached across the table and held out her hand to him. "We loved each other, in whatever way we were capable of at the time. We both suffered from that night," she said gently. "But now we can put it behind us. We loved each other, and we had the moment we were meant to have, and then we had to go live our lives."

He didn't take her hand. He couldn't. *Put it behind them?* It was raging through him right now like a fucking inferno.

Her brow furrowed. "Ryder?"

He cleared his throat and dragged his hand out from under the table and took her outstretched hand in his. Her fingers were warm and soft, and his entire gut clenched at the feel of their hands intertwined. "Yeah. It's good. Move on and that shit."

"Yeah." She took a deep breath. "I can't even tell you how much better I feel. This weighed on me all the time, and now it's just gone." She met his gaze. "The worst feeling in the world was to lie in bed at night, have my thoughts stray to you, and to believe that the person I trusted most in the entire world had betrayed me."

Jesus. "I'm so sorry—"

"No." She shook her head. "You didn't betray me. I wasn't

wrong to trust you." She looked down at their joined hands. "I get to trust you again, and that is the greatest gift."

He nodded. "I'd never betray you, Zoey. Ever."

"I know." She squeezed his hand. "I didn't know why I came home, until now. It wasn't because I wanted to move back. It was because I needed to heal the scars of that night before I could fix anything else."

"And they're healed? Just like that?" Because his scars sure as hell weren't healed. If anything, they were worse after this conversation.

"Not entirely, but it's a start." She held out her arms. "Hug me, Ryder."

With a low growl, he pushed back his chair and stood up. She jumped up, wrapped her arms around him, and buried her face against him.

Ryder took a deep breath as she settled against him. Her breath was warm against his neck. Her breasts crushed against his chest. Her arms tight around him. *Jesus*. He pressed his face into her hair and breathed in. She still smelled like lilacs. He tightened his arms around her, holding her tighter.

She wasn't eighteen anymore.

He wasn't twenty-four.

They were both older, battered, and bruised by life.

But the way he felt when he held her in his arms that night hadn't changed.

No, he was wrong. It had changed. It had become a thousand times more intense.

But what hadn't changed was who he was, a man who even Zoey agreed she was better off without. Poisoned by the Stockton blood in his veins.

"I missed my best friend," she whispered, her voice muffled by his chest.

He closed his eyes. A best friend.

Fuck friendship. He wanted more. He needed more. He needed *everything*.

Swearing, he released her suddenly and stepped back. Sweat was beading on his brow. "So, we're good, then?"

She nodded. "I need you, Ryder. Will you help me?"

"Help you?"

"Help me find my way back." She searched his face. "I need to find myself, Ryder. I don't want to make friends here. I don't want to get involved in a relationship. I need to...I don't know...somehow find a way back to my life in Boston, the one I used to like. I don't know how to do it, but you might. Will you help? You're the only one who knows me. The only one I trust."

She didn't want a relationship. She was glad she'd gone through hell instead of staying in Rogue Valley with him. She wanted him to help her get back to her life. In Boston.

She wanted him to help her leave him.

He let out his breath. He'd helped her leave him once. It had not gone well.

This time?

He stood there, looking into her eyes, as she asked for his help. Those green eyes that used to sparkle with mischief and delight. Those green eyes that used to search for him when he'd climb in her window. Those green eyes that used to follow him around the room whenever they were together.

Where was the sparkle? The light? The one she used to shine on him?

How could he say no? He couldn't. He'd help her leave him, because he had to.

He sighed. "I'll help."

Her face lit up. "Really?"

He froze, shocked by the expression on her face. Relief. Hope. Happiness. The first spark of life he'd seen since she'd been back.

Realization rocked him back. Son of a bitch. *Son of a bitch.* His mind leapt back in time, over the years, to this moment, to that moment, frantically cataloging events until there was no doubt in his mind.

All the sparkles he'd worked so hard to protect over the years? The light in her eyes that made her shine? The only time he'd ever seen it was when she'd been with him.

Son of a bitch.

He was the source of her light. *He* was what made her shine. *He* was what she needed. He, the guy who was poison, darkness, and hell, was her light.

Jesus.

Dane was wrong. He'd been wrong. Ryder wasn't her *darkness*. He was her *light*. How was that possible? It wasn't, and yet...it was.

She frowned. "Ryder? You don't want to help me? I totally understand if it's too weird."

He looked at her, at those beautiful eyes, and he knew. He wasn't going to help her get back to Boston. He was going to help her heal...and then he was going to keep her.

Somehow. Someway. He was going to find a way to become the man she deserved, and prove it to both of them. He'd never trap her, he'd never force her, he'd never take away her freedom of choice, but somehow, someway, he was going to find a way to make it happen between them...and he had to do it fast, because she'd made it clear that she was on her way out the door as soon as she could manage it.

She dropped her hands from his arms. "Never mind—"

"No." He caught her wrist, encircling it gently, so as not to scare her. "I'm here for you, Zoey. You got me."

Her face lit up again. "Really?"

He grinned. "Hell, *yeah*."

She had *no* idea.

CHAPTER TWELVE

WHEN ZOEY AWOKE at five o'clock the next morning to get ready for work, there was a lightness in her heart that hadn't been there in a very long time.

Ryder hadn't rejected her.

Instead, he'd loved her so much that he'd freed her.

She peered at herself in the bathroom mirror, staring into her own eyes. How much sadness she'd seen in them over the years. Loneliness. Fear. Excuses.

But today, for the first time, there was a sliver of hope. The tiniest little sliver of hope. Hope that she could find her way forward. That she could feel better. That she could find her way to the life she'd tried to build for herself, and find the joy that she'd never quite been able to access.

She now felt the tiniest thread of hope that she could become strong enough to stand on her own feet and claim her own life. Not through a man. Not through anyone but herself. She saw now that she'd hidden behind Ryder since she was little. After she'd moved to Boston, she'd hidden behind Nathan.

And now...she needed to learn to stand on her own.

She took a deep breath, and braced her hands on the sink, searching her face. "I am strong," she whispered.

A ripple of energy sparked inside her.

She said it again, this time, a little louder. "I am strong."

More energy. Almost excitement.

"I am strong!" She almost shouted it, and banged her fists on the sink. The words seemed to echo in the bathroom, repeating themselves as they faded.

"Hey!" Someone banged on her door. "Everything okay in there?"

She froze, startled by the unfamiliar male voice. There was a *man* in the house? "Who's there?" she asked.

"Brody Hart. Who are you?"

Brody? It took a few seconds for her to remember what Ryder had told her about the Harts, and that Brody owned the house. Shit. What if he didn't want her there? She quickly pulled her sweatshirt on and hurried out of the bathroom, across her room, and opened her door.

Standing in the hall was a man who was pure cowboy, muscle, and brawn. Brody was tall, well over six feet. His jeans sat loose on his narrow hips, but his tee shirt showed off chiseled muscles in his upper body. He was wearing a black cowboy hat, well-worn boots, and his belt buckle had a logo with two horses entwined around an H and an E, which she was guessing stood for Hart Enterprises, or something like that. He was pure male, and his eyes were dark and assessing as he studied her. "And you are?" he prompted.

"Zoey Wilson. Dane's sister. My apartment burned up yesterday and Ryder offered me a room here. I can leave if you want—"

A smile lit up his face. "Family is always welcome," he said. "It's great to meet you." He held out his hand. "Brody Hart."

She was startled by how friendly he was. His smile was

warm and genuine, his gaze steady and welcoming, although she could see the dark shadows in his eyes, ones that seemed to be etched permanently there. "Thanks." She shook his hand, and his grip was strong and firm, his skin just rough enough to tell her he was a man who wasn't above hard work.

"Want some coffee?" he asked. "I was just heading down to make some."

"Um, sure." She glanced at Ryder's door, which was still closed. "Ryder said you weren't in town. When did you get in?"

"Just arrived about an hour ago."

She blinked. It was five in the morning. He'd arrived in the middle of the night? "Did you drive?"

"No. Flew. It's faster." He grinned at her. "Welcome back, Zoey. I've heard a lot about you."

She smiled back, surprised at how relaxed he made her feel. She didn't usually feel comfortable around strangers, but there was something about Brody that made her feel like she belonged. "It's all lies," she teased. "I'm really not such a bad person."

"No? You're pure trouble." Ryder walked out of his bedroom, wearing only a pair of sweats, as if he'd yanked them on and rushed out into the hall. She caught her breath at the sight of him. She might have thought Brody was chiseled, but Ryder was pure heat. His abs were defined, his stomach completely taut. His hair was tousled, standing straight up, and he looked disheveled and adorable.

He walked right over to her, slid his arm around her shoulders, and pulled her up against his side, so the heat of his body was burning through her sweatshirt. "Brody, this is Zoey Wilson. She's been the love of my life since she was six years old, so don't fuck with her or I'll have to kill you."

She was so startled by his comment that she glanced at

him. He winked at her, which then made her unsure if he was kidding or not.

Brody's eyebrows shot up. "Well, damn, bro. That's good to know." He grinned at Zoey. "Coffee, you said?"

She nodded. "That would be great."

"Excellent. Ryder? You come around yet or are you still in denial that coffee is one of the Seven Wonders of the World?"

"None, thanks."

"Why don't you go get dressed, bro? I'll take care of Zoey." Brody held out his arm. "Let's go drink, Ms. Wilson. You can give me the inside scoop on the Stockton youth so I can ruthlessly manipulate them into doing what I want."

Zoey grinned and ducked out from under Ryder's arm so she could slide her hand through Brody's elbow. "Sounds good. I have lots of stories."

"I bet you do." Brody winked at Ryder as he led her away, and Zoey couldn't help but look back at Ryder.

He was standing there with his hands on his hips, his eyes narrowed thoughtfully as he watched them walk away.

Her heart fluttered. She knew that look. Ryder was planning something. But what?

CHAPTER THIRTEEN

"In love, huh?" Brody nudged him.

Ryder didn't look up from the plans that were spread over Chase's dining room table, ignoring the man who had become family when Hannah had married a Stockton. "I was twelve. She was six. I was from hell. She was sunshine." He was not interested in getting Brody and Chase involved in his situation with Zoey

Once Dane found out he was pursuing her, he risked forever severing his relationship with Dane...and Jaimi. Since the Stocktons had learned about Jaimi only a year ago, he had a lifetime to make up for in getting to know his sister.

Was Ryder willing to risk all of that, his best friend and his sister, to make Zoey his?

The answer had seemed obvious last night.

It had seemed even more obvious when he'd walked out of his room this morning and seen Brody checking out Zoey.

Now? It had taken only driving by Dane and Jaimi's house on the way to this meeting to remind him of what he stood to lose. Family. His sister. His best friend. Potentially driving a wedge between Dane and his entire family.

The cost of pursuing Zoey romantically had loomed large and ugly.

"That's love," Brody said. "*In* love is different. This morning, you said she was the love of your life. That sounds like *in love* to me."

"What are you guys talking about?" Chase looked up from the plans.

Brody grinned. "Ryder. He said he's been in love with Zoey since she was six."

"Oh, that. Yeah, he has." Chase grinned. "He used to sleep on her floor every night. He couldn't sleep if he wasn't near her."

"Really?" Brody raised his brows. "That's adorable."

"She was in a dangerous situation. What else was I going to do? She was my best friend's little sister." Dane had stood by him so many times over the years. Was he really willing to betray him? *Shit.*

"What about now?" Chase challenged.

"She's a friend in need." He pointed to the lower right quadrant of the designs, trying to get their attention off of him and Zoey. He was on edge, big time. What the hell was he going to do? There was something burning inside him, a need for her that was so visceral that he could barely contain it. And at the same time...he'd learned his lessons about what mattered in life. Family. "I'm still not sure about the indoor arena. I feel like we need two smaller ones, instead of one big one. It gives us more flexibility."

Chase ignored him. "How is it going with her?"

"Fine. We had a good talk last night." Ryder tapped the plans again. "I think having some sleeping quarters above the barn makes sense. We need more than that bunkhouse on Chase's property, with all the Harts coming in, along with Logan and Quintin." Logan and Quintin were the only two Stocktons who hadn't moved back to town.

"And Caleb," Chase said. "He'll be back."

Caleb, who no one had heard from in almost nine years now. No one even knew where he lived...or even if he was still alive. "Maybe." Ryder was beginning to doubt it.

"Your family's bonds are strong," Brody said. "Those don't die. If he's alive, he'll be back."

Ryder glanced at Brody. The man had a dark side to him that every Stockton could recognize, because they all had it, too. But Brody was intensely loyal to his family, and that was a trait that every Stockton valued. The Hart family loyalty was what had created that bond between them and the Stock-tons. The Stocktons had survived hell because they had each other's backs. Brody was the same with his family. Ryder and his brothers trusted no one except Dane...until the Harts.

Ryder had met all the Harts at Hannah and Maddox's wedding, but he didn't know most of them well. He knew Brody was solid, though, as were Keegan, Lucas, and Jacob. Those four? He trusted. The others he didn't know well, but he'd be willing to wager they were fucked up, but loyal as all hell. "Are your sisters like you?"

Brody raised his brows. "Like what?"

He shrugged. "Like us."

Brody's face darkened with regret, but he nodded. "Yeah."

The three men looked at each other across the table. All of them had childhoods that had been about pain and survival, instead of love. They'd all fought to live, to survive, to protect those they loved, even though they'd all been in situations where protecting was impossible. Ryder wondered which was worse, living in his dad's house and getting the shit kicked out of him, like he and his brothers had, or living under a bridge and creating a family from survival, like the Harts had.

Didn't matter.

It was what it was.

Chase tapped the plans. "You see anything else you want in the plans? Anything we're missing?"

"No. It's good." It was a modern barn that far eclipsed what they had on Chase's ranch at the moment. They'd have space to train lots of horses, there was a surgical center for Steen's wife, Erin, and they had state-of-the-art facilities in every way. Ryder specialized in high-end barns, but this was the best he'd ever done.

He had money. Chase had money. Travis had money. Some of his other brothers did too, but it was the Harts who had poured funds into it. The Harts had turned street kids into cowboys into billionaires who wore faded jeans, old cowboy boots, and a distrust of everyone...except the start of the bond with the family their sister had married into.

The Harts were a bunch of antisocial bastards who were too fucked up to live any kind of a normal life. Ryder's kind of peeps.

"There's one more thing we need to add," Brody said. "A late addition."

Ryder and Chase looked at him. "What is it?" The excavation was scheduled to start in a week. If it was a major change, Ryder needed to know now.

"Keegan wants a bakery," Brody said.

Ryder blinked. "A bakery?"

"Yeah. He wants to expand to the West, and this is a good base of operations."

"A bakery?" Ryder repeated. "A bakery on a *horse ranch*?"

Brody met his gaze. "Yeah. Baking helps him. He doesn't want a huge one. Just one big enough to do his thing. A boutique bakery. Maybe ten employees max."

Ryder took a deep breath and exchanged glances with Chase. They both knew what Brody meant. When the nightmares came, when the anger became too much, they all had to find something to deflect it, to allow them to stay in control.

As kids, it had been the horses for both the Stocktons and the Harts. For Keegan, apparently, it had also been baking. For Ryder, it had been the horses...and Zoey. She had been that anchor for him, until she'd left.

Zoey. What was he going to do about her?

"I'm fine with a bakery," Chase said. "As long as I can use it, too."

Brody looked surprised. "You bake?"

"I'm a pie genius." Chase nodded at Ryder. "All my brothers are."

"Pies." Brody looked back and forth between them, and then started to laugh. "Jesus. You guys bake *pies?*"

Chase shrugged. "Yeah."

Brody grinned. "Damn. I knew I liked you guys. Now I know why. Fucking *bakers*." He tapped a spot on the plans that was about a good distance from the barn. "I was thinking here for the bakery."

Ryder studied it, then nodded. "That works. We can still break ground on the barn next week while we work on plans for the bakery." A *bakery* by men like them. A *boutique* bakery on top of it. It was irony at its best, but at the same time, it made sense. One of his few decent memories from the house of hell they'd grown up in was when Chase had corralled them all into the kitchen to make a Thanksgiving pie for Ol' Skip and his wife, as thanks to the old couple for allowing a bunch of hooligan kids to run wild on their farm.

A bakery. It made sense.

The three of them spent a while longer discussing the bakery, and then Ryder added to his list to get updated plans from the architect. He was just rolling the plans up when he felt Brody studying him. He raised his brows. "What's up?"

"Zoey."

Chase looked over at them, as Ryder stiffened. "What about her?"

"You got something going on with her?"

His fingers tightened around the rolled-up plans. "Why?"

"Because I like her. If you don't want her, I'm going all in on her."

Something flashed dark and ugly inside Ryder, the kind of darkness that had ruled their lives when their father had been alive. It was hard, angry, and violent, rising up so fast that he stepped back quickly, even as his fist balled.

Shit. *Shit.*

Chase swore under his breath, watching his face.

Brody held up his hand. "It's cool. I get it. I won't move in." But his voice was slightly cooler than it had been.

Ryder ground his jaw and forced his hands to relax. Jesus. How fast had his dad risen inside him at that one remark? Was that what would happen once he decided to make Zoey his? That he'd turn into his dad?

Poison. Dane had said he was *poison.*

What the fuck was he doing, deciding to go after Zoey? Dragging her into his hell? He ran his hands through his hair, trying to catch his breath. There was too much at stake, too much to lose. Too many to hurt.

"Hey." Chase frowned at him. "Take it down a notch, bro."

Ryder stepped back. "I can't do this. I can't—"

"Yes, you can."

Brody's hands went up. "I won't interfere. She's yours—"

"She's not mine. Shit." Ryder gripped the back of the chair, trying to calm down.

Chase leaned over him, resting his hand on the back of his shoulders. "She's always been yours, bro. It's okay."

He looked up at his brother. "It's not okay. Dane said—"

Brody interrupted. "What do you want?"

Ryder looked at him. "What?"

Brody sat down and folded his arms over his chest. "What do you want? It's a simple question."

"I don't know—"

"Yeah, you do. What do you want?"

"Her. I want her!" The moment he said the words, Ryder tensed. They were his truth. His fucking truth. Jesus. "I want her." He whispered the words, his gut clenching as he owned the words that he'd denied his whole fucking life. He looked at his brother in desperation. "Fuck."

Chase grinned. "It's okay."

"It's not." Jesus. Dane. Jaimi. *Zoey.* "You saw what just happened. Brody said one fucking thing and I almost lost my shit." He bowed his head, trying to calm down. "I can't do this to her." But even saying that felt wrong. He was her light. But he was also her darkness. How could he be both?

Brody leaned back and clasped his hands behind his head. "I call it the curse of darkness. We all have it."

Ryder looked at Brody. "What are you talking about?"

"The curse of darkness. We're all so fucked up that we don't believe in light. In love." The lines on his face deepened. "I believe that's crap. That's why I fought for Hannah and Maddox to work out. Because if she can find happiness, if she can find love, then it's proof that we all can." He leaned forward. "We all need to believe there's a chance for us, or the darkness will swallow us up. You're no different, Ryder. We fucking need that light, or we'll all die."

Ryder stared into Brody's face, and he saw a darkness that was even deeper than his own. A hopelessness that mirrored that which stalked him. A belief that there was no way out for people like them.

Chase believed there was a way out, because he'd found

Mira. But Brody was still alone, still being haunted by his past. In that moment, Ryder felt that connection to Brody that he couldn't find with his own brother, because Brody hadn't found his way out yet either.

Brody met his gaze. "We all deserve light, Ryder. Every last fucked up one of us, no matter what we've done to survive. I believe it."

"You're alone. You haven't found light."

Brody shrugged. "Just because we deserve it doesn't mean we'll find it before it's too late to save us. But with Zoey, if you've got a chance, you gotta grab for that life preserver before you drown. For all of us."

Ryder gripped the chair and rocked back and forth. He wanted Zoey with every piece of his soul. But how could he claim her? "I won't drag her down with me," he said. "I can't." But even as he said it, that voice in his head said the same thing. *I am her light.*

But he was also pure darkness.

Brody leaned forward, his voice low. "The shit I have done in my life to keep my family safe would revile you. You were an innocent victim, but I was the one who *did* those kinds of things. That makes me so much worse than you, Ryder, but I did it because I *love* my family. That makes me worthy. If there's someone out there who can handle who I am, I deserve her, and you're no different."

Ryder stared at Brody, something rising to life inside him at his words. Something that resonated at the truth. Something that made him hate the voices in his head that had been haunting him his whole life, the ones who had ruthlessly taunted him, screaming in his father's voice about what a bastard he was.

Tonight, for the first time, those voices felt like lies.

He looked at Chase. "If I pursue Zoey, it may put a

permanent rift between me and Dane, one that could affect our entire family, including our relationship with Jaimi." He put it out there, holding it out there, offering the unspoken. If Chase didn't want to risk that, Ryder would back off from Zoey.

Chase grimaced. "I won't lose you to the darkness, Ryder. Fight for it. For Zoey. We'll work it out."

Ryder looked back and forth between the men, both of whom knew how black his soul was. They matched his darkness, and yet, they nevertheless believed in his light.

"Does Zoey deserve what you can give her?" Chase asked. "Does she deserve to be happy?"

"Yes." He didn't hesitate.

"Then do it." Brody met his gaze. "Do it because you have the chance that the rest of us might never get. Don't be a dick and blow it."

Ryder raised his brows. "A dick? You're calling me a dick?"

Brody shrugged. "I'm just saying that I'm willing to name the name if you deserve it." He nodded at Chase. "Your own brother has your same demons, and he let himself find love. I know I deserve it. What makes you so different from us?"

Ryder looked back and forth between them, and then finally a slow smile spread across his face. "Not a damned thing."

Not a damned thing.

Fuck the darkness.

It was time for him to be the light.

And this time, *this time,* he knew he meant it.

He would find a way. He didn't know how, but he was going to find it.

"So, what are you doing to do?" Brody challenged him.

Ryder grinned as he grabbed his cowboy hat and set it on his head. "Not give you a reason to call me a dick, that's for damn sure. I gotta go see a girl."

Chase grinned. "It's about trust."

He glanced back at his brother as he headed for the door. "Get her to trust me?" He could do that.

"No. Get you to trust yourself."

Ryder paused. Shit. That was the tough part.

CHAPTER FOURTEEN

RYDER WAS ON HIS WAY.

What had he meant by that?

Zoey kept checking the front of the café every time the door opened, in nervous anticipation of Ryder showing up during her shift.

He'd texted her that he was on his way there, but she had no idea why he was coming, or why he'd decided to warn her.

"Expecting someone?" Lissa grinned at her as she plated two burgers, flipping them expertly from the stove to the homemade buns. "You keep looking at the door."

Zoey felt her cheeks heat up. "I don't know what you're talking about."

"No?" Lissa folded her arms and leaned her hip against the counter. "Sweetie, we're both women. We both know how damn hot the Stockton men are. I saw the way you and Ryder were looking at each other at breakfast yesterday."

Zoey cleared her throat. "We've been friends forever. That's all. I would never date him."

"Date who?" The door leading from the restaurant part of the café swung open as a tall, muscular man in jeans, a

102

cowboy hat, and a gray tee shirt walked in. He walked in as if he owned the place, but he wasn't a Stockton. Instead of the Stockton blue eyes, he had deep green ones, and his short blond hair accentuated the strong line of his jaw. He was pretty much a male specimen, though he couldn't measure up to Ryder's darker good looks.

"Keegan!" Lissa grinned at him. "I didn't know you were going to be in town today."

"They're talking bakery with the architect tomorrow, and I wanted to be in on it. You should be there as well."

She raised her eyebrows. "I told you, I'm not going to go in on a commercial bakery. I love my café."

"You can do both." He reached her and swept her up in a hug, then kissed her cheek. "Good to see you, sis."

Lissa whacked his arm. "Get off me, you big oaf. It's busy here." She set the two plates of burgers in his hands. "If you're going to bug me during the lunch rush, then you need to work. We need help."

He flashed Lissa an adorable grin that showcased a dimple that made him look even more appealing. He was funny and charming, a lightness in his manner that none of the Stockton men ever had. Holding the two plates in front of him, he swung around to face Zoey. "Who might your new waitress be?" He bowed. "My name's Keegan Hart, best damn baker in the country, even if the Stocktons and Lissa claim otherwise."

Zoey couldn't help but smile. He was so charming. So, this was one of the Harts. She'd met two of them now. How many others were there? She couldn't remember. "I'm Zoey Wilson. Dane's sister."

"Ah...my bro, Dane." Keegan straightened up, studying her with renewed interest. "I'd like to say that makes you my sister, but I think maybe I don't want to go there with you. You new to town?"

Heat filled her cheeks at the obvious flirtation. Men never

flirted with her, especially drop-dead-gorgeous men, and she wasn't sure how to react. "I grew up here, but I haven't been back for a decade. I'm just in town for a little while."

He gave her a conspiring grin. "Well, then, I think I'll have to stay in town for a little while as well."

Lissa kicked him lightly in the calf. "Shut up and go deliver my food, minion."

Keegan rolled his eyes, winking at Zoey. "As soon as my sister married Lissa's husband's brother, Lissa immediately decided she owns me. I love that." He shot them both a sassy grin, then sauntered out of the kitchen whistling cheerfully.

Zoey couldn't help but stare after him. "He seems so happy. Brody was really nice, but he had the same kind of shadows in his eyes as the Stocktons. I figured all the Harts were the same way."

Lissa shook her head. "Keegan is awesome and hilarious, but don't let the humor fool you. He had the same tough childhood the others did, and that leaves scars." She cocked her head. "Like Travis. Like Ryder."

Heat flushed Zoey's cheeks. "Ryder can be hilarious as well. He used to make me laugh all the time."

"Really? He never shows that to anyone." Lissa studied her. "Seriously. What's up with the two of you, Zoey? You and Ryder?"

"Nothing." She didn't even know how to begin answering that. For so long, she'd loved him. Then for a decade, she'd hated herself for trusting him, and hated him for betraying her. And now...so much of that was gone...and it left her with...what? Her best friend again? But what else? "I don't know. It's complicated."

Lissa grinned. "I love complicated." She plated a grilled cheese and handed the sandwich and a bowl of chili to Zoey. "Let's grab a drink after work tonight. Have some girl time. We can talk Stockton men. It's been a while since you've been around them, and I'm full of advice that I consider pretty fantastic. What do you say?"

Zoey hesitated, startled by the offer. She wasn't used to anyone in Rogue Valley reaching out to her, and she felt a little awkward. "I don't know," she hedged. "I was going to do some research on the internet tonight—"

"Really? You get an offer to hang with the coolest chick in town, and you want to sit home with a computer?" Lissa pointed the spatula at her. "We close at nine tonight, so we'll meet at the Bucking Bull at nine-thirty. I'll get some of the other girls to come. We'll have girls' night out to welcome you back to town."

Oh, man. Others? A legit girls' night? That so wasn't her thing. She'd come here to sort out her issues alone, not get pulled into girl bonding with women she didn't even know. Yet at the same time, a part of her wanted desperately to go, but she had no idea how to do it. Getting together with a bunch of women who all knew each other sounded like the perfect recipe for feeling more lost than she already was. "I'm not that good at socializing—"

"No problem. I'm great at it. No buts. It's done. Now go deliver that food to table sixteen. Don't charge them for the meal. Think of a reason why it's on the house. Now go away. I need to create magic in this kitchen." Whistling cheerfully, Lissa turned away and started flipping the burgers on the grill.

The door swung open, and Keegan walked back in. He grinned at Zoey. "Need some help with that?"

Heat flushed her cheeks at his obvious interest in more than the food she was holding. "No, I'm good." She quickly scooted past him and hurried out into the restaurant as she heard Keegan ask Lissa what her story was, and if she was single.

Single? He was asking if she was *single*?

She wasn't ready for a man to notice her, or want to date her.

Men. They were never around when you wanted them, and sniffed at your heels when you didn't. But as she wove around the tables to number sixteen, she couldn't quite keep the smile off her face.

She might not want to date Keegan Hart, or anyone, but she couldn't lie: it felt really good to be noticed as a woman. It had been a long time since she'd felt pretty, and now Keegan was the third man in twenty-four hours to make her feel attractive, including Brody and Ryder.

Ryder.

She glanced at the front door again, but he hadn't arrived yet. Good. She didn't have time for him. She was working, right?

Dragging her attention off the front door, she headed toward table sixteen. Seated at it were what looked like a grandpa and his grandson, who was maybe seven years old. The man's skin was quite a bit darker than the boy's gorgeous light brown coloring, but there was a similarity in their smile that made her certain they were related. The grandfather was listening intently to his grandson as the boy talked with great animation, his hands gesticulating excitedly as he spoke. The two of them were so focused on each other that it made Zoey smile.

That was family, right there, and it was beautiful. It made her think of the family she'd once had. She had only scattered memories of her parents, but the ones she had were of moments like this. Game night. Baking brownies with her mom. Painting with her mom.

Painting. Like the gift Ryder had given her...brushes and paints that held no magic for her anymore, even though they were from him.

She neared the boy and his grandfather, and as she got

closer, she noticed more details. The old man's boots were worn and old, and his jeans were faded and threadbare. The boy's pants were too short, and he was thinner than he should be. The boy's socks didn't match, and his shoes looked like they'd been found in a dumpster in the eighties. No wonder Lissa hadn't wanted her to charge them.

The old man noticed her, and he sat back with a warm smile as Zoey hurried up. "Well, hello," he said. "You must be Lissa's new waitress."

"Good afternoon. I'm just temporary help," she said cheerfully, embarrassed that he'd caught her inspecting their clothes. She smiled at the boy. "I assume the grilled cheese and fries are for you?"

He stared up at her in silence.

"We haven't ordered yet," the grandfather said gently, as if wanting to protect her new-waitress-ego. "We just sat down."

Zoey hesitated for a moment, wondering if she'd gotten the right table. Then she looked at the way the boy was looking hungrily at the grilled cheese and decided that she hadn't made a mistake. "I know, but the chef is experimenting with a new chili recipe and different bread for the grilled cheese, so we need testers. Do you mind? It would be super helpful."

The old man raised his eyebrows at her. "Is that so?"

"Absolutely." She set the grilled cheese in front of the boy. "My name's Zoey Wilson. What's yours?"

He nearly dove into the sandwich. "Liam Eaton," he said, his mouth already full of his first bite.

She crouched down next to him, remembering the times Ryder had come to her house for dinner, and she'd snuck him food, because they'd had nothing to eat in the Stockton hell-hole. He'd eaten like that, scarfing down food like he hadn't eaten in weeks. "Well, Liam, we have several different kinds of grilled cheese we're testing today. If you have space for more after that one, you let me know, okay? It would be super helpful if you would let us know if you like it."

He sat up a little straighter. "Really?"

"Absolutely." She glanced at the grandfather, who was watching her carefully. "In fact, Lissa, who owns the café, really wants to make the menu more kid friendly, and she needs taste testers. Do you think you might be interested in the job? You come here, and test some food, and let her know what needs to change?"

Liam pulled his shoulders back and gave her a serious nod. "I can do that." He looked at the old man. "Pops? Can we do that? Come back and help?"

Pops raised his brows at Zoey, clearly knowing exactly what she was doing, but he nodded. "We can do that, Liam."

"Awesome." Liam looked delighted as he dove back into his sandwich. "I'll tell you right now that this bread is a little weird tasting," he said. "And I can see brown flecks in it. Kids don't like whole grain weird bread. We like white bread."

Zoey pulled out her notepad and jotted his comments down. "Fantastic. And the cheese? Melty enough?"

Liam took another bite, pulling the sandwich away slowly so a long string of melted cheese stretched out. He looked at Zoey, then burst out into giggles when it broke and drooped down onto the table. "Yeah, that's good."

She grinned. "Awesome. What about the flavor of the cheese?"

Liam chewed his food for a moment, cocking his head as he clearly contemplated how to answer. After a moment, he swallowed. "It tastes like the cheese on those frozen pizzas we get from the store. A little weird."

"Weird. Got it." She jotted it down. "Anything else? Overall rating on a scale of one to ten?"

He cocked his head, thinking. "Six."

"Six." Damn. The kid was a food critic. "That's super

helpful. We'll bring out a revised version in a bit. What do you need to drink to do your job?"

"Root beer—"

"Milk," Pops interrupted. "Water or milk."

Liam made a face, and Zoey giggled. "Milk and water, it is." She stood up. "I'll be back in a few. Let me know how the chili is..." She paused. "What is your name?"

"Frank. Frank Eaton."

She smiled. "Great. Thank you both for your help." She stood up and headed back toward the kitchen, feeling a deep sense of peace that she'd been able to help them. If Lissa didn't want to give them free food forever, she'd give Lissa the money for it.

"Zoey."

She turned around as Frank shuffled up to her. He was old and a little bent, but there was a sass and fire in his eyes that said he was a force to be reckoned with. She tensed, worried that he was going to be annoyed that she'd given them free food. "Yes?"

He said nothing. He just walked up to her and gave her a huge hug.

For a moment, she just stood there awkwardly, not sure what to do, and then she slowly put her arms around him and hugged him back.

"This is for leaving Liam and this old man with some pride," he whispered gruffly into her ear. "Thank you."

Her throat tightened and she nodded. "I've been there," she said.

He pulled back, studying her face. "Sorry to hear that. Sorry indeed."

Tears unexpectedly sprung into her eyes, and she quickly blinked them back. "It was a long time ago. It's all good."

"Is it?" He gave her a long look. "Because I'm not sure it ever becomes all good again." There was a sadness in his eyes that made her heart turn over, but he turned away and headed back toward Liam before she could say anything more.

For a moment, she just stood there, watching as Frank sat down across from Liam, smiling at his grandson. They were strangers, and yet now, she had a connection with them. Something real and personal. Something that mattered.

She'd never had that in Boston. It felt...special. Healing. Beautiful. She realized that maybe she was the one who owed them the thanks.

"Hey, Zoey." Ryder's voice was low and deep, whispering over her shoulder as he slid his arms around her waist.

She closed her eyes for a split second, letting herself lean into his strength. God, it felt good to feel his arms around her...too good. The kind of good that would make her forget that she was here to learn how to stand on her own two feet, not weaken herself by letting him hold her up.

With a silent groan of how sucky it was to have to be strong, she untangled herself from his grasp and turned to face him. "You can't go grabbing me while I'm working. It's much too difficult to carry plates and drag you along behind me."

He grinned, a sparkle in his eyes that made her heart leap. "Yeah, well, I'm sure you could handle it. How's the day going?"

She narrowed her eyes. "You came here to ask me how the day's going?" Out of the corner of her eye, she saw Keegan walk out of the kitchen carrying several plates of food. He looked right over at them, and then headed straight for them.

Ryder didn't appear to notice Keegan. "I came here to invite you to go canoeing with me on Monday. The café is closed, so you'll be free."

She blinked. "Canoeing? Seriously?"

"Yep. The river runs right by the house, and the house

110

came with a bunch of canoes that have never been used." He shrugged. "I thought it might help inspire you to paint."

She tensed. "I don't paint anymore. I just—"

"Hey." He set his hands on her shoulders. "It's okay. No painting. Just canoeing. And a picnic. What do you say?"

She hesitated. Monday was day five of being in town. She was committed only for four days to Lissa. She was planning to be gone by then, but the idea of spending a day hanging out with Ryder was so tempting. Now that their relationship had started to heal, she was deeply tempted to stay long enough to rebuild their friendship. When she left again, it would be beautiful to keep connected to him this time.

"Hey, Ryder, back off. I was going to ask her out." Keegan walked up. "Lissa said she was single."

Ryder's face went from relaxed to dark instantly. His shoulders tensed, and his jaw tightened. *Uh, oh.* She'd seen that look on his face before. It was a look of fury that masked pain, the pain he never shared with anyone. She was shocked by the expression on his face. It was raw, and visceral, too strong for him to hide behind the mask he usually wore.

He didn't look at Keegan. He just stared at the wall behind Zoey, fighting for control.

Was it his protector mode? Something about Keegan that he wanted to protect her from?

"What do you say, Zoey?" Keegan smiled at her, so charming and gorgeous. "I'd love to treat you to dinner tonight. It's the only night I'm in town, but I'll be back again in a week or two."

His intentions were obvious. Even though he was charming and handsome, and clearly adored by Lissa, the thought of dating him made Zoey panic. She was so not in a place to build trust with any man. "I'm so sorry, but I can't."

He raised his brows. "Tonight? Or ever?"

Ryder glanced at her, his face an unreadable mask. There

was something in his gaze, something stark and raw that grabbed at her heart.

She looked over at Keegan, and for a split second, she saw a flash of vulnerability in his green eyes, vulnerability that belied his easygoing manner. This man was like Ryder and the rest of the Stocktons, carrying a load of pain and loneliness, held together by the bond he had with his siblings.

Two men, both of them so strong, so handsome, and so confident...with so many scars buried deep inside, scars that they showed to no one...except the people who could see them despite their best efforts to hide them.

Keegan was waiting for her answer, and the longer he waited, the more she saw his shields go up, expecting rejection, preparing for it. Her heart turned over. "It's not you," she said softly.

He raised his brows. "I'm getting the 'it's not you, it's me' speech already? That was fast."

His tone said that he clearly understood that it *was* him. He was a man who, in his own eyes, would always be the homeless kid who no one thought was worthy, and damn if she was going to let him believe that she was one of those people who would judge him.

She'd been judged brutally enough once her parents had died that she'd be damned if she'd let someone else feel the way she had.

Ryder had always made her feel valued, even at her worst. There was no way she could do less for Keegan, and there was no chance a man like him would believe that she just had a shitload of emotional intimacy issues. He was too ready to wear the label he'd been saddled with since he was a kid. "No, it's really not you. It's...it's Ryder." She said it before she thought about it, and both men's eyebrows went up.

"Ryder?" Keegan looked over at him. "What about him?"

"He's... I..." Crap. What was she supposed to say now?

Neither man helped her out. They both just stared at her, waiting.

Dammit. "Ryder and I are dating," she finally said.

Ryder grinned, but Keegan looked skeptical. "You and Ryder? Really?"

"Hell, yeah." Ryder slung his arm around her neck, hauled her over to him, and, before she realized what he was about to do, he kissed her.

CHAPTER FIFTEEN

Ryder had dreamed about kissing Zoey pretty much every night since she'd left. He'd been pretty damn certain that he remembered exactly what it had been like to kiss her.

But he was wrong.

All his memories, all his fantasies, were absolutely *nothing* compared to what it was like to feel her lips under his once again.

Her mouth was pure angel and heaven, a taste of beauty and peace that he'd never found anywhere else. Her lips were soft as a dandelion mist, and they tasted like the deep, comforting taste of apple pie.

Ten years ago, he'd kissed her half-afraid of what he was doing, of what door he was opening.

This time, the kiss with her was everything he wanted, and he didn't hesitate. This was the chance he never thought he'd get again, and he knew it might be his only one...so he gave her everything he was, everything he had, everything he could offer her.

Yeah, he knew that she'd claimed they were dating just to get Keegan to back off, but he was going to take the opportunity and make the move he hadn't thought he'd ever get the chance to make.

For a split second, she stiffened, her body rigid against his, her hand on his chest, as if she were going to push him away.

So, he deepened the kiss, sliding his hands through her hair, cradling her head in his palms as he coaxed a response from her. He whispered her name into the kiss, barely a breath, before kissing her again. "*ZoeyBear.*"

It was her name that did it. The moment he said it, the resistance drained from her body. She sighed deeply and she relaxed into him, the weight of her body leaning into his chest as she parted her lips and kissed him back.

She was kissing him back.

For a moment, Ryder was too overwhelmed to respond. This moment, what he'd dreamed of for a decade, was really happening. *It was happening.*

He felt her hesitate, so he quickly focused on the kiss again, sliding one hand across her lower back and drawing her to him. She sighed into the kiss, an adorable little Zoey sigh that made him smile as he kissed her, teasing her with little kisses meant to make her laugh.

She giggled, and drew back, her eyes sparkling. "You're such a dork."

"I know. I'm fantastic that way." Her lips looked so tempting that he brought her in and kissed her again, this time a slow, decadent seduction that sent heat rushing through him, the kind of heat that was pure need and desire, for her, simply for her.

Her arms went around his neck, and she pulled him closer, matching his intensity with her kiss. Suddenly, he forgot about silly kisses to make her smile, and it became only about the deep, intense kisses that were a culmination of ten years of missing her—

"Ryder!" Lissa's amused voice broke through the kiss, and

Ryder swore, suddenly remembering they were in the middle of the lunch crowd at the Wildflower Café.

"Shit. Sorry." He pulled back, grinning when he saw it take a moment for Zoey's eyes to flutter open and awareness to return. Yeah, the kiss had affected her too, even if she'd done it just for show.

She met his gaze for a second, her face full of emotions that he couldn't read.

"Damn, all right. I guess you and Ryder have a thing." Keegan held up his hands in defeat. "Lucky man, Ryder."

Ryder grinned. "You have no idea."

Zoey's cheeks turned red, and she stepped back. She pointed at Ryder. "You need to stop bothering me on my shift," she muttered, her voice thick with emotions. "Go away."

His smile faded at the edge of tension in her voice. She'd been unsettled by the kiss, and he knew she hadn't been expecting it. Shit. Had he pushed it too far? She was like a skittish fawn, and he knew he needed to be very careful with her. "Canoeing on Monday, then?" He kept his voice light.

Zoey hesitated, and his tension rose. He couldn't lose her again. He *had* to handle this correctly. "ZoeyBear," he said softly. "I need to make you smile again."

She looked at him, her gaze searching his, so lost that his heart turned over for her. Yeah, Dane could say what he wanted, but Ryder knew that she needed what only he could give her, and he wasn't going to give up so easily.

"Ask her later," Lissa said, sliding her arm through Zoey's. "We have hungry people, and you men are in the way. Either help or vacate, gentlemen."

"I gotta jet." Keegan tipped his hat to them. "I'll report on the bakery, Lissa."

"I'm not doing a commercial bakery!" She rolled her eyes

at Zoey as she led her back toward the kitchen. "Seriously, with men, right?"

As the women walked away, Zoey looked back over her shoulder at Ryder, her brows furrowed in confusion.

He nodded at her and tossed her his most smart-ass grin.

For a split second, he thought she wasn't going to respond, but then she shook her head in exasperation and sighed, her lips curving with amusement as she turned away.

The smile. She'd given him that smile that was meant for him only, the one she used to give him when she was pretending to be annoyed by him, but was actually highly entertained.

Yeah, that's right. He'd gotten *that* smile from her.

He grinned and set his hat on his head, whistling as he strode toward the door. Her barriers were coming down, and he was going to be there to catch her when they did.

He was on his way.

CHAPTER SIXTEEN

ZOEY STOOD in the doorway of the bar and watched Lissa laughing with two women she didn't know. They were in hysterics, laughing so hard that they were nearly in tears. Clearly best friends with shared stories. And all three of them had wedding rings on.

Yeah, she wasn't so sure about this.

Ever since her divorce, she felt awkward around women who were married, like there was something wrong with her, like there was a big sign over her that proclaimed her such a loser that the man who knew her best had decided she wasn't worth keeping around.

So, did she want to skip over there and plop herself down in the middle of three women who are not only married, but also clearly besties? She wasn't really feeling it. Lissa hadn't seen her yet. She could simply turn and leave...except she didn't want to.

A part of her was so incredibly desperate to feel better, to connect with someone, to start to heal the hole in her soul that she'd lived with for so long. Making female friends sounded like exactly what she wanted...if she weren't so freaking uncomfortable doing it. But where else could she start to put her feet down? She didn't want to date, and she really didn't want to think about that unbelievable kiss with Ryder anymore.

Ryder's kiss.

She hadn't been able to stop obsessing over it the rest of the day, after he'd flipped her that sassy smirk and sauntered out the door. The kiss... God. That kiss. It had been incredible. Amazing. So beautiful that it was painful, because it had opened up the parts of her heart that had far too many cracks in it to handle any kind of infusion of old feelings for him.

Going home would put her in close proximity with Ryder...so maybe girls were the answer.

Lissa had been nice, right? Maybe the others would be, too. Did she just walk up there, and say "hey" and start high-fiving everyone—

"Zoey?" A woman standing behind her said her name. "Are you Zoey? Lissa said you were coming."

She spun around to see a woman with dark curly hair, dark eyes, and a warm smile. For a moment she hesitated, trying to figure out why she looked familiar...until she recognized her from the photos Dane had sent her. This woman was her sister-in-law, whose wedding she hadn't even managed to be at. Crap. Jaimi must think she was such a bitch. "Are you Jaimi?"

"I am." Jaimi was beaming at her. "I'm so glad we finally get to meet! I've heard so much about you."

"Really?" Zoey wanted to be anywhere but there. "I'm so sorry I haven't been over to meet you and the kids yet. I just —" She faded to silence. What excuse did she have? She'd been in town long enough. "I'm sorry. I'm just super pathetic, I guess." The apologies started pouring out. "I'm so sorry I missed your wedding. It wasn't about you. I just...I didn't have the capacity at the time. I should have been there, and then I just, I don't know, you and the kids have this nice family, and I don't fit, but I'm really happy for you and Dane and—"

"*Zoey.*" Jaimi held up her palm to stop her, and Zoey faded into silence.

"I'm sorry," she whispered again. "I'm so sorry. I'm just—"

"You're human," Jaimi said gently. "As are all of us."

"But—"

Jaimi held up her arms. "Bring it in, sis. It's all good."

Tears filled Zoey's eyes. "But—"

Jaimi didn't let her finish. She just reached out, grabbed Zoey by the shoulders, and pulled her into a hug.

Zoey crumbled immediately at the kindness, and the tears spilled out as she hugged the woman she'd been so afraid to meet for so long. She held on, unable to stop the tears as Jaimi held her tightly in a hug that was real, not just for show or politeness.

She felt like she clung to Jaimi for an eternity before either of them finally began to let go. Zoey stepped back, wiping her wrist across her teary cheeks. "I really am sorry," she said.

Jaimi shook her head. "No apologies needed, Zoey. I know you've been through some tough stuff." She gestured at the table of women, who were all watching them now. "Every single one of us has. At some point, you hit rock bottom, and then you start to climb back up." She smiled gently. "This is a good place to start the climb. Lots of support, including a bunch of badass women who have been dying to meet you for years." She tucked her arm through Zoey's. "Come meet the gang."

Zoey took a deep breath and managed a tremulous smile. "I'd like that."

"So would all of us." Jaimi patted Zoey's hand as she led

the way through the bar. "You're the first woman to tame these Stocktons. You're a legend around here."

"Me?" Zoey blinked. "A legend? What do you mean?"

Jaimi raised her brows as they reached the table. "The Stocktons are all about brotherhood. They didn't believe in women, or kids, or families. Just each other, and Dane, because he has that male thing going as well, for which I'm super grateful, of course." She winked, and the other women all laughed as they reached the table. "Except for you, Zoey. You were the female that penetrated their inner circle, who showed them that it was possible for a woman to be a decent human being."

"Totally." A woman with curly dark blond hair and brown eyes chimed in. "Without you, I doubt Chase would have been able to see past my oh-so-scary breasts and realize that there was a chance I could save his soul." She held out her hand. "I'm Mira, Chase's wife."

Zoey shook her hand as she slid onto a bar stool next to Lissa. "Nice to meet you. Chase is a good man."

"He is indeed," Mira agreed.

"Thank God for him," another woman said. She was tall and curvy, with long auburn hair and dark brown eyes that were so warm. "Steen never would have been willing to cross that line with me if Chase hadn't already fallen in love with Mira." She grinned. "I'm Erin, Steen's wife. It's so great to finally meet you." She hopped off her stool, jogged around the table, and swept Zoey up in another genuine hug.

"Nice to meet you." Zoey felt herself relaxing as she hugged Erin back. They were all so nice and welcoming.

"Chase has pretty much talked all our men into realizing that they can handle being in a relationship with a fantastic woman," Lissa said. "Travis barely made it over the hump, but he did." She held up her hand to show her wedding ring and a truly massive diamond. "After getting dumped when I was seventeen and pregnant, I honestly believed I'd never get married, but he got me to trust again."

"Me, too," Erin said. "After my divorce, I was so done."

Zoey looked over at Erin. "You're divorced?"

"Yep." Erin rolled her eyes. "Getting divorced sucks, doesn't it? You feel like you'll never be whole again."

Zoey inched forward on her seat. "You felt like that, too?"

"Every day." Erin smiled. "It's really hard, even if the guy you're married to winds up being not worth your energy, it's still hard not to give it to him."

"*Yes.*" Zoey looked over at Jaimi. "And you? You were a single mom as well before Dane, right?"

"I was, and I was happy being single, just like Lissa and Erin were." Jaimi shrugged. "When you've worked hard enough to get your life back on track, standing on your own two feet, it's scary as hell to think about giving away that power to someone else."

"But with the right guy," Lissa added, "it's not giving away your power. It's adding to your own."

The other women all nodded their agreement, and Zoey felt a stab of envy. The women she was sitting with were all clearly strong, badass women. They'd had their lives under control before they'd met their husbands, giving them the ability to be equals. She wasn't there yet. She looked over at Lissa. "How did you pick yourself up after you left home?"

Lissa shrugged. "I started small, waitressing at the Wildflower Café, actually. The owner eventually sold it to me for a bargain, and I've been doing it ever since. Financially, I don't need to work anymore since Travis earns so much money, but I do it for me." She grinned. "It makes my soul happy, so what other reason do you need?"

Well, damn. Zoey loved that so much. Something that made her soul happy? She didn't even know what that was...

but she didn't have to think twice to know that it wasn't being a lawyer.

Erin nodded. "Agreed. We all need something that's ours."

"I agree," Mira said. "It's not so much a job as a sense of self. Like you know what matters to your soul, and you have that compass to keep you focused, and you make sure you honor and respect that, whatever it is."

"Exactly," Erin said. "It's the only way to make the relationship balanced when you're in one with such a strong man."

"And all the Stocktons are strong," Lissa laughed. "God, they can be such pains in the ass."

"Dane too," Jaimi said. "He's the same as the rest of them."

"Well, of course. He's one of them, with a different last name," Erin said.

Zoey couldn't help but get caught up in the infectious warmth as the women began to trade stories about their husbands. They clearly loved them, but they also were able to see how they weren't perfect. Their affection was so obvious, and she could practically hear the starry-eyed sighs of romance as they talked about the men they loved.

I want that.

The thought startled her. She didn't want that, did she? She wanted to be solo and independent, never giving away her power again, once she found it, that thing that made her soul sing. These women who were so amazing had found a way to marry strong men, without losing their own sense of self and integrity. She hadn't even realized that was possible, but now that she did...she wanted it. The "it" she wanted was to find that thing that made her soul dance, and then to take that sense of self into a romantic relationship that was as beautiful as the ones these women had.

She wanted it with every fiber of her soul. To be loved that much. To love herself that much. But it was clear that all these women had gone into their relationships with something that she didn't have, and that was a sense of their own power.

She needed to find that for herself. But how? She didn't even know where to start. But at least right now, for the first time in a long time, she had an idea of what she wanted, and that felt good. It gave her hope, like a light shining at the end of a tunnel that used to be only blackness.

"Oh...look who just walked in." Lissa looked past Zoey, a wide grin on her face. "How totally random that they picked this bar to hang out in tonight. I wonder how that happened."

Zoey and the other women looked toward the door, and Zoey's stomach jumped when she saw Ryder walk in with Keegan and Brody. All three men were wearing cowboy hats and jeans, but she barely noticed the two Harts. All her attention was on Ryder. His hips were lean and fit, and his shoulders were wide and muscular beneath his loosely buttoned shirt. His cowboy boots were worn and perfect, and he'd trimmed his whiskers just enough to look sharp, but not enough that anyone could call him clean-shaven. He looked pure cowboy tonight, raw heat, and dangerous Stockton bad boy.

He was pure man, carrying a lifetime of shadows on his broad shoulders.

He scanned the bar, until his gaze fell on her.

Then he smiled, that same sassy smirk that made her belly jump, a smile without any shadows at all. The smile that was for her, and only for her.

Ryder. Heat rushed through her, and she felt her cheeks turn red. She still had no defenses against him. As a teenager, she'd fallen in love with the older, dangerous cowboy who had been her protector and defender since she could remember. Today, he was still an older, dangerous cowboy who came to her rescue...and her old feelings were quick to roar back to life.

Only now, there was a heat burning inside her that she'd been too young and innocent to understand before.

Not now. Right now, she knew exactly what she wanted from that man, and it wasn't the platonic friendship she'd thought.

Ryder said something to the Harts, and all three men headed toward their table. Her heart started to pound as he neared them. He wasn't going to try to kiss her again, was he? That had been just for show for Keegan, right? A one-time thing. Because they both knew there was nothing romantic happening between them.

"Good evening, ladies," he said as he neared the table. As her tablemates chimed in with a chorus of greetings for him and the Harts, he turned toward her. "Zoey." His voice was low and deep, enveloping her in a warmth that felt both safe and exciting at the same time.

She swallowed. "Hi."

He walked over to her and slid his hand behind her neck, a gentle, seductive caress that made her catch her breath.

"Don't kiss me," she whispered, totally lying.

"I have to." Then he bent his head and brushed his lips across hers. The kiss was different than the seduction in the café. This kiss was tender and sweet, making her sigh with longing. It was the kiss of a man who cared about the woman he was kissing, who thought that she was the sunshine to his darkness, the kiss of a man who would give her anything, and take nothing from her.

Or at least, that's what it felt like, what she wanted it to be, what she wanted to be kissed like.

He paused the kiss, and she opened her eyes. He smiled. "Save a dance for me later?"

"A dance? There's no band."

"There will be in a little while." He rubbed his thumb over her jaw. "One dance, ZoeyBear. Promise?"

She swallowed. "Fine, but only if you'll go away and stop interrupting girls' night."

He grinned. "You got it, babe." He kissed her again, this one long and deep, awakening every bit of woman inside her.

Her body was still humming after he ended the kiss, greeted the other women, and then settled himself with the Harts on the other side of the bar...directly in Zoey's line of vision.

"Damn, girl." Erin let out a low whistle. "Lissa wasn't lying when she said there was heat between the two of you."

Zoey cleared her throat, her cheeks burning. "We're just friends."

"That was not 'just friends.'" Mira propped her chin up on her hands, grinning at Zoey. "I remember my first hot kiss with Chase. I knew he was going to be trouble, the kind of trouble that would last a lifetime." She raised her brows. "Seems like that was the same kind of kiss."

"Totally." Lissa looked delighted. "Ryder is such a great guy. It's so rare to get a smile from him. It makes me so happy to see the way he looks at you."

Something fluttered inside Zoey, something that felt way too much like what it had used to feel like every time she thought of Ryder. "Listen, we've been best friends for almost twenty years. That's seriously all it is."

Jaimi cocked her head. "Why do you say that? Because to us, that kiss had nothing platonic about it. So, I'm curious why you think it meant nothing?"

What? She had to explain it? "I was just protesting so I

didn't have to actually explain the depth of the baggage between us."

The women all burst out laughing, and Zoey felt some of her embarrassment fade. She even found herself giggling when the women started listing everything about the kiss that wasn't platonic, including the length, intensity, the way he'd cupped the back of her neck, and how they'd leaned in to each other. It was hilarious, and at the same time...it made her think.

Finally, she leaned forward, looking around at the women. "Do you guys *really* think he meant for that to be more than a platonic kiss, or a kiss just to get Keegan to back off? I mean...we have so much heartbreak between us, and we've just barely begun to rebuild our friendship. It's so fragile. I just can't imagine he would want to reopen that part of our relationship, to risk losing everything, like we did before."

The women at her table were silent for a moment, exchanging glances.

Finally, it was Mira who answered. "Honestly, I believe that he's not thinking right now. I think he's doing what feels right to him. He's not worrying about outcome. He needs you, and you need him, and that's what's driving him."

"Oh." That wasn't what she'd hoped for. She realized a part of her was hoping that one of them would announce that Ryder was her fairytale hero, and she was going to be lucky, like them.

Jaimi set her hand on hers. "Can I ask you something?"

Zoey nodded at her sister-in-law. "Of course."

"If there was no Ryder, would you consider staying here? Moving back for good? Would it even be possible you might want to do that, just for yourself?" Jaimi's face was serious, as if there was more at stake than a simple question.

She started to shake her head...and then stopped. The answer that had been so clear to her suddenly felt murky. In one evening, she'd already fallen a little bit in love with these women, women who were welcoming her into their lives so completely. She'd loved working at the deli, meeting Liam and his grandfather, making a difference to them. "I always thought I needed to find a way to get back to Boston. Before it was tainted by my ex, I was pretty happy there."

Happy. What was happy? What did it really mean? Had she truly been happy, in the way these women radiated contentment with their lives?

"But now?" Jaimi prompted.

"What would I do here? I can't practice law in Wyoming."

Lissa raised her brows. "You could work at the café."

"I appreciate that, but—" She stopped herself, not wanting to insult her new friends.

"But it's not calling to your soul." Lissa nodded. "I get that." She smiled. "You'll figure it out. In the meantime, you can work at the café for as long as you want. You were great with Liam and his grandpa today."

She smiled. "Thanks. It was fun. What's their story?"

Lissa's smile faded. "Liam's dad, Eddie Eaton, was a single dad in the military. He died in the service a couple years ago. Eddie's dad, Frank, is raising Liam now. It's been really hard on Frank, losing his only son, and then having to provide for Liam. I honestly don't know what's going to happen to them, or how much longer Frank can keep taking care of Liam. I'm worried about them."

Zoey bit her lip. She knew what it was like to be raised by family after her parents died. Her aunt and uncle had not been good people. At all. If she hadn't had Dane and the Stocktons watching out for her, it would have been very, very bad, and she knew it. "Frank's good to him though?"

Lissa smiled. "The best. Frank's one of the loveliest people in the entire world. I adore him to pieces."

"Okay, then." Zoey felt herself relax. If Liam had love, that was enough to get him through anything.

The conversation turned to babies and kids, and Zoey was amazed to hear all the stories about how the Stocktons were all such dedicated dads. It made her smile, remembering the tough, angry loners she'd grown up with, knowing that they'd found their way to being dads and husbands.

They were good men. She'd known it back then, and she knew it now.

She looked across the bar, and saw Ryder watching her. He pointed to her right, and she looked over to see a band setting up.

Her heart skipped a beat, and excitement pulsed through her.

Tonight, they were going to dance.

The first time he'd kissed her had been at her prom. On the dance floor.

And in a few minutes, she would be back in his arms.

CHAPTER SEVENTEEN

ZOEY WAS COMPLETELY ENGROSSED in Jaimi's story about how Dane and Ryder had dressed up as Santa's elves and climbed through the window at Chase's house on Christmas Eve, wearing red tights, green felt shoes, and jingle bells on their cowboy hats when she felt a hand on her shoulder.

She didn't have to turn around to see who it was. The way her belly jumped and her breath caught in her chest told her exactly whose hand was so warm and solid on her shoulder.

And the fact that every woman at the table looked past her with huge grins on their faces might have helped.

"Hey, Ryder." Lissa beamed at him, looking absolutely delighted. "Are you being rude enough to steal Zoey from us?"

"I am. I pride myself on breaking all standards of polite and proper behavior, by doing things like stealing Zoey for a dance." His fingers tightened on her shoulder. "ZoeyBear? May I have this dance?"

Yes. She took a deep breath, then turned around to face him. His blue eyes were heated and intense, then he smiled,

130

that amazing smile that had always made her want to smile back, regardless of how tough her day was going.

Like now. Her smile came to life on its own, and she grinned at him. "You're such a pest. Clearly, dancing with you is the only way to make you go away."

"Damn straight it is." He slid his hand down her arm and encircled her wrist with his fingers, a gesture both gentle and commanding, the dichotomy that defined him. "Until later, ladies."

Zoey shot an apologetic look at her brand-new friends. "Sorry about this—"

"Oh, babe, don't be sorry," Erin said. "We are all highly familiar with the irresistible temptation that a broad Stockton chest presents. You go right ahead while we fantasize about what's waiting for us when we get home tonight."

Lissa grinned. "Yes, enjoy, for sure."

Heat flared in Zoey's cheeks, but before she could think of an adequate retort about Stockton chests, Ryder had already pulled her away from the table, his hand sliding down her wrist to her hand. As his fingers entwined between hers, Zoey's heart started to hammer.

What was he doing? What was she doing? What were *they* doing? "Ryder—"

"My favorite song." They reached the dance floor, and he turned and pulled her into his arms in a single, seamless move. "You remember this?"

The first notes dropped into her heart, and she nodded, clasping her hands behind his neck as she let him pull her against him. His chest was indeed broad, and it seemed to pour heat into her body where they were touching. "It's from my prom."

"It is." He locked his hands on her hips, not quite on her ass, but very close. "You recall dancing to it?"

She looked up at him, surprised by the subtext to his question. "You remember?"

"Our first kiss? The song that was playing when I kissed you for the first time? Fuck yeah, I remember. For the last ten years, every time I've heard that song, I've danced that dance with you again, and shared that first kiss with you."

"Oh." Her throat tightened. That was incredibly romantic. "I didn't think you would have paid attention to the song."

"Ahh...ZoeyBear. You were my sunshine. I noticed everything about you." He smiled. "I need to kiss you again. This song requires it."

Her heart was racing so fast now that she was certain he would feel it thundering. "Okay."

"Okay," he repeated, with a grin. "That's it? Just an okay?"

She raised her brows. "For the last ten years, whenever I heard that song, it made me hate you for kissing me and then leaving me."

He blinked, clearly startled by her comment, that had taken a flirty, fun conversation and sent it right into an ugly past that she'd thought she'd sealed away.

Regret flicked through her. "I didn't mean—"

"You did, and that's okay." He palmed her lower back. "Hate isn't a healthy emotion, and it's a popular song, so you need a new association with it."

"Like what?" She issued the challenge, knowing full well what he was going to do about it, because he was right. She did need a new association with it, and she knew what she wanted.

"Like...this." He bent his head and kissed her. Deep. Unhesitating. The kiss of a grownup seduction, not a tentative prom date kiss.

Need raced through her, need that had been building all

night. Need driven by stories about the Stockton men, romance, and living life with passion. She threw herself into the kiss, holding on tightly as the kiss turned from hot to scalding. His hands slid down to cup her butt, tongues got involved with decadence and temptation, and suddenly, she couldn't get close enough to him.

He pulled her more tightly against him until her breasts were pressed against his chest, making her nipples tighten with need and desire...and maybe a little bit of pure lust.

She lost track of the music, if it was even still playing anymore. All her senses became consumed with Ryder, with the raw strength of his muscles, the delicious scent of his aftershave, the prickle of his whiskers against her face, and the way his hands romanced her ass, her lower back, and her shoulder blades.

Ryder was hers. He'd always been hers. Her bedroom floor was where he'd slept so many nights. She was the one who crashed in his room. She'd been the one to elicit that beautiful smile from him. No other girls had ever had the intimacy that she'd had with him, for as long as she'd known him.

He'd made her leave town for her own good, not because he didn't want her.

He'd wanted her. He'd wanted to keep her. And now...the way he was kissing her...it made her feel safe again. It was safe to give herself to Ryder. He wouldn't cheat on her like her ex had. He wouldn't steal from her. He wouldn't do anything, *anything*, that he thought might harm her.

She pulled back, searching his face. "Do you remember when you asked me if I still trusted you?"

He nodded, sliding one hand through her hair. "I do. You said you weren't sure anymore."

"I wasn't."

"But now?"

Her heart tightened. "I believe in you, Ryder."

His face lit up. "Thank you."

He looked so happy that her heart seemed to fill with sunshine. "I needed this. Us. To heal what was between us," she said, not quite able to stop herself from running her hands over his upper arms, over his biceps. "I needed to feel safe in your arms again."

His smile faded into seriousness. "You will *always* be safe in my arms, ZoeyBear."

She nodded. "I know." She wanted to ask whether she'd be safe outside his arms, outside this intimate moment, but she didn't dare. She didn't want to look past what they were sharing. She didn't want to think about life, and how she still had so many things to fix about herself, so many things she had to figure out, so many scars she still had to heal.

Right now, she just wanted that feeling that Ryder gave her. "I even forgive you for crashing girls' night."

He grinned and nodded past her. "Looks like it was coming to an end anyway."

She looked over her shoulder just in time to see her dates nearly sprinting out the front door. They all waved cheerfully at her, and then they were gone. She shook her head. "Those women are trouble."

"Thank God for that. My brothers couldn't handle any other kind." He nodded at his table. "Looks like my ride took off. Can I get a lift with you back to the house?"

She saw then that Keegan and Brody were gone as well. Manipulative bastards, the whole lot of them. She sighed melodramatically. "I'll give you a ride, I guess."

"Great." He slid his hands around her waist. "Just one more dance before we leave?"

She grinned. "Just one."

"One is all I need."

She raised her brows. "For what?"

"To seduce you." Then he kissed her, fast and hot, the kiss of a man with a purpose, who had no intention of giving her room to resist.

Which was fine with her, because right now, all she wanted was him.

CHAPTER EIGHTEEN

ZOEY KNEW what was going to happen before they got home.

She knew what was going to happen before they'd walked into the quiet house, with Brody and Keegan already retired to their bedrooms.

She knew what was going to happen when Ryder walked her to her bedroom door.

But the fact she knew didn't do a damn thing to keep her hands from trembling and her heart from pounding as she turned to face him in her doorway. "Thanks for a great night, Ryder."

He smiled, trailing his finger down the side of her face. "My ZoeyBear," he said softly. "You smiled tonight."

She was still smiling. "I did."

"You feel better?" There was an undercurrent to his question, a subtext she couldn't quite decipher. "Better than when you first came back to town?"

She cocked her head, considering the question. "You know, I do, actually. My heart feels so much lighter than it has in a long time." She smiled. "Lissa, Erin, Jaimi, and Mira are so great."

He nodded. "They are." He moved closer, his eyes searching hers. "And?"

She breathed deeply, well aware that his hips were less than an inch from hers. His chest, too. They were so close, so connected, hovering beside each other. He smelled so good, like warmth and safety and man. "And what?"

"Anything else about the evening meet your fancy?" His lips were almost on hers, so close she could almost taste them.

"You mean the band? They were good."

"Yes, they were." He nuzzled the side of her neck, just barely skimming with his lips. "Anything else?"

She closed her eyes, pressing back against the doorframe. Her bed was only a few feet away, and they both knew it. There was no way she could initiate, though. Would he? Neither of them would be that stupid, right? To take this thing that was sizzling between them and take an irreversible step, like they had so long ago. "Keegan and Brody are nice."

"Fuck them." He gently bit her collarbone. "I want you thinking only about one man when I'm this close to you."

She opened her eyes. "What man is that?"

He met her gaze. "Me, ZoeyBear. *Me.*"

"Ryder, my best friend?" The question hung in the air. *Friend.*

He went still.

She waited. Not sure what to say. Not sure what she wanted to say. Not sure what she wanted from him.

Finally, he pulled back far enough to look at her face. "Answer one question for me, Zoey."

She nodded, her heart pounding at how serious he looked. "Sure."

"Do you feel happier when you're with me, or when you're not with me? Truth."

"With you." The answer was instant. She didn't even have

to think about it, and it tumbled out before she had time to consider whether she wanted to admit that, either to herself or to Ryder.

It didn't matter, though, because the moment she said it, he smiled, a gorgeous, heart-melting smile that seemed to reach inside her and ease all the pain that still lived there. "That's what I thought." Then he slid his hand behind her neck, drew her to him, and kissed her.

She had no chance to summon resistance. Her need for him had been building since she'd first seen him at the Wildflower Café. And tonight, in his arms, laughing with him...her need had reached a point where all it would take was one tiny spark for it to explode to life.

His smile was that spark.

She melted into the kiss, her arms going around his neck, her heart aching with need for him.

He leaned into her, so her back was sandwiched between his body and the doorframe, trapped... No. It felt more like she was protected, instead of trapped. It was exactly where she wanted to be, exactly whose arms she wanted to be in.

Ryder's hands went to her hips, and then he slid them up to her waist. She knew before he did it that he was going to lift her up, and she moved with him, wrapping her legs around his hips without breaking the kiss.

He supported her, his arms solid and strong around her as he carried her across the room to her bed, easing them both onto the soft comforter without breaking the body contact between them. The mattress sank beneath them, inviting them into the safety of her bed.

He grabbed the hem of her shirt and pulled it swiftly over her head. For a split second, she was embarrassed, highly aware of Ryder's gaze on her body. Then she saw the look of complete reverence on his face, and her tension vanished. "No one has ever looked at me the way you do," she whispered, unable to take her gaze off his face as he ran his hands over her ribs and stomach, reveling in each touch.

"No one knows you like I do," he said, bending down to kiss her belly button. "No one but me knows the fears that haunt you. No one else knows just what to say to make the nightmares leave you. No one else can get that smile out of you when the tears are trying to crush you."

Her throat tightened, and she had no words. He was right. Of course he was right. She'd let him get closer to her than she'd ever let anyone get, even her ex-husband.

He kissed his way along her ribs, and then pressed a kiss to her nipple through her bra. She gasped and arched into the kiss, as spirals of fire rippled through her. "Ryder," she whispered.

"Yes?" He pulled off his shirt, and her heart caught at the sight of his body. When she'd seen him naked before, she'd been so in awe of the experience that she'd barely taken time to notice him, but he'd been leaner then, more sinewy.

Now, he was chiseled muscle and strength. His abs were ripped, and his biceps were pure temptation. "Holy crap," she whispered. "You're like a Greek god."

He laughed, the rich, deep sound making her heart lighten. "I'm *your* Greek god, baby. Take advantage."

"I might have to." She sat up, and pushed him onto his back. He rolled over easily and clasped his hands behind his head, crossing his ankles in a position of complete submission.

"God, you're like the ultimate dessert." She sat on his hips, straddling him, and flattened her hands on his stomach. "I can literally feel your six pack beneath my hands. Every ridge of muscle."

He grinned. "For the last ten years, I've been trying to think of the best way to get you into bed. I figured you're super shallow and superficial, so a chiseled set of abs seemed to be the best plan."

"It totally is. If I'd known you had these, I would have jumped you that first night in my apartment when we were unpacking." She ran her hands along his ribs and then to his shoulders. "What the hell, Ryder? Your shoulders are incredible. And your biceps?" She ran her hand over them, desire mounting in her belly. "You're completely out of my league. I think I need to go sleep in the garage or something—"

"No." His face darkened, and before she knew it, he'd flipped her onto her back, pinning her arms to the bed above her head. "Listen to me, Zoey. You are an incredible woman. Smart. Beautiful. Capable. But that's not why I'm in bed with you right now. I'm here because there is no one but you in this world who matters to me. You could weigh six-thousand pounds and have purple skin with bumps all over it, and you would still be the most beautiful woman to ever exist."

Her throat tightened. "Ryder—"

He didn't pause to let her speak. Urgency coursed through his words. "I need you to understand this, Zoey. Your heart and your soul are like sunshine, pure, gorgeous, and flawless. That makes everything about you a treasure. Never ever put yourself down like that. Never doubt your worth. Never doubt who you are. Do you understand?"

His beautiful words reached inside her and broke something open. Something that had been locked away for years and years, something that hurt to open, that made it hard to breathe. Tears started streaming down her cheeks, tears she had no chance of stopping.

His face softened and he swore under his breath. "I'm sorry, baby." He sank down beside her and brushed his thumb over her cheek. "I didn't mean to make you cry."

She caught his hand and pressed it to her face. "Kiss me,

Ryder. Please. I need you. I need your soul to be a part of mine tonight. I need what only you can give me."

He hesitated. "You're sure? As much as I want you, I can't hurt you again—"

She grabbed his face and pulled him toward her, kissing him fiercely.

Ryder let out a low groan, and then rolled on top of her, pressing her body beneath him as he unleashed ten years of separation into their kiss. Yearning rose between them, and suddenly, there was too much fabric between them.

Almost frantically, she grabbed at his pants, desperate to get them off, and he did the same for her. They fumbled, they laughed, Ryder almost fell off the bed, but finally they were both naked, totally bare, with nothing between them except passion and desire.

She gasped as he stretched out on top of her, and she felt the warmth of his skin along her body. His chest against hers, his belly, his thighs, his calves, all of him, against all of her. It made her feel alive and vibrant, as if life itself was coursing through her cells.

He kissed his way down her body, his hands stroking fires inside her as he ran his palms over her hips, her thighs, her legs, as if every part of her was a treasure he was desperate to unearth. Then he locked his arms around her thighs and used his tongue to rip away her self-control. Heat poured through her. Need. Desire. A crushing *need* for him, and only him.

"Make love to me, Ryder." She ran her fingers through his hair, begging him to come back to her, to make her his, to bring them together in the way that she longed for.

He kissed his way back up her body, until he could see into her eyes. He met her gaze and held it captive while he slid his knee between hers, parting her legs. "My ZoeyBear," he whispered. "I'll always be yours. Always."

She held onto his shoulders. "My Ryder," she whispered.

"I—" She cut herself off, just before she said she loved him. She'd told him that a thousand times over the years, but the words felt different now. If she said them, they would mean something different, something she wasn't ready to feel...or say.

Ryder kissed her again, deep and hard, a promise of a thousand forevers as he shifted his hips. She could feel him against her, and she flashed back to that that moment so long ago, the one when everything had changed for them before... and she knew that if they made love now, everything would change for them again. How would it change? She didn't know. Not yet.

"Baby."

She opened her eyes to see Ryder's blue ones watching her face.

"I need to see you when we make love. I need you to see me. I need you to see how I feel about you. Do you see it? Can you feel it?"

Her heart tightened at the pure reverence on his face. She nodded.

He smiled. "My girl," he whispered. "My sweet girl." And then he slid inside her, easily and deliciously, as if they were made for each other.

She sucked in her breath at the feel of him inside her. "God, that feels so perfect."

He grinned. "It does, doesn't it?" He tangled his fingers in her hair as he moved inside her. "Like there's nowhere else we belong, except right here, with each other, making love."

Desire rippled through her, radiating out in all directions as he moved. "Exactly," she whispered. She stretched beneath him, her body aching for more of him. "I—" She stopped herself, almost saying it again. She wasn't ready to love him, not like that. Not now. This moment had to be just this moment, his love as her best friend healing so many of the broken bits inside her.

He kissed her again, deep and intoxicating, as he intensified his rhythm. Faster and faster, adjusting his angle, his fingers dancing across her, stoking the fire even more, until she was completely lost to him, free-falling into the magic he wove, surrendering completely to him.

The orgasm came fast, sweeping over her with a glorious thrill that made her scream. He responded instantly, bucking against her as the orgasm leapt into him with a fire that tore her name from his throat as he held onto her, keeping her safe, giving her an anchor so she didn't have to hold onto anything herself.

She just let herself take flight, because she knew she would land safely in his arms.

Always safe in his arms.

Always.

CHAPTER NINETEEN

ZOEY DIDN'T WANT to fall asleep.

She wanted to stay awake forever, inhaling Ryder's scent, feeling the weight of his arms around her as he held her, listening to the rhythm of his breath.

He nuzzled her neck, and she smiled, wrapping her hand around his wrist. "That was beautiful," she said.

"It was." He didn't lift his head, but she felt tension beginning to take root in his body.

She tapped his arm. "Ryder? What's wrong?"

He said nothing.

"Ryder!" She hit his arm this time, fear starting to grip her. "Talk to me." Last time they'd made love, this was exactly what had happened. She'd felt him start to tense almost as soon as they'd finished making love, and then he'd walked out of her life. "Are you having regrets? You have to tell me if you are. Don't just walk away like before—"

He lifted his head quickly, his eyes turbulent. "I'm not walking away."

"Then what's wrong?"

He swore and rolled onto his back, away from her, leaving her feeling cold and vulnerable.

She grabbed his shirt and pulled it over her, needing clothes, seeking protection. She could feel her heart closing up already. "Listen, I know that we're just friends and this didn't mean anything, so don't feel like you owe me—"

"No!" He sat up, grabbed her, and rolled on top of her, pinning her to the bed. "Don't even say that. It did mean something. It meant everything."

"Well, I know it meant something, but I know it's not a forever thing—"

"I want forever. I want forever with you."

She froze, her heart stuttering at his words. *"What?"*

His blue eyes were vibrant, roiling with emotion. "I wasn't going to tell you. I don't want to freak you out, but I can't have that look on your face, when you think that I'm going to walk away again, like you're not worth wanting. That's not okay. You deserve more, and I can't stay silent. If it freaks you out, then it freaks you out. It's worth the price to take that look off your face and that pain out of your heart."

She swallowed, her heart starting to pound. The words were so fierce, so unexpected, so breaking all the rules she'd laid out for them. Of course, making love had broken a big rule, so yeah, there was that. But the way he said it, the raw emotion in his voice stunned her. She wasn't used to that from him. He was always the stoic male, holding his emotions tight to his chest. And he had *never* said anything like that to her. She could barely even grasp that those words had been spoken by the Ryder she knew.

"Here's the thing, ZoeyBear." Ryder tangled his fingers through a lock of her hair. "I've always loved you. You know that, right?"

She nodded. "I've loved you forever, too. Since the first time you snuck into my room and promised you'd keep me safe. I'd only seen you from a distance before then, but you were like this giant grizzly bear protector."

He grinned. "I'd seen your uncle, and I didn't like him. None of us did. I think I wanted him to try something, so I'd have a reason to beat the shit out of him."

She smiled and relaxed slightly. "Such violent tendencies you had."

"I still have them." His smile faded, and pain flickered through his eyes. "Which is why I probably shouldn't be telling you this."

"What?" She smacked him in the arm. "You can't not tell me now that you've started. My image of you as a hard, cold villainous rebel has already been shattered. There's no going back from that, so tell me the rest."

He cocked an eyebrow. "Villainous rebel?"

"As if you could ever deny that."

"True." There was a bit of regret in his voice, but he didn't elaborate on that point. "Fine, I'll finish, but no freaking out on me."

"I might freak out. You'll be fine."

He grinned. "Okay, fine. So, as I said, I've loved you forever, right? As my best friend's little sister, as the little sister I never had. Platonic. Protective. That kind of thing. Right?"

She nodded slowly. "Okay." Was this going to be a let-her-down-easy speech? Because if it was, she was going to seriously regret goading him into continuing.

"But the night of your prom," he said, "when I kissed you for the first time, that love changed irrevocably. I fell *in* love with you that night, and I've never fallen back out."

Her breath caught. "*What?*" In love? He was *in love* with her? Her childhood knight in shining armor who had broken her heart and left her shattered for a decade was *in love* with her and always had been? "That's not possible."

"It is." He framed her face with his hands. "I held it back all this time because I didn't want to trap you into staying in Rogue Valley. I still don't want to trap you. But I can't live any longer with that look in your eyes, the one where I see that pain of you believing you're not worthy of being loved. You need to know, to understand, that there is someone in this world who loves you fiercely and unconditionally, and that person is me."

She blinked back sudden tears, and her throat ached so badly that she didn't know if she could breathe. She could feel his truth in every word, and she knew he wasn't lying.

He took her hands and tucked them against his chest. "ZoeyBear, I love you as a friend, as my best friend, yes, but I also love you as the woman I want to spend the rest of my life with. I want to be the one who makes you smile when you want to cry. I want to be the one who puts a ring on your finger. I want to be the one whose arms you fall asleep in every night of your life. That's what I want, Zoey. I never said anything before, because I believed the Stockton blood that runs through my veins tainted me and made me unworthy. Honestly, it might make me unworthy, but I also believe that I'm the man who can make you happy, and you deserve to be happy. Maybe it's your bad luck that I'm that guy for you. You're free to decide you don't want me. But you need to know that you bring out the light in me, and give me the strength to be the light and love that you deserve." His face softened. "I love you, Zoey, and you deserve to know that you're loved deeply, unconditionally, and forever."

She stared at him, speechless, too overwhelmed to even begin to respond. Silent tears rolled down her cheeks, and she felt like her chest was cracking in half.

He waited for a moment, then he nodded and rolled off her. He pulled her into the curve of his body, holding her tight as he pressed himself up against her back. "You don't have to say anything," he said softly. "I know it's a lot."

She closed her eyes against the tears squeezing out of her eyes, holding tightly to his hand, where it was on her belly. There was so much she wanted to say, but she didn't know where to start, or how to start, or even what she should admit to herself, let alone him.

He kissed her shoulder. "I can feel you trembling," he said softly, tightening his grip on her, tugging her more securely into the curve of his body, as if he could protect her from the world. "I'm sorry it upset you, but I had to say it, Zoey. You needed to know how deeply you are loved. You don't owe me anything."

Tears clogged her throat. "For years, I dreamed of you," she whispered. "I dreamed of you coming after me, telling me you loved me, and sweeping me away from the ache in my heart that followed me everywhere."

He pressed a kiss to her hair. "I had the same dream. If I had known you were struggling, I would have come after you. Dane never told me."

She shook her head, still gripping his hand tightly. "It's not Dane's fault. I told him not to tell you. I didn't want you to love me because you felt sorry for me. I wanted you to love me because you did, not to rescue me. But you never came."

Regret hit Ryder hard, deep in his gut at her words. She was right. He never followed her. "It wasn't because I didn't love you. It was because I did."

"I know. You explained that." Her voice was so full of tears that Ryder felt his own chest ache.

All he did was bring her pain. If he loved her. If he didn't love her. Somehow, he never got it right. "I'm sorry you're hurting, baby." But he wasn't sorry he'd said it. He needed her to know. He'd needed to tell her.

She raised their entwined hands to her lips and pressed a

kiss to his knuckle. "I wish I was still the woman who could live that fairytale," she whispered. "But I'm not. I would say that part of me that could love like that is broken, but I'm not sure I ever had it."

Ryder tensed. "What are you are talking about?" She was the definition of love. She poured love out everywhere she went.

"I can't remember ever telling anyone I loved them," she whispered. "I guess I told my parents, but I don't remember. Dane never said it to me. No one ever said it to me, not even my ex. I..." She pressed their entwined hands to her chest. "It hurts so much in here," she said softly. "I feel like there's this vice clamping down on my chest, trying to suffocate me." She rolled over so she was facing him, her cheeks streaked with tears. "Ryder, all I ever dreamed of was being loved the way you just told me you love me. But...the only thing I want to do is run away. Why? Why can't I just say, yay, kiss you back, and enjoy it?"

Ryder smiled gently and kissed her softly. "The same reason I never told anyone I loved them until just now. I didn't believe in romantic love or family or any of that, until Chase broke that barrier with Mira."

She nodded. "That's what the women said tonight. That Chase showed his brothers the way."

"Not just Chase. Each one of my brothers, as they've fallen in love, become dads and husbands...I've watched. I've watched my brothers, none of who believed in love or women or families, find their peace. I've watched their wives make my brothers happy. And more importantly, I've watched my brothers make their wives and kids happy. They made me believe we have a chance. With the right woman, our fucked-up Stockton genes have a chance."

Zoey's brows furrowed. "You're not fucked up."

He raised his brows. "Really?"

She sighed. "Okay, you are. But you're a good person."

"I know that." God, it felt good to say that. It had taken him a long time to be able to see the good in himself through the shadows that still haunted him. "But you're the one that makes me whole." He was so glad she was still talking to him. When he'd first opened this conversation, the look of panic on her face had shaken him. He'd thought for a moment that he'd totally blown it, but right now, he felt like he had a window of a chance to make this right. "Am I wrong that I make you happy?"

"Ryder." She sat up and hugged her knees to her chest. "We haven't seen each other for a decade. We've never even been on a date. This doesn't even make sense."

"So, let's go on a date."

She looked over at him. "It's not that simple."

"It can be. We just start." As he said it, anticipation rippled through him. Was he really going to do this? Go all in on Zoey? Dane would kick the shit out of him. He knew that. But he was going to do it anyway.

"You don't understand." She turned to face him, her arms still wrapped around her knees. "I don't have the capacity for this."

"Why not?" He encircled her ankle with his fingers and rubbed the top of her foot gently. The bruises from her fall had faded now, still visible, but definitely healing. "Talk to me, Zoey. Help me understand."

She sighed, watching his thumb move across her foot. "My ex and I had a law practice together. He was the finance expert, so he ran that side of the business."

Ryder closed his eyes, easily able to predict where the story was headed.

"After he left me for that other woman and the divorce proceedings got underway, I learned that he'd lost all our money. Our firm had to file for bankruptcy, and I even temporarily lost my license for mismanagement of client funds. That's why I stayed in Boston longer. I was trying to get it back."

Ryder ground his jaw, trying to contain his anger at the bastard who'd fucked her over so badly. "Did you?"

"Yes, right before I came back here. I had given up at that point, accepted that the career I'd worked so hard on was gone. I came out here, planning to start over. To stay. To retreat." She inched closer to him, so her hip was against his side. "Then earlier today, I got a call that I'd gotten my license restored, and a friend of mine offered me a job at her firm. So, now, I could go back to Boston, to the life I built."

"Or you could stay here." He grasped her waist and gently tugged on her.

She let him pull her down onto the bed into his arms. "With what? I have no money, no safety net. But if I go back, my reputation is shot. I worked so hard for everything I had in Boston, Ryder, and I lost it all. Because I was stupid. Because I trusted him. With my career. My heart. My money. Everything."

"Oh, baby, I'm so sorry." He stroked her hair gently, trying to comfort her when all he wanted to do was get up and beat the shit out of that asshole. His father's genes ran hot through him, but he shoved it aside, focusing instead on Zoey, and what she needed from him.

"But here's the thing," she said, still holding his hand tightly. "I thought I'd be so happy to get my license back, and to receive that job offer. All I have to do is accept her offer and get back to work, but when I got it back, I just started to cry. Not from happiness, but because I didn't want to have that choice to practice law anymore. I wanted someone else to take it away from me so I couldn't do it anymore, so I didn't have to decide what I wanted."

Ryder's heart ached for her pain. "You don't want to be a lawyer?"

She rolled over in his arms to face him. "I don't know, Ryder. I don't know anything. I worked so hard for that career, and now...I don't know. Do I hate it because of him? Or did I spend years pursuing something I didn't actually want? I have to let my friend know in two weeks if I'm taking the job, and I don't know what to do. All I know is that I *have* to say yes to the offer because I'm broke, but that feels like a terrible reason to choose a path in life. But what else would I do?" She looked at him, her eyes so lost. "I don't know, Ryder. I'm just so lost, too lost to even think about being able to invest in a relationship with you, or to promise you anything."

The thought of her going back to Boston made something dark grip Ryder's heart, but he kept his voice light. "You have two weeks, right?"

She nodded.

"Take those two weeks here. I'm the one who knows you best. Let me help you find your way."

She gave him a skeptical look. "You're not exactly impartial."

"I am." He took her hand and pressed a kiss to her knuckle. "I love you, Zoey. I want you to be my forever. But I loved you so much that I was willing to let you go once before because I thought it was best for you. I'd encourage you to go back to Boston if that was right for you." He met her gaze. "But if starting over with me is right, I'm going to fight like hell for it."

Fear flickered in her eyes. "Ryder, I'm not ready for a relationship. I can't promise that."

"No promises necessary," he said. "Just spend your two weeks here. Go on a date with me. Let the people in this place heal you, and then see where you end up."

She took a deep breath, and his heart started to pound as he waited. Two weeks. That was all he wanted from her. If, in two weeks, he was convinced she was better off in Boston, he'd make her go. But if not...he was going to do everything he could to show her that he was the one she was meant for. She couldn't lie, it sounded perfect. She hesitated. "Can I stay here? I can't pay much, but I can pay something."

"You bet. No rent, though. Friends and family discount." He grinned, his heart feeling lighter than it had in a long, long time. "Being a general contractor has been great for my bank account, so I'll even give you an allowance...if you do your chores, of course."

"You're such a pain in the ass." She pointed a finger at him. "And you won't sneak into my room every night? I need space to find myself, and I can't do that if you're taking up my world with your massive shoulders and huge biceps."

His smile widened. "Sneaking in? No. Striding right in without apology? Maybe." He raised his brows. "Kiss to seal the deal?"

"No. I already said no biceps or naked shoulders allowed." She flipped the covers back to get out of bed.

He locked his arm around her waist, dragged her back toward him, and then proceeded to show her exactly what other parts of him besides his shoulders and his biceps were tempting.

When she giggled in protest, he knew he'd done the right thing.

Because he was bringing laughter back to his woman.

CHAPTER TWENTY

"YOU'RE SUCH A DORK." Zoey couldn't stop laughing when Ryder missed the frying pan with his third pancake in a row. At least this one landed on the counter and not the floor, so progress was being made. "Stop trying to flip them. You clearly suck at it."

He grabbed the pancake and hurled it at her, scoring a direct hit on her forehead. "I used to be able to do this. I'll get my mojo back."

Zoey grinned and took a bite of the pancake. "It actually tastes pretty good."

"Of course it's good. I'm a master chef." Ryder ladled another dollop of batter into the frying pan. "You want chocolate chips with this one?"

"No, I'm good." She propped her chin on her hands, giggling as she watched him dancing to *Crocodile Rock* while he cooked. "I don't remember you being this silly."

"Never?"

"You were always serious, sometimes angry, but always protective, and cynical about the world." She took another bite. "I don't know what to do with this Ryder. I'm not sure I've ever met him before."

"Just fall madly in love with me, and we'll be good." He eyed the pan. "I think I've got it this time."

"Do you? I tend to doubt it." Zoey knew she should be tired, because Ryder had kept her up much of the night showcasing his excellent love-making skills, but she was totally wired on adrenaline and giggles. He was such a considerate lover, really talented, and fun. Even though it was basically like starting with a new lover, their long history gave her a level of comfort she hadn't experienced before. With Ryder, she could just be herself, and it felt so good. She'd never felt as happy as she had spending the night in his arms. Her entire soul had been at peace, and it still was. "Thank you for accepting me as I am."

He shot a glance at her. "Baby, the only thing I want is for you to be you, whoever you want to be. You can change your mind a thousand times, and it's all good. Because it's your soul that I love, and that never changes."

Her heart tightened. "How do you come up with such beautiful things to say? Do you sign up for daily win-her-over emails from Howtogetagirl.com?"

"Nope. It's all me. But I'm considering being offended that you think I couldn't come up with that kind of shit by myself."

She cocked her head. "Okay, apology sent your way. But seriously, how do you come up with it? You're so...kind. You've always been my protector, but now there's something else to you as well. Something...more introspective, I guess?" This new side of Ryder was intriguing. A little unsettling, because he was changing the rules, but at the same time, she kinda liked it.

Oh, who was she kidding? She freaking loved it. The guy was an amazing lover, and he made her feel like the most special person in the entire world. What woman wouldn't completely melt for that?

He shrugged. "It's a side effect of a long life of hating myself and my genes, I guess, and trying to figure out how to get past it. It was tough trying to come to terms with my brothers finding happiness, which didn't make sense to me for a long time."

She frowned. "Why didn't it make sense? I think it's beautiful."

He raised an eyebrow. "Baby cakes, we all had the shit beat out of us on a regular basis by our bastard pig of a father. Every woman he brought into the house was a bitch, and we have a string of different mothers, none of whom stuck around or gave a shit about us once we were born. None of us know a damned thing about being a husband or a dad or any kind of remotely acceptable member of society. So, when my brothers started finding happiness and love, it didn't make sense to me. We didn't get those things, and yet, apparently, we did. So, I had to figure out how to understand that."

Sadness filled her at the honesty in his voice. "You always had loyalty to each other. And to me and Dane. That's family."

He nodded. "I think our loyalty to each other is what enabled my brothers to connect with their wives. We don't trust many people, but with the ones we let in, the bond is deep. It took a long time for me to understand that." He tested the pancake, then glanced at her. "I have a monster inside me, Zoey. All the Stocktons do. I didn't think it was possible for any of us to become more than what our dad was. And yet, I'm surrounded by proof that it can happen, which made it hard for me to keep lying to myself that it wasn't possible." He pointed the frying pan at her. "And you, my dear, are part of the reason I learned not to hate myself so much. I figured if you thought I was worthy of your sunshine, I must not be half bad, right?"

Her throat tightened, and she wasn't sure which part was most powerful. The part that he hated himself for so long, or that she was part of the reason he learned not to. "I always saw beauty in you," she said softly.

He met her gaze. "I know you did. You never stopped seeing a hero when I saw nothing but shit. I think that's maybe one of the reasons I declared myself your protector. I needed your sunshine more than you needed to be protected."

She raised her eyebrows. "With my uncle?"

He laughed. "Okay, so maybe you did need protection, but after all this time, I'll finally confess that my motives weren't completely altruistic. You were my lifeline, Zoey, and when you left, I wasn't sure I'd be able to find my way without you."

Why did you let me go, then? The question bubbled up inside her, but she didn't ask it. He'd already given her his answer, and she knew hearing it again wouldn't change anything. She had to deal with what had happened, to find her way back, just as he had.

She watched as Ryder slid his spatula under the pancake, flipped it, and executed a perfect landing in the pan. "Voila!"

She applauded him, laughing at the sparkle in his eyes. She'd never seen him so happy, which made him even more handsome than ever. His good mood was infectious, and her heart felt lighter than it had in a very long time, even now, despite their brief trip to the past and his horrible, horrible childhood.

She knew this happy, relaxed moment with them was temporary. Real life hovered just outside the walls of the kitchen. He'd already told her he had to leave town in a couple hours for a one-night trip to another site. She had to get to work at the café, and start to think about what her life could look like without law in it, and how she felt about that possibility. She still wasn't ready to turn herself over to the demands and stresses of a relationship, especially with Ryder, who could so easily make her forget about anything but him.

But right now, watching him with flour on his cheek and the floor littered with failed pancake flips, she was so relaxed, and so happy, and it felt great. "When are you coming back to town?"

"Tomorrow evening." He carried the surviving pancakes over to the table and gave her a long, delicious kiss before setting them down. "I promise to make it back in time to kiss you goodnight, sweetheart—"

"Ryder? What the fuck are you doing?" Dane appeared in the doorway, his voice hard and cold.

Ryder immediately tensed, and she saw his jaw flex. "Dane." His voice was hard, and he set his hand on Zoey's arm as if to claim her, and then he slowly turned around. "So good of you to stop by unannounced and uninvited."

"You piece of shit." To her shock, her brother leapt across the kitchen, grabbed Ryder, and punched him right in the jaw.

RYDER REELED BACKWARD. Not from the punch so much, which he'd seen coming and hadn't tried to evade, but from the fact that his best friend had just hit him for kissing the woman he loved. He hit the counter hard, staggering to stay on his feet, stunned that Dane had actually hit him.

"Dane!" Zoey leapt between them, her voice elevated with shock. "What are you doing? What's wrong with you?"

His fists bunched by his sides, Dane didn't even look at his sister. He just glared at Ryder. "What the fuck, Ryder?"

Ryder fought to keep his anger in check. He was so pissed

he could barely think. "So, that's what you think of me? I'm so unworthy of your sister that you'd *punch* me to keep me away from her?" The man who had stood by him his whole life, since they were kids, thought he was nothing more than scum. Dane had told him as much the other night, but to actually see Dane so angry that he *hit* him was surreal.

He'd never seen Dane hit anyone or anything in his entire life. The man had no violent streak, no anger issues, no need to get physical, which showed exactly how much he hated the fact Ryder was kissing Zoey.

"What?" Zoey looked back and forth between them. "What are you talking about?" She grabbed Dane's arm. "What's going on?"

Dane finally dragged his gaze off Ryder and focused on his sister. There was so much pain in his eyes that Ryder almost felt sorry for him. "I gave up everything for you, Zoey," he said, his voice raw with emotion. "I gave it all up so you could get out of here and live the life you deserved."

She stared at him. "What are you talking about?"

Ryder swore. "Don't go there, Dane. Don't do that to her."

"Do what?" Zoey stiffened and pulled back from Dane, her body tensing. "What are you guys talking about?"

Dane answered her. "I had an athletic scholarship to the University of Wyoming," he said. "I had a chance to get out of town, but I stayed here to take care of you. I knew I couldn't leave you with our bastard uncle. I was going to stay until you left for college, but then, you needed spending money. So I stayed in this town so you could get out."

Her mouth dropped open. "You never told me that. I thought you wanted to stay in town."

Ryder swore at the shocked guilt on her face, and he walked over to her, sliding his arm around her shoulders, because he had a feeling she'd need it.

"I didn't tell you because it wasn't your burden to carry." Dane's voice softened, even as he glared at Ryder's possessive stance. "I never regretted it, Zoey. You were worth it, and I'd do it a thousand times over." He scowled at Ryder, new anger simmering in his eyes. "But I didn't do all that so Ryder could fuck it all up. He promised he wouldn't keep you. He promised to keep his hands off you, not trap you here just because he wanted to get his jollies with you—"

"What the fuck?" Ryder couldn't let that one pass by uncontested. "That's not fair, and you know it. I love her and—"

"No! Don't!" Dane was almost frantic. "Don't you get it? Zoey deserves everything, and you don't get to steal it from her! Don't fucking love her!"

"Wait a minute!" Zoey held up her arms to silence them. She turned to Ryder. "What is he talking about? That you promised to keep your hands off me and not trap me? When?"

Ryder ground his jaw at the pain in her eyes. "It was just before the prom, when he said you were falling in love with me. I told you, remember?"

"Yes, but that was ten years ago, and he just punched you *now*." She looked back and forth between them. "Did you have the same conversation again since I came back?"

Ryder ground his jaw, and Dane said nothing.

"You did, didn't you?" Zoey felt like her heart was shattering all over again. She looked at her brother. "You told Ryder to stay away from me again? You kicked me out of this town ten years ago, and now you want me gone again," she said, her voice starting to shake. "You didn't want me here then, and you treated me the same way this time."

"Because you deserve better," Dane said.

"Better than living with the man I loved?" *The man she loved.* The words had slipped out, but she knew she meant them. She had loved Ryder back then...and now? She was so afraid to admit to herself what she was feeling for him.

"You were eighteen!" Dane said. "You didn't know what love was!"

"And now? You think that after living in Boston for ten years, going through marriage, divorce, a miscarriage, and bankruptcy, that I'm not capable of handling my own life? Because that's how you're treating me, like I'm some pathetic idiot!"

"Miscarriage?" Ryder sounded shocked. "You had a miscarriage? When?"

Shit. She hadn't meant to bring that up. Her throat tightened at the memories of that horrible time. "I lost the baby the week after Nathan announced he was leaving. He never knew I was pregnant."

Ryder swore, and she felt his arm tighten around her. It was a subtle move, but it seemed to reach inside her and steady her as the old grief tried to well up.

"I don't think you're an idiot." Dane took a deep breath. "I just want you to have a beautiful life, and Ryder's not it."

"I don't understand." She wedged herself tighter against Ryder's side, needing his support and his grounding. "Ryder's always been your best friend. Why on earth are you so angry about me being with him?"

Dane ground his jaw. "Because I know his demons, Zoey. I know his darkness. I've seen the sides of him you never have." He gave a hard look at Ryder. "He's my best friend, but if he decides to go after you, he's not anymore. You have to choose, Ryder."

Zoey felt like her heart was breaking. She couldn't believe Dane was trying so hard to come between her and Ryder. Yes, she wasn't ready to declare her love for him, but she needed him in her life. He was her strength, her peace, her laughter, her salvation, and she'd just now finally gotten him back.

"And me? I have to choose between the two of you as well? Is that what you're saying?"

Dane sighed. "You'll always have me," he said softly. "Always. I'd give my life for you. I already have."

Guilt clenched around her heart. "But if I were to choose to be with Ryder, what then? Would you accept him?"

Her brother didn't hesitate. "No. Never. It would be the ultimate betrayal by him to be with you." He looked at Ryder. "Do the right thing, Ryder. If you love her, you will let her go. If you keep her, then you're the selfish bastard you've tried your entire life not to be, just like your dad."

Ryder sucked in his breath as if he'd been punched, and Zoey felt like she was going to cry. "Why would you say something like that to him, Dane?"

Tears brimmed in his eyes. "Because you're all I have left of my family, Zoey. I have to protect you, the way I couldn't protect Mom and Dad. Come to dinner tomorrow night. Meet my kids. Jaimi loved you so much. Be a part of my family, sis, until you go back to Boston."

Then he spun around and strode out of the kitchen, slamming the front door as he left the house.

CHAPTER TWENTY-ONE

THERE WAS silence between Ryder and Zoey after Dane left.

Ryder was so pissed at Dane he could barely even think. He wanted to go after him, haul his ass back into the kitchen, and beat the hell out of him...and the fact he was even thinking that scared the living shit out of him.

Zoey pulled away from him, and he let her go, flexing his jaw as he tried to pull himself together.

She put the table between them before she turned to face him. "You let my brother talk you out of going after me?" she asked softly. "I know you already told me, but I didn't really understand. You actually let him talk you out of being with me?"

"I made the choice myself," he said again. "I believed you deserved Harvard. I did not, however, understand until a couple days ago that part of the reason he spoke to me back then was because it was *me* he wanted you away from. Not the town. *Me.*"

"What made you realize it now?"

"Because he told me two days ago, when he found out I'd been at your place helping you unpack. He told me to stay away from you again." He shrugged. "I thought about it, because I do believe you deserve to be happy."

"But...?"

"I decided I'm the one you need in order to be happy. So, I ignored him. It went over well, as you saw." Did he regret it? He probably should, but he couldn't summon any regret. If anything, Dane's reaction made him more certain that Zoey needed him.

She searched his face. "Why? What's so bad about you that he'd actually *hit* you to keep you away? I thought you were best friends."

Ryder rubbed his cheek where Dane had hit him. "I did, too."

"What does he see in you that scares him so badly?" she asked, her voice a raw whisper. "Because I don't see it. What do I not know about you, Ryder?"

Ryder ground his jaw. "I don't know," he answered honestly. "I feel like you know me pretty well. I don't know what he sees in me that scares him." But even as he said it, he realized it wasn't true. He did know, because that's how he'd perceived himself for so long. "I saw myself as a monster for almost my entire life," he said. "Maybe I can't blame him for seeing me as I believed I was."

"That doesn't make sense." She was still watching him, still looking wary. "There has to be *something* you did, something that scared him."

The fact that there wasn't anything was the part that bothered Ryder the most about Dane's rejection of him. He'd never lost his temper. He'd never beat anyone up. He'd never had even so much as a drop of alcohol. He'd lived his life under a brutally tight rein, unwilling to take a chance on what would happen if he relinquished even the slightest bit of control on his emotions. "It's just me, Zoey. He just saw me, day in and day out. Exactly as I am. My father's son. Apparently, that's enough."

She let out her breath. "He fears the demon inside you. The one you never let out."

Ryder stiffened. "My demon?"

She nodded. "I see it in your eyes all the time, Ryder. Haunting you. Stalking you. It never scared me because I knew you would never hurt me. But for him to react like that...am I wrong to trust you?"

Ryder felt like she'd just kicked him in the gut. She doubted if she could trust him? She was the only one who had believed in him, and he *needed* her to believe in him. "No, you aren't wrong to trust me." He strode across the kitchen and took her hand. "You know me better than anyone, Zoey. You *know* me."

She pulled her hand free, a movement that felt like it struck a dagger right through his heart. "I thought I did, until you abandoned me after the prom. I know you wanted me to go to Harvard, but there were a thousand ways you could have made that happen without rejecting me like that. You could have come with me. You could have told me that you loved me, but you couldn't let me stay. I would have listened to you. I worshipped you, Ryder. *Worshipped* you. If you'd simply told me to go, I would have listened. But you didn't choose that path. The path you chose was—"

"I know what path I chose, and I'm sorry." She was right. He'd never considered any other options, any of the ones that would have given her Harvard and still allowed them to be together. It had never even crossed his mind. "I guess I didn't think I deserved you," he said slowly. "I was afraid of my demon. Maybe I wanted you away from me as well." Saying the words felt like a betrayal to himself, but as he said them, they felt true.

Hell, he'd almost walked away from her again two days

ago. If it hadn't been for Chase and Brody, he might have quit the barn project and left town completely. He'd been that close to leaving her again.

He let out his breath. Maybe he'd been lying to himself by believing he could give her what she needed. Dane was a good man, not a fool, and he loved the hell out of his sister. Maybe he did know what was right. "Maybe I'm not the man you need," Ryder said slowly. "I have no experience with good relationships. Maybe I can't give you what you need." He looked at her, barely able to think over the pain those words caused in his heart. "Because you deserve everything," he said softly.

She didn't argue with him, which said more than he wanted it to say.

They stood silently, staring at each other.

"I already told you I don't want a relationship right now," she said, her voice shaky. "I can't deal with this."

"I understand." He wanted to promise they could just be friends, that he could just be her platonic buddy, but it would be a lie. It was impossible. "All I wanted to do was make you smile again. A real smile. One with your heart." He searched her face, looking for any sign that she believed he could be the one for her, but there was nothing. Her face was a mask of pain and walls. "I thought you needed me, but maybe I was deluding myself, because *I'm* actually the one who needs *you*."

"You don't need me, Ryder. You never did. You couldn't have let me go if you did. And the same with Dane."

"Jesus. Is that what you think? That because I let you go, I didn't need you? I—"

"No." She held up her hands to stop him. "I have to go to work. You need to go to your other job site. Let's just take a day apart and get some perspective, okay? We can talk when you get home tomorrow night."

He didn't want to walk away. He was terrified she'd sneak

away while he was gone, and he'd lose her forever. "Promise me you'll be here when I get back?"

She hesitated. "Ryder—"

He grabbed her wrist, trapping her. "*Promise me you'll be here when I get back*. I won't leave until you promise me."

"Why do you care?"

"Because I fucking love you. Maybe I'm not the right guy for you. Maybe Dane's right that I'm a fucked-up bastard, but I love the hell out of you, ZoeyBear, and if you walk out of here while I'm gone, I will lose the one thing, the one person, who makes my heart whole. This isn't over. *Promise me*."

She stared at him for a long moment, then she nodded. "I promise," she whispered.

"Okay." He paused for a split second, then locked his arm around her waist, pulled her against him, and kissed her hard. Passionately. Pouring every last bit of his soul into her safe-keeping. He kissed her until she melted into him, her body sagging into his in complete capitulation and acceptance.

It was only then that he felt safe enough to let her go.

CHAPTER TWENTY-TWO

ZOEY SAT on her bed later that evening, her knees pulled to her chest, tired. Drained. Lost. It was almost midnight, and she hadn't been able to fall asleep, despite a double shift at the café. Everything in her brain and heart was a jumble that she couldn't sort out. Ryder had texted a few times, just to make sure she was still there, and she was mad at how much she looked forward to his texts.

A light knock sounded on the door, making her jump. Was Ryder back a night early? She wasn't ready to see him. She didn't know what to say.

"Zoey? You still up?" Brody's voice was quiet, drifting through the door just loud enough for her to hear only because she was listening.

Brody. Relief rushed through her. "Yes, I'm up."

"Can I come in?"

She pulled the covers over her lap, feeling awkward and exposed sitting in her bed, but she nodded. "Yes, sure."

He nudged the door open, just enough to lean in. He glanced around the room, no doubt noticing she'd dropped her clothes from work in the middle of the floor, too tired to care where they went. "Keegan and I are going on a late-night kayak ride. Want to come?"

She blinked. "It's after midnight."

"Yeah, it's a full moon. Gorgeous. You want to join us?"

"I need to get up early for work."

"Who the fuck cares? Life is not all about work." He opened the door the rest of the way, showing that he was already in water sandals, shorts, and a tee shirt that showed off impressive amounts of muscle. "Come on, Zoey. You need to get out of here. See you by the water in five minutes. Kayak vests are in the closet by the front door." He winked and left before she could argue, leaving her scowling after him.

"You're a pain in the ass," she called out.

"I know!" He sounded amused, not annoyed, and his feet thudded down the stairs as he headed out.

For a moment, Zoey considered pulling the covers over her head, but she didn't want to be alone with her thoughts. She'd spent way too much time alone with her thoughts over the course of her life, and they weren't helping her right now. Why not a midnight kayak ride?

With a sigh of resignation, she flipped off the covers and went in search of midnight kayaking gear...whatever that might be.

TEN MINUTES LATER, with some guidance from Keegan and Brody, she was in the kayak, afloat, and gliding out onto a magically still river. The moonlight was so bright that its silver rays lit up even the darkest shadows, as if it were midday. It was absolute peace and beauty, and within moments, she felt something inside her relax, and her tension began to ease away.

Neither Hart brother said anything as they paddled, allowing her to sink more deeply into a space of peace and calmness. She watched the ripples as night creatures swam just beneath the surface, and the chorus of night sounds included frogs, owls, and even a distant howl. Her heart turned over with sudden joy. "I haven't heard a coyote in forever."

"It always makes me feel like home. I love that sound." Brody rested his paddle across the front of his kayak, letting it drift as they listened to the coyotes talk to each other across the river. "I might have to move here permanently," he said. "I fucking love this river."

"Me too," Keegan said. "It reminds me of sitting on the riverbank as kids, watching the auto barges go past while we kept an eye out for cops. I liked that time. It was the only time that life seemed to make sense."

Zoey looked over at Brody as he nodded. Both men hadn't shaved for a few days, and they looked hard and strong, with their muscles flexing, and the craggy lines of their faces. They were both incredibly handsome, but there was a realness, a roughness to them, that only a tough life could create. "You guys are so lucky you found each other," she said softly. "I can't imagine a childhood of living on the streets."

Brody looked over at her. "I think you can. You had it rough."

She shrugged, knowing she could never compare her childhood to the Harts. "I had my aunt and uncle."

"Good people, were they?" Brody asked skeptically, making it clear that he'd heard plenty about them.

"They weren't my parents, but they were okay."

Keegan swung his kayak around so he was facing her.

"What happened with Ryder and Dane today?" he asked, changing the subject. "We heard it even upstairs."

She frowned. "Nothing. It's fine."

The Harts exchanged glances, then Brody spoke. "Zoey, when we were kids, the only way we survived was because we were a team. Loyalty was the *only* thing that mattered. We had nothing...except each other. And that was enough, because we could count on it, no matter what."

Keegan nodded. "Brody was the one who pulled us all together, and he had this iron-clad rule that we never, *ever* kept anything from each other. If one of us were scared, we had to share it. If we did something stupid, we had to share it. Every single night, he made us sit together on the bank of that river, no matter what the weather, and each of us had to say how we were feeling, and what we needed. And then we'd try to help. Usually, we had no solutions, but it helped to get the shit out from inside us, where it was ripping us apart." He looked at his brother. "Those meetings were what saved us. Without those, the loneliness and fear would have destroyed all of us."

Zoey was embarrassed at the pang of envy that rippled through her. The Harts had had nothing as kids, and she'd had a home and food and the Stockton boys, and Dane. She knew she should be grateful for how much more she'd had than they had, but she couldn't stop the envy for their connection, for the fact that every single night, each Hart had gone to sleep knowing they had each other. "That's beautiful," she said softly, watching the ripples from her paddle slide across the water.

"My point," Brody said, "is that we consider you family now, Zoey. That means you don't get to sit and suffer in silence. Talk it out. It's what we do."

She tensed. "Talk what out?"

Keegan tapped the front of her kayak with his paddle.

"You're trapped out here with us, Zoey. There ain't no going back until this shit is flayed open and exposed."

Brody leaned forward, bracing his forearms on the kayak. "We've seen it all, Zoey. Every single Hart has been to hell and back. There's nothing you can say or feel or do that we can't handle."

She bit her lip and trailed her finger though the cool water. "I'm not used to talking things out." The only one she'd ever talked to was Ryder, and that had been somewhat sparing. He'd been her protector, more than her deepest confidant. She'd tried to be brave and strong around him, around everyone, although Ryder seemed to be incredibly astute about what she was feeling and what she needed, despite her attempts to pretend to be strong.

"That's fine. It's not supposed to be pretty," Brody said. "I've heard a lot about you from Dane. We know a lot of background already. So just start in the middle."

Zoey felt her chest tighten, and she picked up her paddle and started to blindly paddle. "I'm fine. Really."

Keegan swore and paddled across her path, so her kayak collided with his with a thump. "For hell's sake, Zoey. Stop with the bullshit. What the fuck is going on?"

"What's going on?" Sudden anger swelled inside her. Anger that these two men who she'd barely met were prying into her business. "You want to know? Fine. I'll tell you. I spent the last ten years fighting for a life that I'm not sure I even want anymore. I think I still love Ryder, but I don't even know if I know who he is anymore, and maybe I never actually knew him. My brother is being an asshole. I feel like I don't fit in anywhere, and I don't even know where I want to be! I tried so fucking hard my whole life! I'm so tired of the struggle and trying so hard, only to have every good moment be wrecked as soon as I have the tiniest minute of being happy!"

Her shouts echoed across the water, and then silence fell, the kind of silence that only happens at night, when everything in the world seemed to be asleep.

Brody grinned. "You even dropped an f-bomb. That's a good sign."

She glared at him. "And I'm mad at you for taunting me into exploding."

"That's fine." He drifted closer. "Anything else?"

She sighed and set the paddle across her boat. "I'm lonely," she said softly. "When I go to bed at night, I feel like this darkness is closing in around me. I have plenty of friends and colleagues in Boston, but I still feel so deeply alone." It was so embarrassing to admit, like she was a loser, but in the darkness of the night, the truth came out.

Keegan nodded. "Have there been any moments when you don't feel lonely? Think back. Any times over the years?"

Two things immediately popped into her mind. "Yes."

"What were they?" Brody asked.

"Painting. Creating art, rather. It didn't have to be painting. Just anything to do with creating art. And..." She hesitated. "When I'm with Ryder."

The Harts looked at each other, and Brody raised his brows.

Keegan swore. "Damn. If Ryder hadn't been one of your answers, I was totally going to risk his wrath and go for you."

Brody snorted. "Fuck that. You'd never do that to him." He grinned at Zoey. "That's one of our codes. We never do shit like that to each other. Ever. So if you have the hots for Keegan, you gotta shut it down right now, because he's not going there with you."

Heat flushed her cheeks. "I don't have the hots for him," she blurted out, then laughed when Keegan put his hand over his heart and feigned agony. "Oh, shut up," she laughed. "You know you don't mean that."

"Actually, I do on some levels." Keegan's smile faded. "You have no idea of the light you shine, Zoey. I saw it the moment I met you, and I completely understand why Ryder needs you. We all need light like yours, and he's a lucky son of a bitch that he's the one you chose."

"I didn't choose him—"

"Your light did." Brody let his kayak drift closer. "I believe in love, Zoey. Romantic love. It's what makes our souls safe enough to breathe and thrive. I see that in the way you and Ryder look at each other. You have that chance with him, so fight for it. Not everyone gets that gift." There was no mistaking the edge to his voice, the almost desperation.

She tried to remember if any of the Harts were married, but she didn't recall Ryder mentioning it. "Are any of your brothers and sisters with someone?"

"Only Hannah. But the rest will all find someone." Brody's tone was hard and unyielding. Accepting no other future.

"The Stocktons give us hope," Keegan said. "Some of them found it, and they're as fucked up as we are."

She looked at them both. "You guys don't seem fucked up. You seem like you totally have your shit together, honestly. So much more than I do."

Brody gave her a half-smile. "There's darkness in each one of us that's twisted so deeply that every day we have to fight a battle to keep from being consumed by it. Don't be fooled, Zoey. The Harts are a bunch of completely fucked-up individuals, and we always will be."

Her heart tightened as Keegan nodded in agreement. "I'm sorry."

Brody shrugged. "It's what we are. We can't change it. So, we learn to live with it." He glanced at Keegan. "But somewhere out there, I believe there's someone for each of us, someone who can handle our shit and the nightmares we bring."

Zoey stared at him, startled by the absolute conviction in his voice. She didn't know the details of his story, but he'd clearly been the leader of the gang of street kids who had all taken the last name of Hart and created a forever family. She had no doubt he'd been through hell and back, and yet he believed that he, and all his siblings, still deserved to be loved.

Envy flickered through her.

"Zoey." Brody tapped her kayak.

"What?"

"You deserve love as well. Everyone does. No matter how screwed up you are, no matter how many bad decisions you've made, no matter how much carnage you've left strewn behind you, no matter what an asshole you are...you still deserve to be happy."

Tears filled her eyes, and suddenly she couldn't breathe. "You're such a romantic."

He shook his head. "I believe in survival. And you can't survive without love."

"And excellent baked goods," Keegan said. "Everyone needs dessert."

She burst out laughing. "Dessert?"

"Yeah. Sugar heals all wounds." There was the slightest edge to Keegan's voice, and Zoey wondered if he believed as strongly as Brody that there was someone out there for him. What was his story? And Brody's? And all the rest of their siblings? Her heart ached for all of them, for all the pain they'd endured, and probably still did, because she knew the past would always be a shadow haunting all of them.

But maybe, just maybe, the shadow could fade.

Zoey suddenly noticed lights on the bank of the river, and she realized they had floated almost all the way back to the house while they'd talked. Sadness drifted through her. She didn't want to go back inside. Being with Keegan and Brody made her feel less alone, and she wasn't ready to let it go, to go back into her own mind and her own thoughts. There was something about being outside, on the water, that soothed her spirit.

"What are you going to do?" Keegan asked. "About art and Ryder? Find a job using your art?"

Longing rushed through her, but she shook her head. "I need money. I have to find a job soon. I have no training in art. No one would ever pay me for it. And I have to find my own space before I can share myself with him, or anyone."

Both Harts were quiet for a moment, and she looked over at them. "What? You think I'm stupid not to just run for him and beg him to take me? Because I can't do that."

Brody shrugged. "No. It sounds like you know what you need to do, then."

Zoey frowned at him. "You just told me not to give up on a chance for love."

"Are you giving up? Or are you taking the path that you need to follow to get you there?"

She frowned at him. "I don't know."

Keegan tapped her kayak with his paddle. "If you need time to sort stuff out, you can always come to Oregon. We have a huge ranch, and our brothers and sisters would be thrilled to meet you."

She stared at him. "Move to *Oregon?*"

"Sure. There's always a space for you there if you want it," Keegan said as his kayak bumped against the shore. "To us, family isn't about blood ties, obviously. It's about the soul. And you're family. We take care of each other, including you."

Brody nodded. "There's always a space there for you, Zoey. A spare room, plenty of food. You can take whatever time you need."

Her throat tightened. "That's a beautiful offer." She could

tell they meant it. Oregon? She'd never considered it. But something about it called to her. It gave her hope. "Maybe."

Keegan nodded. "We're heading back on Monday evening. You can come with us then, or we can send the jet back for you whenever you want."

She blinked. "The jet? You have a private jet?"

Brody grinned. "Not bad for a bunch of homeless kids, right?"

She smiled back, her heart suddenly feeling lighter. "Not bad at all," she agreed. If the Harts could go from being homeless street kids to a big, solid family with a freaking private jet, then why couldn't she find her own way as well?

The Harts had given her hope by showing her their path, a path that had started in loneliness and desperation, and ended up with a bunch of loyal siblings and a private jet.

She grinned at them as her kayak bumped gently against the shore. "Thanks, guys. Tonight helped."

They both grinned at her, looking deeply satisfied. "You got it, sis," Brody said.

Keegan held out his hand. "Want some help out?"

She grinned. "Sure." She took his hand and started to stand...and then Keegan grinned and gave a hard yank to the left. She screeched as the kayak rolled, dumping her on her ass in the water.

Water streamed down her face as she tried to glare at him, but his eyes were sparkling with such mischievousness, that she burst out laughing. "You're in such trouble, Keegan."

He blinked innocently. "Never. It was a total accident—" Before he could finish, Brody snuck up behind him and swept his feet out from under him in one swift move that wound up with Keegan down in the water beside her.

Both brothers were laughing now, and she realized that this was how they'd survived. Creating joy in whatever way, whatever moment they could.

Brody held out his hand to her, still laughing. "My brother's an ass. Want some help up?"

She smiled. "No thanks. I got this."

And she knew she did.

Because for the first time in a long time, she felt like she actually had a chance.

CHAPTER TWENTY-THREE

SUNDAY EVENING, Ryder pulled up in front of Dane's house for the second time in less than a week. It was almost nine, not as late as last time.

After he turned off the engine, however, he didn't move. He just sat in his truck in the driveway, staring up at the house.

He'd wanted to drive right home to see Zoey, but he hadn't been able to make himself do that. He'd spent the last thirty-six hours thinking a lot about Zoey, Boston, and Dane's absolute conviction that Ryder would destroy her.

Destroying her wasn't an acceptable option.

Chase believed he was good for her.

Dane believed he'd destroy her.

He didn't know what to think anymore.

But he had to know before he walked back into that house and saw her. If he was going to fight for her, for them, he had to know, without a doubt, that it was the right decision for both of them.

He had to be certain.

After a long moment, he opened the door and got out.

His legs felt heavy as he walked up the stairs and knocked on the front door.

It was Jaimi who answered, holding little Justin in her arms. She raised her eyebrows in surprise. "Hey, Ryder. It's good to see you. What's up?"

He gave her a quick hug. "Is Dane here?"

"No, he's out on a call. Why?"

He swore. "Nothing." He started to turn away, but stopped when Jaimi put her hand on his arm.

"Ryder."

He turned back toward her. "What?"

"Dane told me what happened at your house yesterday morning."

He nodded once.

"Was Zoey really upset?"

He shrugged. "It wasn't a real feel-good moment," he admitted. "She feels like Dane has been rejecting her for a long time."

"Damnit. I'm so sorry to hear that." Jaimi sighed. "I really enjoyed meeting her and hanging out the other night. She has a beautiful soul."

He smiled. "That she does. I'm glad you two were finally able to get together. I know it was hard for her."

"I could tell, but she got through it, and it was a great night." Jaimi cocked her head. "Do you love her?"

He sucked in his breath at the unexpected question. "*What?*"

"Do you love her?"

He cleared his throat. "Dane thinks—"

"I know what Dane thinks. That's not what I'm asking. Do you love her?"

He stared at the wall behind her, gritting his teeth. "Yes." The tension dissolved from his body the moment he admitted it, putting it out there into the world, his deep, dark secret that he hadn't been able to shake for ten years. "Yes, I love her. Completely."

She beamed at him. "Then ignore Dane."

He looked at her. "Really?"

Jaimi shifted her baby to her other shoulder. "Dane is a beautiful man, Ryder. You know that. But he carries a tremendous amount of guilt over his parents' death. He has tried to make the pain go away by protecting Zoey. It's not about you. It's about trying to undo his past. Like you, he's a protector, and in his heart, he feels he failed, both his parents and Zoey."

Ryder closed his eyes briefly, his chest heavy for his friend. "He never said anything."

She shrugged. "He's just now beginning to understand it." She grinned. "Sometimes it takes a woman to sort out you men."

Ryder leaned against the doorframe. "My past is a hell of a lot darker than his, Jaimi. I don't want to bring that down on Zoey—"

"Uncle Ryder!" Jaimi and Dane's daughter, Emily, came sprinting down the hall. She took a flying leap at Ryder, and he caught her easily, swinging her around while she shrieked with laughter.

"Hey, shortcake." He chuckled when she pulled his hat off his head and set it on hers. "What have you been up to?"

She looped her arms around his neck. "Did you see the new foal over at the barn? I've been taking care of it with Chase. He's showing me what to do."

"There's a baby over there?" Ryder was surprised. He hadn't spent much time at the ranch since Chase had taken over. Were they breeding horses now? He felt a stab of guilt that he'd stayed away from the ranch, even though it had started to become a family compound since Chase had bought it. Zane, Travis, Steen, and Maddox had all joined

Chase on the property with their wives and kids, but Ryder had stayed away.

He, Logan, and Quintin were the only holdouts who weren't living there. Plus Caleb, but no one had heard from him for years. Chase was adamant that they'd hear from Caleb again someday, but Ryder was a little worried. It had been too long, and the silence had been so complete.

Since the Stocktons had started taking over the ranch that had once been their salvation when they'd been kids, and the property had been owned by Ol' Skip, Ryder had kept his distance. He knew Chase had hired him for the new barn to try to draw him back in, but Ryder had kept his focus on building the new barn, carefully keeping a distance so he didn't get pulled back into the world that haunted him so badly.

Apparently, it had worked well enough that he didn't even know they had babies at the barn...and that felt weird to him, to not know what his family was up to. How much had he missed out on by keeping his distance?

Emily hit his chest, drawing his attention back to the moment. "You have to come see her! She's so cute! I named her Moana. Come tomorrow and see her! We're having a picnic at the ranch, and you can meet her."

A picnic? Hmm... "Who's coming?"

"It's just sort of grown organically since Monday is a holiday, but I think everyone is coming now," Jaimi said. "It would be great if you'd come."

He wanted to join them. That fact surprised him, but it also felt good.

"Uncle Ryder?" Emily poked his jaw. "Promise you'll come?"

He grinned. "Yes, I promise I'll come."

"Yay!" She threw her arms around his neck and hugged him, then put his hat back on his head, leapt down, and raced back upstairs singing what sounded like the newest Taylor Swift song. "Bye!"

"See ya, kiddo!" Ryder was grinning when he looked back at Jaimi, who was watching him with a bemused smile on her face. "What?"

"My kids adore you."

He nodded. "They're great kids."

"They are great kids," she agreed. "They're also smart kids, and they know who's worth their time." She cocked her head. "And as I said, they adore you. Go figure, right?"

At that moment, the baby woke up. He blinked sleepy eyes at Ryder, then his face lit up and he extended his arms to Ryder.

Jaimi immediately handed Justin to him. "Ryder Stockton. Baby whisperer."

Ryder took the baby and lifted him high, grinning at the goofy gurgles of laughter echoing from that tiny body. "What do you think, kid?"

Jaimi folded her arms over her chest, watching them. "Ryder," she said, her voice gentle. "You're a good man. Dane knows it. He's just struggling right now with the fact that Zoey has come home. He feels like he failed her. It's not about you. He loves you."

Ryder looked over at her. "That's not the issue, Jaimi."

She raised her brows. "He trusts you with his children. What stronger statement is there than that?"

"If he trusted me with his sister."

She let out her breath and nodded. "In time." But there was a faint hint of doubt in her voice, and he knew that Dane might never, ever come around to believing Ryder was worthy of his sister.

Maybe it was because of his own guilt. And maybe it was because of Ryder.

But either way, it was clear: he would not be able to get Dane's blessing, or his belief that Ryder was good for Zoey.

Silently, he handed the baby back to Jaimi. "I need to go."

She tucked Justin against her hip. "What are you going to do?"

He took a breath. "I don't know."

She nodded. "Trust your heart, Ryder. It will show you the way."

He gave her a quick hug, knowing damn well that his heart was ripping him apart, not laying down a well-lit yellow brick road for him. "Maybe. Give Em a kiss for me."

She nodded, stepping back to make room for him to leave.

When he got in his truck, Jaimi was still standing in the doorway. She and little Justin were watching him, cast in the soft yellow glow of the light by the front door. Something inside his chest turned over at the sight. He wanted someone to stand there like that for him when he drove into his own driveway.

And he wanted it to be Zoey.

CHAPTER TWENTY-FOUR

WHEN RYDER GOT HOME, he found Zoey sitting in the family room, surrounded by the painting supplies he'd given her.

She had headphones on, and didn't turn around when he walked in, so he paused in the doorway, watching her.

She was sitting with her back toward him, perched on a bar stool she'd placed in front of the easel. She'd set up a card table beside her, and her paints and brushes were arranged in haphazard order. Her hair was up in a ponytail, and she was wearing cut-off shorts and an oversized gray sweatshirt. He recognized it as one of his, and he smiled at the thought that she'd gone into his room to get it.

Her hand was resting on her thigh as she studied her painting, and he could see bright blue paint on the end of the brush. His heart turned over. *She was painting again.* The easel was angled away from him just enough that he couldn't see what was on it, but it didn't matter.

She was painting again.

She was beautiful. The kind of beautiful that made all the

darkness inside him fade away, until all that was left were feelings of hope, potential, and light. His need for her was so strong that it actually made his chest cramp.

He didn't just love her.

He *loved* her, every single part of her soul, her body, and her spirit.

Was that enough? Was the fact he loved her so deeply enough? Did it make him worthy of her? Would it make her happy, the kind of soul-deep happy that she deserved?

She turned suddenly, as if she'd heard him, and he was shocked to see tears streaming down her cheeks.

"Shit." He hurried over to her. "Hey, ZoeyBear, what's wrong?"

She pointed at the canvas as she pulled off her headphones. "Look what I painted."

He glanced at the canvas, and then swore. She'd painted the house that she'd grown up in, before her parents had died and she'd had to move in with her aunt and uncle. She'd captured it with incredible vividness and passion, and he could feel the energy almost vibrating off the canvas...including the wrecked pickup truck she'd painted in the front lawn.

The car that her parents had died in.

"Oh, baby." He wanted to pull her into his arms, but she was holding her body stiffly, so he sat down beside her on the arm of the couch.

"Every time I paint, I paint pain," she said. "Art used to be my respite, and now it's just pain." The tears were still trickling down her cheeks. "I need to create, Ryder. I need to paint. But it's not the same anymore. It feels like it's just going backwards into the past, when I need to move forward into the future." She looked down at the brush. "This isn't mine anymore," she said quietly. "It's not me, not the me I need to become."

He nodded. "Okay."

She held out the brush. "Take it."

He lifted it from her hand and set it on the table.

Zoey watched him do it, and as he set it down, she felt a deep relief rush through her, as if she were finally letting go of something that had been weighing her down for so long. "Thanks."

"Sure." He hesitated, and then nodded at the painting. "Want to talk about it?"

She looked over at the painting she'd been staring at for hours. "I don't know why I painted it. I just started painting, and it just happened." She brushed her finger over the truck, smearing the paint. "At first, I was so happy I was painting again... And then I painted pain."

"Did you?" He indicated the front porch. "This part isn't pain. This part, the home, the yard, the porch, those are good memories, right?"

"It started out good until I killed it with the truck." She bit her lip. "Every time I'm happy, it twists into pain. Like the other morning, when I was so happy with you, then Dane came in with his rant. Then I start painting earlier today, and I wind up with this. I was so proud of my accomplishments at Harvard, and then I chose a husband who was a douchebag."

He chuckled slightly, and she couldn't help but smile a tiny bit at his amusement. "He *is* a douchebag," she said.

"I know." Ryder rested his palm on the arm of the couch. He looked relaxed and muscular, and so freaking tempting. His cowboy hat was tipped back, his shoulders were so broad and strong, and his forearms were sinewy strength. He looked like a cowboy god, actually.

"God, you're so beautiful," she whispered. "You're like one of those Greek statues, only you're actually hot."

He grinned. "Thank you, my dear." He cocked an eyebrow. "Paint me."

A thrill raced through her. "You? I can't. I don't paint people—"

He tossed his hat on the couch behind him and pulled off his shirt, revealing ripped abs, sculpted pecs, and the same shoulders she'd spent half the night digging her fingernails into. "You need to create art, right? So, the human body is the highest form of art."

She was surprised by how much she wanted to take him up on his offer. He was so beautiful, a perfect specimen on both the outside and inside, and the man who had held her up so many times for so long. "What if I paint you being mauled by a grizzly? I'm pretty sure I just finished telling you how I ruin everything good. So, what if I paint all those luscious parts of you strewn across a forest clearing in a pool of bloodied remains?"

He raised his brows. "Is that how you fantasized my death after I acted like an asshole after your prom? Shit. That's a little frightening. It's a good thing I didn't fall asleep in your bed the other night, or I might have been missing body parts by morning."

She giggled. "How can you make me laugh about that? I've held tight to that night as my reason for tears for a decade."

"Because when the tears stop serving a purpose, it's time to let them stop." He held up his arms and flexed his biceps. "How about this?"

"Shit." She grabbed her brush. "Are you kidding me with that? How can I possibly not paint you?"

He grinned. "You can't resist me, my darling. Concede defeat now."

"I can resist you." She pulled out her paints and started mixing a tone for his skin. "In fact, I had a lovely midnight kayak trip with Brody and Keegan—"

"What?" He lowered his arms. "I distinctly recall inviting you for a river trip on Monday. With me. Not them. How the fuck did they get you out there first?"

"Arms up." She pointed the paintbrush at him. "I want to see those muscles."

He left his arms down, and she could feel that his energy was suddenly off balance. "What happened on the kayak ride?"

"I'm not telling you until you pose for me."

With a scowl, he raised his arms again, and she couldn't help but giggle at his irritated expression. Not that she wanted him to suffer, but the fact he was clearly a little upset that she was out with two handsome guys made her feel good. "Did you know Brody is a romantic?"

His arms came down again. "Did he hit on you?"

She set her hands on her hips. "I swear to God, Ryder. This is the first time I've been excited about painting in ten years. Are you going to let me paint or not?"

He glared at her, but raised his arms again. "Did he hit on you? Did Keegan?"

She couldn't believe how good his annoyance felt. He was actually jealous. "Do you know that after you dumped my vulnerable teenage heart after my prom, I actually believed it was because you didn't care about me?" She began to outline his right biceps, because honestly, she couldn't look anywhere else. "I convinced myself you didn't care about me at all. How ridiculous is that?"

"It may surprise you to know that I'm aware you just tried to change the topic from what happened with Brody and Keegan on the river." His biceps flexed, and she almost felt like whimpering. "You already know I love you, so I'm thinking this is just distraction tactics."

She grinned. "God, you're cute when you're jealous."

"Jealous?" He frowned, then sighed. "Yeah, I guess I am." His blue gaze bore into hers. "What the fuck happened out there, Zoey?"

She hummed under her breath as she painted. Ryder was *jealous*. She loved that so much. "They told me that there was magic between you and me, and that it was a special gift we need to fight for."

His eyebrows shot up. "Really?"

"Yep. And then Keegan offered to have me out to Oregon and stay on their ranch until I figured out my next steps."

He went still. "Are you going?"

She bit her lip. She'd actually decided that she would go. Oregon was beautiful, and it would be a chance to be away from all the influences of her past, to find herself. But with Ryder in front of her, tempting her, making her laugh, the thought of Oregon didn't sound quite as appealing. "I don't know," she finally said.

He let out a breath. "Don't go."

Her gaze snapped to his. "What?"

He lowered his arms. "Don't go. Stay with me."

She bit her lip. "Ryder, I have literally no foundation to stand on right now. How can I possibly be in a relationship if I can't stand alone?"

"How can you possibly walk away from the man you love? The one that got away ten years ago?"

She closed her eyes against the need to throw the paint brush down and fling herself into his arms. "Shut up." She took a deep breath and dipped her brush in the paint again. "Arms up."

He didn't move. "What do you really need, Zoey? What are you really looking for?"

She glanced up at him and met his gaze. *You.* The word jumped into her head, but she didn't say it aloud. Because there had to be more to her than being the woman who loved Ryder, right? Didn't there have to be more? "Me."

"You're looking for you?"

She nodded slowly. "Yes. I think I am." And him. She couldn't lie about that. She wanted him so desperately, so desperately in fact, that it terrified her. It terrified her because until she found herself, she'd never feel safe enough to trust again, not the way he deserved.

He nodded. "I get that."

"You do?" She narrowed her eyes. "Does that mean you'll support me going to Oregon?"

He didn't answer her question directly. "It means I'll sit here in this pose for as long as it takes you to paint me, my dear artiste." He met her gaze. "Find your art, Zoey."

She relaxed slightly, relieved that he wasn't actually telling her to go. As much as she wanted her freedom, she didn't want him to *ever* tell her to leave him again, no matter how much it would benefit her. Everyone she'd loved had ditched her, and she desperately needed Ryder to refuse to be pushed away, no matter how hard she tried. She might decide to leave anyway, but she *needed* Ryder to fight like hell to keep her. She wasn't sure that made sense, but it was her truth. "Arms up, then, Ryder."

He did as she directed, settling more comfortably on the arm of the couch, clearly committing to staying there for as long as it took. "Take all the time you need, ZoeyBear."

She smiled, relaxing. "It'll take a while."

He met her gaze. "I can wait."

RYDER WAS MESMERIZED by the expressions on Zoey's face as she lost herself in her painting. He knew the moment she'd forgotten he was there, the moment she'd pulled him into her world, allowing him to become a part of her art, instead of an outsider.

Being the subject of her painting was an incredible experience. The way her gaze traveled over every inch of him, seeing him so deeply that he felt as if she was stripping him bare. The way she'd focused on his jaw, her brow furrowed as she studied the shadows along his whiskers. She'd worked in silence for the first hour, and then she'd started humming to herself.

The humming was magic to him. The humming was what he remembered from years ago. Her voice was beautiful, filled with light and love and freedom. Her breath mingled with the notes, enriching them. He'd watched her paint in the past, but never had he been a part of the process before.

He felt as though he'd been given a gift, this moment of participation in her world. The deep sense of peace emanating from her seemed to envelop him in a cloak of protection, sealing them both off from the outside world, leaving them floating peacefully in an alternate realm where colors were life, and shapes were the soul.

He saw her look right into his eyes, without even seeing him watching her. She frowned, and looked at the blue paint on her brush, and he knew she was trying to find the right shade for his eyes.

Zoey was seeing blue the way he'd never see the color blue. She was seeing shadows and light in a way he'd never known. She was experiencing texture on a level he never would.

And yet, being her subject, he could share it with her on the deepest level.

He could tell she was completely aligned with herself, maybe for the first time in a very long time.

And he was the one who'd given it back to her.

Yeah, he was a keeper...for her, at least. And no one else mattered.

He watched her rub her wrist over her forehead, leaving behind a blue streak that matched his eyes. Let her go to Oregon? No chance.

I'm not letting you walk away this time, Zoey.

I promise.

CHAPTER TWENTY-FIVE

She was finished.

Zoey finally sat back, gazing at the painting that had flowed out of her with such magic. She'd painted Ryder leaning against a wooden fence, the kind that had surrounded Ol' Skip's ranch when they were kids. He was shirtless, his plaid shirt draped over the top rail. His jeans were low on his hips, revealing the beautiful shadows of his lean, hard stomach. His jaw was perfect, and his eyes... God. His eyes...

She leaned forward, studying her painting more carefully. His eyes were so full of depth. Pain. Love. Passion. Humor. They were truly alive, and they made her heart turn over just looking at them. So many hours of her life had been spent gazing into those eyes.

"Finished?" Ryder's voice was gentle, lightly brushing over her to draw her attention back to the room.

She looked up at him, and her heart leapt when she saw those same blue eyes gazing at her so intently...full of all the same emotions she'd painted into them. "I love it so much," she said. "I love what I painted."

He smiled. "Can I look at it?"

She nodded.

Ryder stood up slowly, stretching with a small groan, making her glance at the clock. "It's almost four in the morning?" He'd been sitting there for almost seven hours?

"I loved watching you." He rotated his shoulders as he walked up next to her. He rested his hand on her shoulder as he leaned in to look at the painting.

For a long moment, he said nothing, and the longer it took for him to say anything, the more nervous she became. She'd thought it was amazing, but maybe it wasn't.

Then he looked at her, and the look of absolute awe on his face made her heart swell with pride. "Really?" she asked. "You like it that much?"

"It's incredible." He crouched beside her, resting his forearm on her thigh as he studied it. "It's truly breathtaking. The mountains. The details on the grasses. And my eyes..." He swore under his breath. "You made me come alive, Zoey. I've never seen anything like it."

She smiled with more than a little bit of pride. "Thanks."

He raised his brows. "Have you been taking classes since I saw you last?"

"Since earlier today? No."

He laughed. "Always my sassy girl. I love that so much about you." He stood up and slid his hands through her hair, sending chills down her spine. "I meant since you left here ten years ago."

"I took a few classes in college, before I focused on pre-law stuff." God, his hands felt so good. So gentle, yet strong at the same time.

"I saw the way your soul came to life when you were painting." He smiled. "The painting shows it, and so did your face. This is where you belong, Zoey. This is your magic. Can't you feel it?"

She smiled. "I did feel it. It was amazing." She wrapped

her hand around his wrist. "Thank you for giving it back to me. I needed you to be a part of it in order for it to come back to me."

"See how much I add to your life?" He grinned. "Baby, you need me. I need you. We're good for each other." Then, before she could decide whether to summon a protest, he kissed her.

The kiss was so tender, so beautiful, so intimate that her heart seemed to sigh with contentment. She closed her eyes, basking in the feel of his hands in her hair, in the heat of his body as he moved closer, in the taste of his kiss.

She surrendered to him, clasping her hands behind his neck, allowing herself to let down her guards this one time, just for a moment, just to let herself feel how amazing it was to turn herself over to him.

He kissed his way down the side of her neck, and she sighed in pure heaven at the feel of his kisses dancing across her chest, and then over the swell of her breasts—

Her phone suddenly rang, startling her.

"Ignore it," Ryder said between kisses.

She had no idea who it could be. "It's four in the morning. Anyone who calls me at this hour needs something." She slid out of his grasp and grabbed her phone off the table. It was a blocked number, which she didn't usually answer, but this time, for some reason, she felt like she needed to.

Ryder came in behind her and slipped his arms around her waist, nuzzling the back of her neck. She smiled and wrapped her hand around his strong forearm as she leaned back into him. "Hello?"

"Hello. This is Mountain View Regional Hospital. Is this Zoey Wilson?"

Ryder tensed against her, and her breath caught. "Yes. What's happened?"

"Do you know a Frank and Liam Eaton?"

For a split second, Zoey couldn't place the name, and then she remembered the grandfather and grandson that had been at the Wildflower Café, the lovely duo who she'd given the free lunch to. She remembered the way little Liam had so proudly given feedback on the grilled cheese sandwich, and Frank's quiet but genuine appreciation that she'd given them a way to maintain their pride while accepting the food. "Yes, why?"

"They were in a car accident tonight—"

She didn't hear the rest. Panic knifed through her, and her legs suddenly seemed to give out on her. She was back in that moment with her parents, when the hospital had called. She couldn't breathe—

"ZoeyBear." Ryder's arms were strong around her, his voice low and reassuring. "It's okay. I've got you. Breathe, baby, breathe."

She gripped his arms in raw panic, leaning back into the strength of his body as she fought for breath.

"Hi." Ryder took the phone from her and put it on speaker. "This is Ryder Stockton, Zoey's partner. Are Frank and Liam okay?"

Zoey closed her eyes as the woman from the hospital answered. "Frank has been admitted with moderate injuries, but Liam will be released tonight. He will need someone to take care of him tonight. Frank listed Zoey as their emergency contact. Are you able to come to the hospital now to take Liam home?"

Zoey grabbed the phone from Ryder. "They're okay? They're not dead?"

"Dead? No. But the boy needs to be picked up tonight, or we will have to put him into a temporary foster home."

Dear God. A foster home? *No.* Zoey's hands started to

shake at the thought of Liam left all alone in the hospital. He'd already lost his parents, and now his grandfather was injured? How badly? *Please let Frank be okay.*

Liam would be terrified right now. Alone. No one to take him home. No safe place to sleep. She knew what that felt like. She'd been the one in that white hospital room, terrified, waiting for someone to tell her it was going to be okay, which of course, no one had been able to do, because it wasn't ever going to be okay.

And now Liam was in that situation? She didn't even care how or why Frank had given them her name and number. All that mattered was getting there and making sure Liam knew he was safe, and Frank was getting the care he needed.

"Are you able to come pick him up?" the woman asked again.

"Yes! Yes, of course. We're on our way." She looked at Ryder, who was already grabbing his car keys and wallet. "How long will it take to get there?"

"Twenty-five minutes max," he said.

"We'll be there within a half-hour," she said as she grabbed her purse. "Don't send Liam to a foster home. We're coming."

"Excellent. Check into the main desk when you arrive, and they will direct you."

"Okay, great. We'll be there soon." She shoved the phone into her pocket and ran for the door that Ryder was holding open for her. She sprinted through it, and the two of them raced for his truck.

It was just like that night so many years ago, and as soon as she was in the truck, she started to panic. "How fast can you drive?"

Ryder didn't put the key into the ignition. Instead, he turned to face her. "Zoey. Look at me."

"Drive! Oh my God! Why aren't you driving? I'll drive. Do you need me to drive?" She lunged for her door handle, but Ryder caught her arm.

"Zoey. Look at me." His voice was urgent and commanding, dragging her out of her panic just enough for her to hear him.

She spun toward him, her heart pounding. "What is it? We need to drive."

He took her hand, sandwiching it between his two larger ones. "This isn't your parents. Say it. Say it out loud."

She stared at him, her heart pounding. "What?"

"I'm not driving until you say it. This isn't your parents. Say it."

She blinked. "This isn't my parents," she repeated quickly. "Can we go?"

He shook his head. "Say it again."

"This isn't my parents," she said louder. Suddenly, her lungs seemed to release, and she sucked in a huge breath. "It's not my parents," she whispered, tears suddenly filling her eyes.

"That's right." He brushed her hair back from her face. "Frank has moderate injuries. Liam is being released tonight. They're not going to die from this, okay? We're going to go help them, and it's going to be okay. Got it?"

She stared at him, searching his blue eyes. "You think so? That it's going to be okay?"

"Yes." He smiled. "You don't have to handle this alone, ZoeyBear. I won't leave your side. We're going to take care of both of them. Together. Okay?"

"Okay." She nodded and took another deep breath. "We got this. Together. Right?"

"Right." He kissed her gently, then sat back. "Now, let's go. Ready?"

She put on her seatbelt. "Ready."

As Ryder started the truck and pulled out, she closed her eyes and leaned her head back against the seat, trying to calm down. She had to pull herself together so she could be there for Liam and Frank, especially little Liam. This wasn't about her past. Not about her parents. This was about Liam and Frank, who, according to Lissa, had no one else to help them. In fact, they were so alone that Frank had given the name of a woman they'd met only one time as their emergency contact.

Tears filled her eyes. She'd felt so alone for so long, and yet she'd had people to turn to all along, even if she hadn't wanted to. If she'd had an emergency, she had a long list of people she could have called at any time. Dane. Ryder. Any of the Stocktons. And now she knew she could add Jaimi, Lissa, and all of the Stockton wives she'd met to her list. And even Brody and Keegan Hart. She barely knew them, and they'd already shown that they were there for her. So many people to ask for help if she needed it.

But Frank and Liam actually *were* alone. Truly alone. No one to ask for help except a stranger.

It made her realize that despite years of feeling alone, rejected, and isolated, she *wasn't* alone, not by any stretch. And she never had been. All she'd needed to do was look around, and she would have realized it.

She opened her eyes and looked at Ryder, his jaw flexed as he drove. "Ryder?"

He glanced over at her. "Yeah?"

"Thank you. For everything."

He flashed a grin at her. "I love you, babe. I'll do anything for you, and you never need to thank me. It comes with the territory." He raised his brows. "You'd be there for me the same way, right?"

She didn't have to even think about it. "Of course I would."

His smile widened, and he reached across the console and took her hand, squeezing it gently.

She didn't let go of his hand for the entire ride to the hospital.

CHAPTER TWENTY-SIX

WHEN ZOEY SAW Liam sitting in the hospital chair beside his grandpa's bed, his knees pulled up to his chest with his chin resting on them, she thought her heart would break. Frank was clearly asleep, with too many tubes coming out of him, and Liam was sitting silently, watching him breathe. "Liam?"

He looked up, and his face lit up when he saw her. "You came!"

"Of course I came!" She hurried over to him and, without thinking, swept him up in a huge hug. His arms wrapped around her, and he held on, gripping so tightly she thought he'd never let her go. "I got you, babe," she whispered. "It's okay now."

He nodded and buried his face in her shoulder, and she felt him start to tremble. God, how hard he must have tried to hold himself together after they'd arrived and Frank had been carted off. She kissed the top of his head and sat down, holding him tightly on her lap as she rocked him gently. She guessed he was around seven, which on some levels, he probably considered himself old, but at the same time, he was a tiny, vulnerable child who had already lost so much. "Are you hurt?"

He shook his head, still keeping his face buried in her shoulder. Tears started to burn in her eyes, and she looked over Liam's head at Ryder, who was standing in the doorway. Ryder looked so big and strong that she knew he would make Liam feel safe as well. "Liam, honey? I brought my best friend with me. He's going to take care of you, too. You have both of us."

Liam lifted his head slightly. "Who?"

She nodded behind him. "Ryder Stockton. He's a cowboy."

Liam twisted around in her arms and inspected Ryder.

Ryder immediately walked over and crouched in front of them, so that he was lower than Liam. He smiled, his beautiful smile that had calmed her so many times. "Hey there, Liam." He held out his hand to shake it. "It's good to meet you. Zoey tells me that you're great at grilled cheese testing."

Liam smiled tentatively and shook Ryder's hand. "Are you a real cowboy?"

"I am." He tipped back his hat. "We're actually going to a picnic at my brother's ranch tomorrow. They have a new baby horse there. Want to go with us and see it?"

The little boy sat up straighter. "Really? A real ranch?"

"Yep." Ryder grinned at him. "My brother has a lot of horses. They actually have a program to teach kids how to ride. You ever thought about riding horses?"

Zoey had heard about the program that Zane and his wife had started. It was a program to give inner city kids or kids with a rough home life the chance to work with the horses, learn to ride, and even stay there if they needed to...giving kids the same chance that the Stocktons had been given when Ol' Skip had opened his ranch to the troublesome boys so long ago.

Liam was staring at him now. "I don't know how to ride."

"It's no problem. They'll teach you to ride and take care of the horses. You'll get your own assigned to you."

Liam's mouth dropped. "No way."

"Way."

Then the youth's face fell, and he looked down at his hands. "We don't have any money. But thanks."

Ryder glanced at Zoey, then he inched closer to Liam. "It actually doesn't cost money," he whispered. "No one has to pay to go to it."

Liam's head snapped up. "Seriously?"

"Yeah. All you need to get into the program is to have an adult recommend you. Want me to recommend you?"

Liam stared at him for so long that Zoey wasn't sure he understood. Until he nodded once. "Thank you," he whispered, his voice shaky.

Ryder grinned. "You got it, Liam. We can check it out tomorrow and see if it's something you want to do. No pressure to do it. Just if you want to."

"I want to," he said so quickly that Zoey smiled. "But we have to ask my grandpa."

"Grandpa says it's okay," a rough, grizzled voice said.

They all turned to see Frank was awake and watching them, a weak smile on his face. There was a bandage across his head, and an IV running from his arm. His leg was in a cast, and he looked old and worn out. His gray beard stood out against his dark skin, and Zoey's heart turned over. "Frank. It's so good to see you awake."

"Thank you for taking care of Liam." He moved his hand, and she reached over to squeeze it.

"I'm honored you had them call me."

He grinned. "You're a hard woman to track down. They had to find the home number of Lissa, and then get your phone number from her."

"Well, I'll write it down for you." She grabbed a pen from her purse and jotted her number and Ryder's number on a napkin. "This is Ryder Stockton."

"One of the Stockton boys, eh?" He eyed Ryder. "I remember your Dad. He was a right bit of work. Liked to drink, didn't he? Used his fists a bit much?"

Ryder stiffened. "My father wasn't a good man."

"But his sons are," Zoey said quickly, sliding her hand around Ryder's arm, pressing her fingers over the scars in his forearm from the cigarette burns, the same scars all his brothers had. "Every single one of them is a good person, including Ryder. I've known them my whole life. I'd trust them with anything."

Ryder didn't smile. She could tell he was on edge, as the same old story about his youth circled back again to try to drag him down once again. God, she was so tired of the noose that sat around the neck of every Stockton male all the time, just because of who their father was. "Ryder." She touched his arm again, and this time, he glanced over at her, but his jaw was strained.

Frank continued to study Ryder. "Are you one of the twins?"

Ryder nodded. "Maddox is my twin."

"You recall a boy named Eddie Eaton?"

Ryder narrowed his eyes, and for a long moment didn't answer. Then he said, "I remember Eddie. He was brilliant. One of the smartest kids I ever met."

Frank's smile lit up his face. "That's my boy, Liam's dad. He got his smarts from his mama, God rest her soul." His smile faded. "Eddie got beat up a lot as a kid for being too smart and too gentle. Until one day, two boys with massive chips on their shoulders took down the bullies that had been dogging him. No one ever bothered him again. I'll never forget the name of those boys. You know who they were?"

Ryder shifted. "Yes, sir. I remember that."

Frank glanced at Zoey. "It was the Stockton twins, Ryder and Maddox, who came to the defense of my son."

Zoey's heart turned over at the story that didn't surprise her at all. "He's always been a protector."

Frank nodded, returning his gaze to Ryder. "You saved his life that day. You two boys were the roughest, most dangerous boys in school, and you showed him that he mattered. It changed his life."

A slow redness rose on Ryder's cheeks. "No one should get beat up."

"No, they shouldn't. That's why he joined the Navy as a nuclear engineer. To do what you boys did, on a bigger level."

Ryder stared at him. "He joined the military because of us?"

"Because you were his heroes. You boys showed him that strength and power can be used for good, and he wanted to be a part of that." The pride was evident in Frank's voice. "He sacrificed his life for a mission he believed in, and I will always be grateful that you gave him the courage to be the man he wanted to be." Frank looked at Liam. "Your dad was a good man. A brave man. Never forget that."

Liam nodded, even as he leaned heavily against Zoey. "I know, Pops."

Frank looked back at Ryder. "I watched you and your brothers after that. I knew what was going on at home, but I couldn't stop it. I watched each and every one of you rise above that and become men of honor."

"Thank you." Ryder cleared his throat, and Zoey could see he looked wildly uncomfortable with the compliments, even though he so deserved them. "I think you're probably the only one in town who saw us that way, but thanks."

"I saw you that way, Ryder. I still do." She took his hand and squeezed it gently.

He glanced at her, and gripped her hand tightly, as if she were his only lifeline. "I know, ZoeyBear." His voice was rough and raw.

She could see the resistance on his face, the refusal to accept that nomination of hero status, and she took mercy on him, gently redirecting the conversation to give him room to breathe. "What are your injuries, Frank?" Zoey asked, still holding Ryder's hand. "Are they severe?"

Frank shook his head. "Broke my leg. A few bruises. Nothing much. I'm having surgery on Tuesday, and then I'll be good to go."

Zoey frowned. "Will you be able to go home?"

Frank glanced at Liam. "They were barking some shit about a rehab facility, but they don't know what the Eaton men are made of. I'll be heading home and have that cast off in no time. We got it covered, don't we, Liam?"

The boy nodded, but Zoey glanced at Ryder, who met her gaze and nodded, clearly thinking the same thing. There was no way the older man would be able to live at home and take care of Liam after surgery for a broken leg, no matter how quickly he expected to heal.

Zoey turned to Frank. "So, Ryder and I live in a house with ten bedrooms. Only four of them are occupied. We'd like to invite you and Liam to stay with us until you're back on your feet."

Ryder nodded. "Yeah, it's way too quiet. We'd be honored if you'd stay with us while you heal, so it's not so damn empty all the time."

Surprise flickered over Frank's face. "That's nice of you, but we'll be fine—"

"You'll be on crutches for a while," Ryder pointed out. "Or maybe even in a wheelchair for a bit."

Defensiveness flashed across Frank's face. "I can handle it—"

"But you don't have to." Zoey leaned forward and took his hand again. "Frank, my parents died when I was a kid. Ryder grew up in a terrible, terrible home situation, as you know. We both had it rough as kids, so we know what it's like to fight difficult battles. We know it's hard for you and Liam right now, and we know that, because we've both been there. Let us help you. We want to."

Ryder leaned in. "We *need* to help you," he said quietly.

Frank started to shake his head, but Zoey squeezed his hand. "For my whole life, I've refused to accept help or even love from the people who love me. I've stood on my own, when I didn't have to. It almost broke me, but tonight, when the hospital called, you gave me the chance to finally see that, to understand that we all need each other, and it's a gift to be able to support each other. Let us do it for you and Liam."

Frank looked back and forth between them, and she saw the weight in his eyes, the weight of an old man who had been trying to hold things together for himself and his grandson all on his own for far too long, with far too few resources. He finally looked at Liam, at the way he was snuggled up in Zoey's lap, his head on her shoulder. His face softened. "Liam? What do you think?"

Liam looked up at Zoey. "Is it a nice house?"

She grinned. "It feels like a mansion to me, honestly. And Ryder's a great cook. He'll feed us all really well."

Liam grinned, and then looked at his grandpa. "I want us to stay with Zoey and Ryder."

For a long moment, Frank didn't say anything, then finally, she saw the tension leave his shoulders. Tears glittered in his eyes as he nodded. "Okay. Thank you. We accept."

"Yay!" Liam grinned, and hugged his grandpa so fiercely that the older man winced in pain. Frank looked at her over Liam's head and mouthed *"thank you"* to her and Ryder.

"No, it's me who needs to thank you, for teaching me what I couldn't see on my own." She hugged him gently.

He cleared his throat gruffly. "You all get on out of here. This old man needs to sleep."

Zoey smiled. "We'll bring Liam back tomorrow to visit and check on you, okay?"

"Sounds good." Frank leaned back against the bed, and she saw a faint half-smile on his face, a smile that had a little more peace than it had before.

"Well, then it's settled." Ryder crouched in front of Liam again. "What do you say we stop by your house and get your things, and then head on over to our place. Want a shoulder ride?"

Liam gaped at him. "Yes!"

Ryder winked at Zoey, then turned around. "Climb on."

Zoey helped Liam get squared away on Ryder's shoulders, and then bit her lip as Ryder stood up. "Watch the door-ways," she said. "Liam's head is pretty high right now." She would have thought he was a little big for a shoulder ride, but Ryder was so strong that he had no problem supporting him.

Ryder grinned as Liam wrapped his hands around his head, nearly blinding him. "Zoey worries about our safety. I love her for that."

Liam grinned. "Me, too."

Zoey's heart turned over. "Well, I love you guys, so we're all even." She patted Liam's back.

Both boys grinned cheekily at her, and she rolled her eyes at them, trying to hide her smile. She couldn't believe how quickly Frank and Liam had accepted her and Ryder...and how Ryder had jumped in so quickly and so naturally. She'd already known he was good to her, but seeing him with Liam and Frank was different. It was beautiful.

She smiled at him as she walked beside them, and she was

rewarded with a wink from Ryder that made her heart swell with warmth.

She glanced back at Frank. He was smiling widely as he watched them, and he gave her a wink very similar to the one Ryder had given her. "Come by after the picnic at the ranch," he said. "I want to hear all about it."

"You bet." She hesitated in the doorway. "You're going to be okay, right?" She couldn't keep the vulnerability out of her voice, and nearly teared up when Ryder took her hand and squeezed it.

Frank's smile widened. "You bet your ass I am. I got a lot more shit to do in my life before I kick the bucket. Got it?"

Relief rushed through her. "Got it."

And she did, on a lot of levels, in a way she hadn't in a long, long time.

CHAPTER TWENTY-SEVEN

PROTECTIVENESS SURGED through Ryder as he glanced in the rearview mirror to check on Zoey and Liam. She had decided to ride in back with Liam, and they had fallen asleep leaning on each other, Zoey's arms around Liam.

The boy had clung to her fiercely when they'd gotten in, and Ryder had felt the strongest sense of need to keep them safe. He hadn't been able to stop thinking about the incident with Eddie Eaton the whole ride to Liam's house. He'd completely forgotten about it, until Frank had brought it up.

He remembered Eddie. Scrawny. Nerdy. Poor, like the Stocktons. But a nice kid. A good kid. One of the few in the school who didn't look at Ryder as if he were pond scum, and he'd never forgotten that. The day he'd seen those kids drag Eddie behind the school, he'd known what they were up to. After a lifetime of having his dad beat the shit out of him and his brothers, none of the Stocktons had any patience for bullies. Maddox hadn't hesitated to go with him, and they'd gone back behind the school, not sure how many kids they'd have to take on.

His raw anger and burning hate for the bullies had

unleashed something in him that had made those bullies back off without either of the twins having to throw even a single punch.

He'd taken that day as a statement that he was so tarnished that people feared him even without him doing a damn thing. Proof of his taint.

Frank and Eddie had seen it as him being a hero.

It was such a different interpretation that it had thrown him completely. He wanted to talk to Zoey about it, but she'd fallen asleep with Liam almost immediately. He'd talk to her tonight. He needed her insight to untwist everything for him, to help him sort it out. She was his light, and he needed her.

He turned onto a battered dirt road in a section of town he hadn't been to for a very long time...a section of town much too similar to the one he'd grown up in. Sudden weight settled in his gut.

When he'd entered Frank's address in the GPS, he'd suspected what kind of neighborhood he'd be driving into, but seeing it, experiencing, and feeling it was completely different.

He drove past a ramshackle house with half the shutters gone, dead cars littering the yard, and decades of weeds growing along the broken walkway...and a light on...which meant someone lived there. The house was eerily similar to the one he'd called home.

Swearing under his breath, he drove another couple hundred yards, and then eased to a stop in front of number twenty-five. The house was a two-story, a decent size. A house that at one time was probably nice. In the early light of dawn, he could see that the paint was a decade overdue for an update. The porch was slanted down to the right. The lawn was mowed, but barren. A single pot of flowers sat by the front door, an attempt to bring hope. It was neat, but worn out. Exhausted. Out of time. Love was fighting to keep it afloat, but there was so little left.

He rested his wrists on the steering wheel, remembering night after night in the hellhole he'd grown up in. The house had been like this, only worse, because this house still felt like hope. Like someone cared. Like Frank had been pouring love into this home he'd held together for Liam, held together by love, which was a hell of a lot better than money.

"Ryder?" Zoey's sleepy voice drifted over him, and he inhaled deeply, breathing in her presence.

He twisted around to look at her. Liam was still sleeping, so he kept his voice low. "This reminds me of my street growing up."

She looked out the window, and he saw the sadness of her face. "It kind of does. Does it feel weird to be back here?"

He nodded. "Yeah. I don't like to come back to town or stay at the ranch because it reminds me of when I was a kid, but being here makes me realize that *this* is the part I don't want to remember."

She stroked Liam's hair gently. "Well, if Frank, Eddie, and I are any indication, you were a lot of good even back then."

He bit his lip. "I don't remember it the way they did."

"It's okay." She leaned forward and set her hand on his shoulder, and he grabbed it instantly, holding tight. "Dane's wrong, you know."

His throat tightened, and he looked back at her.

She smiled. "Eddie, me, and Frank. The way we see you is the truth." She smiled gently. "You were so lovely tonight at the hospital with Liam and Frank."

God, he wanted to hold her right now. He *needed* to hold her. But there was a seat and a little boy between them...and the wall that Zoey always kept so carefully erected. "Thanks." He took a breath. "Thanks for always believing in me."

"Except for the last ten years, you mean?"

He laughed softly. "Yeah, except for then."

She rubbed the back of his hand. "You know, Eddie and Frank are right about you. You are a hero. A man of such beauty and honor. The way you defended Eddie was beautiful."

He shrugged. "I don't like bullies."

"It's not just that." Zoey took a deep breath, drawing his attention to her face. There was an expression on her face that he'd never seen before, one he couldn't read. "You're pure love, Ryder. Love in a world where no one is about love. You pour it into me, and also Frank, and Liam and anyone else who needs it. You're a gift, Ryder, to all those around you."

At her words, he looked back at the houses around them. "I'm from such darkness, Zoey," he said. "It's in my soul. Dane sees it."

"No." She shook her head, even as she tightened her arms around Liam. "It's in your past. It was in your surroundings. In the judgments of others. Not in your soul. It's never been in your soul. Don't you understand? You're the one who is making me believe in love, the kind of love that's real, that I've shut out my whole life."

Love? His breath caught, and he slung his arm over the seat, as if he could climb over and pull her into his arms. "What are you saying?"

She met his gaze. "I—" She hesitated, leaving him on the edge. "It's just that—"

"Are we here?" Liam sat up, rubbing his eyes.

Shit. A part of Ryder wanted desperately to tell Liam to go to sleep for another thirty seconds, but it was only the selfish, desperate man who loved Zoey who wanted that. The other part of him, the part of him that lived and breathed to protect others from the life he'd had, smiled gently at the boy. "Yeah, we're at your place. We'll go in and pack whatever you want to take to our house, and some of your grandpa's stuff, so it'll be there when he gets out of the hospital. You don't need to take everything. We can come back and get whatever you forget. Sound good?"

"Yeah." Liam scrambled out of Zoey's arms and almost vaulted out of the truck, racing up to the house with the enviable energy of a pre-teen boy, leaving Ryder and Zoey alone in the truck.

"Zoey." He caught her arm as she started to get out.

Her breath hitched noticeably. "Yes?"

"Finish this, talk later? After we get Liam settled?"

She looked back at him, searching his face for a long moment, before she finally nodded. "Yes. I'd like that." She scooted to the edge of the seat and lightly kissed him, her lips soft and warm against his.

The kiss was over almost before it had begun, but the sensation of her kiss lingered after she climbed out of the car and headed after Liam...just as it always had.

She'd never left his soul. Not now. Not when she'd been gone for ten years. Not ever.

He got out of his truck and followed the two of them up the broken walkway into the house, watching the line of her body sway with each step she took.

His need for her was so strong it almost hurt. Had she been about to tell him she loved him? Not as a friend, but as so much more?

Or was she never going to come to him?

He had a feeling tonight he was going to find out, either way.

CHAPTER TWENTY-EIGHT

ZOEY SAT on the edge of Liam's bed, watching him finally fall asleep as the sun's morning rays stretched across the comforter. He'd chosen to sleep in Ryder's bed, and he was so little in the king-sized luxury. He'd been in awe when they'd driven up to the ten-bedroom house, literally stunned speechless when he'd realized that was where they'd be living.

The magic he saw had made her see the house through his eyes. Beautiful. Luxurious. The latest in all technology. And yet, it still was warm and homey, a place where kids could track in mud and boys could be boys. A place where kids were safe.

Where she was safe.

With a sigh, she stood up and walked over to the window and braced her hands on the windowsill as she looked out. Ryder's room was on the river side, and she could see it winding through the fields and trees. A few other houses dotted the river, but there was so much space.

In the distance were the mountains.

It was beautiful. It felt like freedom. A place to breathe deep and follow whatever path she wanted.

"ZoeyBear?" Ryder's whisper drifted across her neck like a warm caress, and she turned to see him standing in the doorway. "You want to catch a few zzz's before the picnic?"

The picnic. The one with all the Stocktons...and her brother. "You want to go?"

He nodded. "I promised Liam." He raised his brows. "You don't want to?"

The picnic would be full of all the people she'd wanted to avoid when she'd first come back to town. All the people she'd cut out of her life after she'd left a decade ago. All the people who she'd used to cause herself so much pain because she convinced herself she didn't belong. But now... "I want to go so much," she whispered.

He smiled and held out his hand. "Come sleep. I'm sure we have only a couple hours before Liam is up. He saw the kayaks and wanted to go for a ride before the picnic. The resilience of kids, right?"

"Yeah." She took one last glance at the sleeping boy as she walked over to Ryder. Liam was sound asleep, hugging the ratty teddy bear he'd brought from home. Her heart turned over. "We're going to make sure he's okay, right? Not just today, but always?"

Ryder took her hand. "Absolutely. Him and Frank. Always. My brothers will take them on as well. They're in our circle now."

So, even if she left town, Liam and Frank would be all set.

Leaving town?

Leaving town.

She looked at Ryder's broad back as he led the way toward her bedroom.

Leaving town.

When she'd arrived, all she'd wanted to do was get the hell back out of town. She'd wanted to run and hide, and the only reason she'd stayed was because she didn't know where to go.

Ryder looked back at her as he opened her bedroom door. "You okay?"

She nodded, her throat tightening at the expression on his face. "You always look at me with such love," she whispered.

His face softened, and he drew her inside the room before closing the door. "Because I love you." He slid his hand around her waist and pulled her against him. "I've always loved you." He hesitated for a moment, then pointed to the bed. "Wait here. I'll be right back. I have to show you something."

Before she could answer, he was gone, leaving her alone in her room.

Instead of going to the bed, she walked over to the window to look out. But when she got there, she just braced her hands on the windowsill, bowed her head, and closed her eyes. What did she want? She had so many choices. She could go to Oregon. Go back to Boston. Go talk to Dane to try to sort things out. Keep working for Lissa. Be a starving artist and live in a shack like Liam and Frank's.

She could tell Ryder she loved him, or she could let him go, soldier onward in a solo quest to figure out what she wanted to do with her life.

Because she did love him.

She'd always loved him. But she'd been scared of herself, of her life, of everything—

The door opened and she turned around as Ryder stepped inside. He was holding something in his hand, something small enough that she couldn't see what it was. "Zoey—"

"I love you." She blurted out the words before she was ready, but the moment they were out, she felt the hugest sense of relief.

Hope flickered across his face. "Love me, how, exactly?"

"Capital L."

He raised his brows. "So, you Love me, not just love me?"

"Yes, definitely." She grinned, feeling slightly giddy at the experience of telling him. "God, I had a crush on you for so long, and I could never tell you. And then I was mad for a decade. And then I was scared. And now..." She held out her arms. "I love you, and it feels amazing to admit it— Ack!"

Ryder caught her around the waist and swept her up into his arms as he kissed her. With a happy sigh, she wrapped her arms around his neck, kissing him back as he carried her over to the bed. She thought he was going to lower her down and turn it into an incredible lovemaking affair, but instead, he dropped her onto the soft mattress and stepped back.

She frowned, propping herself up on her elbows. "Seriously? I honestly thought you'd have a different reaction than dropping me on the bed and running away."

"I'm not running. I need to give you something." He crouched in front of her, his blue gaze intent. "When I managed to drive you away from Rogue Valley when you were eighteen, I thought you would come back when college was over. I believed that you would find your way back, because I knew I couldn't live without you."

Zoey sat up. "I'm sorry, I didn't—"

"No." He held up his hand to silence her. "No apologies, *ever*, for how you need to be and how you need to live. That has to be a rule of our relationship, okay?"

A relationship? A future? Her heart started to pound. Telling him she loved him was one thing. A future? A forever? That was different. So different. But the idea of it made something inside her come to life with hope and excitement and a kind of delirious level of euphoria. She took a deep breath. "Okay."

He nodded. "A couple years after you left, I was making great money in construction. It was before I owned my own business, but I was doing really well. I bought you a present for when you came back."

Her heart lurched. That was the sweetest thing she'd ever heard. She looked at his closed hand. "And you kept it all this time?"

He nodded. "Long ago, I gave up believing you would ever come back here, but I kept it because every time I looked at it, it reminded me that there was someone in this world, someone with a beautiful soul, who thought I had value as a human being. I needed to see that reminder every day. I kept it in my wallet during the day, and on my nightstand at night. Every night. And now, I want you to have it."

How could she ever have doubted this man? "Ryder..."

He took her hand and pressed something into her palm, something cold and hard. "You saved my soul and changed my life, Zoey. When you came back here this time, and I saw the shadows in your eyes, I knew I had to do the same for you." He smiled, brushing her hair back from her face. "The spark is back. I see it. You're going to be okay, whatever you choose to do with your life. You can feel it, can't you?"

"Yes," she whispered. She was different. She was on a path she'd never been on. A path of love, and hope, and joy. And people. So many people to love.

He squeezed her hand, the one with his gift. "Keep it, ZoeyBear. It's for you. It's always been for you."

She looked down and opened her hand, and her breath caught at the shiny circle on her palm. "It's a ring?"

"Not just a ring."

She saw then that there was a single stone on it. A diamond. Stunned, she picked it up and looked at it. A single, solitaire diamond. "You bought me an engagement ring?"

"Yeah. Eight years ago."

Tears filled her eyes, and she clenched her fist around it. "All this time, for all these years, I thought you didn't care about me, that you didn't love me, and you were carrying this?"

"Yeah." He dropped to his knees and took her hands. "Even if you'd come home before this, I'm not sure I would have given it to you. I didn't believe I was worthy of you. I was so crushed under the darkness of my dad, and all the shit I lived under. It's been changing over time, watching my brothers get married, but it wasn't until now, when Dane told me to back off, and I couldn't, that I finally was able to understand that my love for you could heal us both. I deserve a chance with the most incredible, most wonderful woman, the one who has filled my heart since the day I first met her." His blue eyes searched her. "And you deserve a chance at love with the man you love, who loves you with every single fiber of his soul."

She didn't know what she would do for a career yet. She didn't know what she'd do with her art. There was so much she hadn't figured out yet...but she finally understood one thing, and that was love.

His love for her.

Her love for him.

The love of family, of all kinds, through everything life can throw at you. Stocktons. Harts. And now the women who had married Stocktons, and Liam and Frank.

Ryder took her hands. "ZoeyBear, I'll buy you a much bigger diamond now, but the question is the same. I need you to be my forever, and I'll be yours. It's fine if you want to take time to sort things out before we get married. If you want to go to Boston, I'll go with you this time. Same if you need to go to Oregon. But let's do it together. As best friends. As lovers." He took the ring from her hand and held it out to her. "As partners who promise a forever for each other." He looked at her. "Will you marry me, ZoeyBear? It doesn't have to be tomorrow. It can take as long as you want.

But let's start on this road together, always together, forever *together*."

She couldn't keep the tears from streaming down her cheeks. "I don't want to move back to Boston."

He grinned. "Good. I didn't really want to go there."

"I don't want to go to Oregon."

He raised his brows. "I sense a 'but' on the way."

"I want to live in Rogue Valley. I want to get to know your brothers again, and their wives. I want to watch Liam grow up, and Emily and Justin, and all the next generation of Stocktons. I want to watch the new barn go up and see Keegan's bakery come to life." She searched his face. "I don't even know what town you actually live in, Ryder, but I don't want to live there. I want to live here. I want to be a part of this family and I want to do it with you. Can you do that?"

"Even two weeks ago, I couldn't have said yes, but now?" He smiled. "We've chased away my demons, Zoey. You and me, and Frank and Liam. I can come home now. With you. I'm ready. We'll heal the past and make new memories here."

Love seemed to expand inside her chest, and she grinned, unable to keep the smile off her face. She held her left hand out to him. "Then my answer is yes."

"*Yes*." He slid the ring over her finger, and the fit was perfect. He swore under his breath, then grinned. "I'm never letting you go this time, ZoeyBear. And I mean it."

"You better mean it. I'm so done with you making these grand overtures and then bailing on them."

He tackled her onto the bed, and she giggled as he ripped his shirt off. "Forever, ZoeyBear. That's the way it is now. Got it?"

She wrapped her arms around his neck and drew him down to her. "I definitely got it. Now kiss me, you beast."

He did. And it was so beautiful...beautiful enough for forever.

CHAPTER TWENTY-NINE

ZOEY NERVOUSLY PULLED the sleeve of her sweatshirt down over her left hand, all the way to her fingertips, as Ryder pulled his truck up behind Chase's house, where there was chaos and craziness with all the Stocktons, their wives, and kids. There were two grills going, a badminton net, an obstacle course, a lesson on roping happening, and four picnic tables of food.

This was going to be her family. For real. On paper as well as in her heart. She was nervous, but at the same time, she wanted to cry. *She belonged.*

Ryder clasped her and Liam's hands, because both of them were hanging back. "They don't bite, you two," he said gently. "They'll love you both."

"How many kids are there now?" she asked.

"Seems like several hundred, but it's possible I'm counting some of them twice." Ryder gently urged them both forward, his grip solid and unyielding, but comforting at the same time.

"Is Dane here?" Zoey hadn't seen his truck when they'd pulled up, and she didn't see him in the middle of the festivities. But she knew he'd be there, because Jaimi was a Stockton.

"I don't see him." He glanced at Zoey. "It'll be fine with him."

"Will it? You won't ditch me again if he—"

"There's nothing he could do or say to get me to walk away from you." He raised her left hand and kissed the ring through the fabric of the sweatshirt. "You got me, baby."

She took a deep breath. "Okay."

Liam tugged on his hand. "I know them."

They both looked to see he was pointing at a boy with dark skin who looked about his age, and a girl with blond hair and a Stockton nose. Ryder nodded. "That's Toby, one of Zane and Taylor's boys. And Emily." He glanced at Zoey. "Your niece."

Her heart skipped a beat. *Her niece.*

"They're both in my class at school." There was no mistaking the longing in Liam's voice, and Ryder immediately beckoned to Zane, who was standing near the kids. He didn't look quite like the motorcycle-riding rebel she'd known from her youth, but he still had the earring and the swagger that would always brand him as the rule-breaker. His cowboy hat and boots, however, suggested that he might have traded in his bike for something more four-legged.

Zane immediately scooped up both kids and carried them over. "Afternoon, Ryder." He flashed a grin at Zoey. "So good to see you again. Taylor loved meeting you."

Her heart warmed. "I loved meeting her, too." She smiled at Emily, who was studying her curiously. "Hi Emily. I'm your dad's sister. My name's Zoey."

Emily nodded. "Mom said you're super nice."

Zoey let out a breath she didn't even realize she'd been holding. "I thought she was super nice, too."

"Want to come see my foal? I named her Moana." She looked at Ryder. "You promised you'd come."

"We will, definitely." Ryder nodded at Liam. "I'd like to introduce someone to you all, first, though."

Zane immediately crouched in front of Liam. "Who do you have with you today?"

"I'm Liam Eaton. My grandpa and I live with Ryder and Zoey."

Zoey's heart turned over, and she looked over at Ryder, who didn't correct the youth's description of their living arrangement.

Zane glanced up at them, then nodded in complete acceptance. "That's great. I'm Zane. I'm Ryder's brother. This is my son Toby, and my niece Emily. They said they know you."

Liam nodded. "Yeah. We're in the same class."

Emily cocked her head. "Do you want to come see my baby horse? Toby and I were going to go see her."

Liam's face lit up. "Yeah."

"We'll catch up," Ryder said. "Why don't you guys go on ahead?"

"Okay." Emily and Toby freed themselves from Zane, and then the three of them took off across the yard toward the barn, shouting and laughing.

Zoey watched them go, her heart so full of joy at the way Liam had been seamlessly welcomed into the family. "Should we be worried about them?"

"Nah. Dane's at the barn. He'll watch them." Zane stood up and pulled Zoey into a belated hug. "So good to see you again, Zoey. You look great."

She grinned and hugged him back. "I feel great."

Zane pulled back and eyed her, and then looked at Ryder, then he broke into a grin. "Well, damn, bro. You finally won her over, did you?"

Ryder grinned. "Yeah. I think so." He put his arm around

Zoey's shoulders and pulled her close. "I asked her to marry me."

Zane's grin widened. "Did you let him down easy, Zoey? Or just trample his heart ruthlessly?"

She smiled. "I decided to keep him." She held up her hand and let the sleeve slide down her wrist, showing the ring. "He's kept it for eight years. How could I say no?"

"You can't." Zane's grin widened. "No woman in her right mind would turn down a Stockton man—"

"Oh my God!" Lissa ran up and grabbed her hand. "You were right, Taylor!" she shouted. "It's an engagement ring!"

Zoey's cheeks heated up, but before she could panic, they were swarmed by men she'd last seen a decade ago, their amazing women, some she knew, and some she didn't. But when she saw Jaimi's huge smile, she knew it was going to be okay.

Her sister-in-law pushed through the crowd, and pulled her into her arms, hugging her fiercely. "I'm so glad, Zoey. Ryder's been waiting for you for so long. You guys will be so happy."

She hugged Jaimi back just as tightly. "I know we will." And she did. No matter what happened with Dane, they'd find a way.

～

RYDER WAS WATCHING Zoey and Jaimi hug when Chase walked up and pulled him into a hug. "Way to go, little brother."

Ryder grinned and hugged him back. "Thanks for all your advice. I'm not sure I would have made it here without it."

Chase shrugged. "You would've. You guys are meant for each other."

"I thought I'd lost her for a long time." Even now, he still felt the urge to go grab her and hold on tight, afraid he'd lose her again. "She said she'd marry me only if we live in Rogue Valley."

Chase seemed to go still, holding his breath. "And you agreed?"

"I did." One by one, Chase had been pulling each Stockton back to Rogue Valley, back to the family that they'd once had. "You finally got me back, too."

"Well, *shit*." Chase punched him lightly in the shoulder, clearly pleased. "There's plenty of space on the ranch to build."

Ryder grinned. "Thanks. I'll check with Zoey." But he had a feeling he knew what her answer would be. Every Stockton who'd gotten married had built on the ranch, a ranch that now housed a program for kids, a state-of-the-art equine surgery facility for Steen's wife, Taylor, training facilities, and soon a bakery. And it had kids, and family, and picnics, and everything else she deserved. "Only three of us left to get back here."

Chase nodded. "Logan and Quintin will cave."

"And Caleb?"

"Still can't find him. No one can."

Regret flickered through Ryder. Was Caleb even still alive? He had to be. If his own brother was dead, surely they would know, right? "Zoey came home, and so will he. The call of this place is too strong."

"Yeah." Chase folded his arms as they watched Zoey being escorted away, surrounded by the women. "It is." He nodded suddenly. "You need to talk to him."

Ryder followed his glance and saw Dane walking their way. He was moving fast, his arms stiff and his fists bunched as he scanned the crowd. "Shit. I need to get to him before he reaches Zoey."

He broke into a jog, reaching Dane just as he neared the edge of the lawn. "Dane."

The sheriff stopped and spun toward him. "You're engaged?"

Damn. News traveled fast. "Yeah."

"You didn't check with me first?"

"No, because you're being a complete ass about the whole thing." He took a breath, reining in his emotions. He *needed* Dane to understand. To believe in him, in them. Zoey needed it, and he needed it. "I love the hell out of her, Dane. She's my world, and despite what you might think, I'm good for her. I'm the only one for her. She loves me, and we're keeping each other."

Dane's scowl deepened. "And Boston?"

"It's not what she wants, Dane. I told her I'd go with her wherever she wanted, but she said she'd marry me only if I was willing to live in town."

Surprise flickered across Dane's face. "Really? She said that?"

"Yes. She wants to be here, Dane. She wants family, both mine and hers." He gestured at the gathering. "This place gave Jaimi a family. We gave you a family. She wants the same thing, Dane. If it's good enough for you, Jaimi, and your kids, why wouldn't it be good enough for her?"

Jaimi walked up then, sliding her hand into Dane's. "I keep telling him that," she said softly, leaning her head on Dane's shoulder. "None of us are trapped here. We *want* to be here, and I can't think of a more beautiful place to be than this town, with all of you."

Dane tangled his fingers with his wife's. "She's my little sister—"

"And she needs a family just as much as you do," Ryder said. "I'm her choice. The Stocktons are her choice." He met his gaze. "And you're her choice. She needs her brother to love her."

Dane scowled. "I do love her."

"She thought we both didn't love her when we sent her away to Harvard." His voice softened. "She needs you, Dane, just as she needs me. You can't stop us from being together, so get on board. Please." He hesitated. "Hate me if you want, Dane, but don't make her suffer for it."

Pain flickered across Dane's face. "I don't hate you."

"I know, you just think I'm not good enough for her. But you're wrong. I am." He gestured toward the melee surrounding Zoey. "Look at her," he said softly. "She's happy again. The spark is back."

Dane glanced at the gathering, and Ryder saw the moment his gaze found Zoey. She threw back her head and laughed, and the sound of her laughter carried across the grass, filling Ryder's heart with joy. "Do you hear that?" he asked.

Her brother nodded. "I didn't think I'd ever hear that again," he said softly. "She...she looks happy. Genuinely happy."

Zoey glanced their way, and the smile vanished when she saw them together. She said something to Lissa, and then hurried their way.

"This is your chance," Ryder said. "This is your chance to make it right with the only sister you have."

Jaimi squeezed his hand. "You wanted to make her happy, Dane. That was your goal. To give her the life that would fill her soul. You did it. Look at her. *You did it*."

Dane glanced at his wife, then at Ryder, and then at Zoey as she came to a stop in front of them. "Dane," she said. "I love him."

Ryder's heart turned over at her claiming of him. "I love you, ZoeyBear."

Her gaze flicked to him, and she smiled, a smile so full of love and warmth that he knew he'd dream of it for the rest of his life.

He walked over and put his arm over her shoulders, pulling her against him. "We're together, Dane. And it's right."

For a long moment, no one else spoke, until Dane finally reached out and touched her cheek. "The spark is back," he said softly. "My little sister is back. God, it's been forever. After Mom and Dad died, I thought I'd never see you sparkle again."

Tears filled her eyes as she nodded. "I was so lost for so long. But not anymore. I know what I want. Ryder. The Stocktons. The Harts." She met his gaze. "And you, Dane. You're the only brother I have. Please let me back in. Please."

Dane suddenly let out his breath. "I'm so fucking sorry, Zoey. I fucked it all up. I tried. I wanted to do right by you, and I fucked it up."

Tears trickled down her cheeks. "I'm sorry, too. I'm sorry I never came home to meet Jaimi, or go to your wedding or any of it."

"You're here now, and that's all that matters." Jaimi pulled her into a hug. "Welcome home, sis."

While the women hugged, Ryder looked at Dane. "Well?"

Dane's eyes looked a little shinier than usual. "She's really okay, isn't she?"

"Yeah, she is."

He nodded and turned back toward his wife and sister. "Zoey—" His voice broke, and suddenly, he grabbed his sister and pulled her into his arms. She flung her arms around his neck and hugged him back, clinging to him as if they'd never let each other go.

Ryder felt a sudden thickness in his own throat, and he

saw Jaimi's eyes were shiny as well. He grinned at her, and she smiled back.

Then Zoey and Dane grabbed them both and pulled them into a four-way hug, the hug that Ryder felt like he'd been waiting a lifetime for. His future wife. His long-lost sister. And his best friend.

Hell, yeah.

∼

Do you want more small-town romance? Check out the quaint Maine town of Birch Crossing, where love always finds a way!

After a midnight tryst results in a marriage-of-convenience, hearts ignite and chaos ensues when an ex-military specialist and his sister's best friend must make their fake marriage real in a way they never intended.

Find out more by grabbing your copy of Unintentionally Mine, and fill your heart with this wonderful story of love that was always meant to be.

Get your copy here!

"One of the best books of the year! I was absolutely blown away."
~Tapnchica (Amazon Review)

∼

SNEAK PEEK: HER REBEL COWBOY

A Rogue Cowboy spinoff

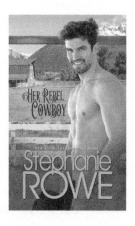

"**WOW, what a knockout!... packs one heck of an emotional punch...wonderfully endearing.**" ~Judy L. (Amazon Review)

When a struggling mystery writer's accidental house swap sends her to the ranch of a sexy bull rider with a murderer on his tail, the sassy city girl finds herself in the middle of a high stakes romantic murder mystery where it's her own life and heart at risk.

~

SO, YEAH, APPARENTLY there was a reason why people read novels instead of actually trying to experience the life they were reading about.

Because fantasies had no place in real life. Ever.

Especially fantasies that involved romantic, soul-enriching excursions to ranch country out west.

Noelle had been dreaming about cowboys and the Wild West since she was a kid, and not a single one of those fantasies included driving her rental car off the road and into a flooded ditch during a thunderstorm. Granted, she'd been driving slowly when she'd hit the brakes to avoid a coyote, and the slide down the embankment had been gentle and danger-free, but that didn't change the fact that her car wasn't getting back on the road by itself. And the part about not having any cell service? Yeah, that hadn't made it into even a single fantasy, and for good reason apparently.

Because it kind of sucked.

Noelle sighed, resting her wrists on the steering wheel as she watched the rain hammer onto her windshield. The din of pounding rain sounded like a herd of cattle stampeding across her metal roof, which, again, wasn't exactly how she'd envisioned her first cattle experience.

She'd been sitting in her car for two hours and six minutes, and not a single car had driven by. Not one. She was on some dirt road, not that far from her destination, and apparently, none of the other residents of Eastern Oregon had any business along this particular stretch of road.

So, yay for finding a place where she wasn't going to be harassed by having to deal with people, right? Go her.

She glanced at the dashboard on her car. Almost seven o'clock. It would be getting dark soon, and she so didn't want to spend the night here. She looked again at her directions. How much farther could the ranch be? She was almost there. She could sit there in the car until someone found her clean-picked skeleton, or she could use her body that she was lucky enough to have, and hike the rest of the distance.

The idea of hiking made energy hum through her, a surprising burst of energy that she hadn't felt in a long time. It made her feel powerful, no longer a victim. Taking action felt so much better than waiting to become roadside carnage. Grinning, she quickly leaned into the back seat, dug through her bags for her hiking boots and her raincoat. Within five minutes, she'd changed her shoes, zipped the ranch house key, her phone, the directions, and her wallet into the inside pocket of the coat, and chowed a granola bar.

Thunder rumbled just as she was reaching for the door handle. She hesitated for a split second, then looked around at the car. Another prison, just like her apartment. Suddenly, she couldn't take another second of it. She had to be outside. She had to be moving. She had to be breathing in fresh air. *Now.*

So she shoved open the door, stepped into six inches of muddy, raging water, and got out. The wind hit hard, and the rain thundered down, and she realized it was really brutal out. She hesitated, one hand on the door frame, suddenly unsure what to do. What if it was longer than she thought to the ranch? What if she got lost? There was literally no one to come to aid. No cell service. No cars going past. But, there were coyotes, or at least one. They didn't attack people, though, she was pretty sure. *Crap.* Was she a total fool to get out of the car and start hiking? Or would she be a bigger fool to sit in her car until someone came past?

Probably hiking was the worse choice.

But dammit. She didn't want to sit around anymore. She wanted to move. To live. To feel her body work again.

Screw it.

She was hiking.

With a renewed sense of power, she slammed her door shut and headed up the embankment toward the highway. She made it halfway up the incline, then she felt her boots start to slide. She yelped, and fought for purchase, leaning down to brace her hands on the ground, but as she stood there, her feet slid all the way back down, she lost her grip and landed on her knees, and rode the muddy gravel all the way back down, landing with a sploosh in the muddy river that had trapped her car.

Noelle looked up at the ten-foot embankment of mud and gravel, and suddenly, she started to laugh. Oh, God. This was too insane. Her first day of replenishing her soul, and she was trapped by a hill of shale and mud? Energy rushed through her, a fire that made her entire body feel stronger than it had in years.

She backed up several steps, set her gaze on her goal, and then charged the hill. She made it halfway up again, and then her boots started to slide. She lunged forward, digging her hands into the mud as she fought to scramble up the side. She made it another few feet, sliding backwards almost as often as she made it forward.

Her breath was heaving in her chest, and she fought harder, her feet sliding down almost as fast as she was able to take a step forward. Rain poured over her, running down her neck and under her coat, and mud coated her hands to her wrists. Her jeans were soaked, there was cold mud oozing over the top of her boots, and her hair was glued to her cheeks by the mud and the rain. She was filthy, soaked, exhausted, and hadn't felt so alive in years. Grinning even as her fingernails were scraped by the gravel, she fought against gravity. Inch by inch, she scrambled higher, until she was almost at the top...and then her feet started to go again.

"Crap!" She lunged for the top of the embankment, and just missed it...and started to slide back down again—

A strong hand suddenly grabbed her wrist, jerking her to a stop mid-slide.

She looked up quickly to find a drenched, muddy cowboy in a long jacket, a dripping cowboy hat, and icy-blue eyes staring down at her, his fingers locked around her arm.

Noelle froze, shocked by the sight of him, by the way her belly leapt, by the sudden heat rushing through her body. Dear God, he was straight out of her teenage fantasies. A hot cowboy coming to her rescue?

No, not hot. Calling him hot was like kind of like calling a wild, fully grown male mountain lion a cute little kitten. It was a supreme injustice to both the lion and the kitten. The man before her was pure, rugged male...the kind of male that made her want to drop everything, sprint over to him, and surrender every aspect of herself to his raw masculinity.

There was something about the way he was standing there with his duster flapping in the heavy wind, his legs braced against the weight of her body, while the rain dripped off his hat that was just so primal. Delicious. Surreal. Hot. Like he was made of testosterone, old West charm, and danger...with just a hint of cocky arrogance curving his mouth so seductively that a shiver went down her spine that had nothing to do with the fact she was soaking wet and closing in on hypothermia (yes, it was fifty degrees, but hypothermia wasn't choosy, was it?)

She couldn't quite believe how good it felt to stare at a man and notice how wide his shoulders were beneath his black jacket, or the way his quads bulged beneath his jean-clad thighs as he braced himself, as if his body was made for a life of outdoor roughness. She took a deep breath, wishing that he was close enough for her to catch a scent of him, a heady masculine scent that would make her stomach curl and her belly flutter like it had back when she used to feel alive. But all she could smell was the damp earth, the fresh rain, and the murkiness of the swampy river she'd just waded through...which was just as well. One more assault to her senses would likely send her romantically barren soul into testosterone-induced shock.

He lifted one eyebrow slowly, amusement flickering in his eyes, and suddenly, she realized she was gawking at him. Like, literally *gawking*. Heat flooded her cheeks, but she had nowhere to hide, nowhere else to look, not when it was his grip on her arm that was keeping her from tumbling back down the embankment to the muddy, bubbly water.

"Ready?" His voice rolled through her. Deep. Masculine. Rich. Her stomach literally vibrated in response.

"Ready? For what?" She had no idea what he was talking about. All she could think of was how kind and warm he sounded, a hint of gentleness in his voice that contrasted so sharply with the strapping strength of his frame, and the ease with which he was keeping her from sliding down the hill.

The amusement in his eyes deepened. "For me to haul you up here so you don't slide down again. I can let you go, if you prefer."

"Oh, right." She'd totally forgotten she was still standing at a forty-five-degree angle, several feet below him, on an embankment that was becoming increasingly unstable in the heavy rain. "Hauling me up would be fantastic, thanks."

He flashed her a grin so devastatingly charming that she forgot to breathe, and then he stepped back, using his body to counterbalance her as she scrambled up the last few feet and over the edge. She landed in front of him, her boots thudding on the even ground...and she realized that he was even more solid and tall when she was on his level than he'd looked when he was above her.

For a long moment, she didn't move, and neither did he. His hand was still locked around her arm, and she didn't pull away. They just stood there, the rain hammering down on them, sliding over her face, and down her neck.

She was close enough now to see the heavy whiskers on his face, a beard that he didn't quite allow to grow in. His jaw was hard and strong. His face angular. And his eyes...she forgot about everything else but his eyes. They were deep, turbulent crystal blue that were so intense they literally took her breath away with the intensity burning with them. She knew then that he wasn't simply a sinfully hot cowboy. He was more, something infinitely more complex, burdened by a weight so raw that he made her heart speed up. This man was *alive*, fermenting with power and passion that made her heart clench.

God, how long had it been since she'd felt alive like that?

His gaze traveled over her, across her face, over her muddy, soaking body, moving with a languid interest that made heat burn in her belly. His gaze flicked to her car, angled down in the ditch, and then back to her. "City girl?"

The way he said it didn't sound like an insult. It sounded like a seduction that made him promise to show her exactly how wild the cowboy life could be. She nodded. "Boston."

"Boston." He repeated the word, rolling it ever so slightly with a cowboy twang that made her belly tighten. "So, you must be Noelle Wilder." His gaze settled on her face. "I've been expecting you."

Like it? Get it now!

239

SNEAK PEEK: IRRESISTIBLY MINE

"I can't find the words to adequately express
how much I loved this book." ~Elizabeth N.
(Amazon Review)

When an ex-military hottie and a spunky social worker
discover they've accidentally rented the same lakeside cabin,
things get complicated in a hurry.

∾

IN THIS MOMENT, Blue knew exactly what he wanted. He wanted to help her. "Give me a chance to make it up to you, Chloe." The moment he said her name, Chloe's face softened, as if the sound of him saying her name had meant something to her.

Still watching him, she put the phone back to her ear, resuming the conversation with her friend. "Hi, Emma. Blue said that he'll fix my car or drop me off, so I'm all set. But if he can't fix it, I'll need the name of a mechanic for the morning."

Something inside Blue loosened when he heard her accept his offer, almost as if the chance to be with her for a little while longer made the tension inside him ease its relentless grip on his gut.

She listened for a moment. "Okay. I'll stop at Wright's for some food on the way. See you soon. And... Emma? Thank you. I don't know what I would've done without you." Her voice choked up, and Blue looked at her sharply. Her eyes were shiny, and she was gripping the phone so tightly that her knuckles were white. She cleared her throat, and nodded, clearly listening to something Emma was saying. "Right, I know. I'm fine. Really, I am. I'll see you soon. Bye."

As she hung up the phone, she closed her eyes, bowed her head, and pressed her phone to her forehead. She took a deep breath, and then another, as if she'd forgotten she wasn't alone. Blue watched her, noting the paleness of her skin, and the way her shoulders were tucked up toward her ears ever so slightly, in the protective posture he'd seen many times when a newly rescued kidnap victim had hunched in the corner of the helicopter, unwilling to believe the nightmare was really over.

Instinctively, Blue walked over to her and crouched in front of her. "Hey."

She opened her eyes and quickly lowered the phone,

sitting up straighter in a posture clearly designed to make sure no one knew the weight she was carrying inside. She met his gaze for a split second, then her attention dropped to the beer he was holding. "Is that for me?"

Silently, he handed it to her, still watching her. "It'll be okay," he said. "Whatever the nightmare is, it can't get inside you unless you let it." Of course, he knew all too well about the damage nightmares could do, but just because he couldn't shield himself from his own baggage didn't mean he was unaware of how it could work if someone had their shit together better than he did.

She narrowed her eyes. "It's that easy to let it go? Really? I had no idea." She sounded a little annoyed, as if insulted he would reduce all her problems to some philosophical resolution.

He got that. He inclined his head in acknowledgment. "Theoretically, yeah, it's that's simple. In reality, it can eat away at you until you're so dead on the inside that life stops mattering. Until all you can do is run as hard as you can, hoping that you can escape the darkness before it consumes you."

She froze with the bottle of beer halfway to her lips, her eyes widening in surprise. Belatedly, he realized what he'd said and what he'd revealed about himself. Grimacing, he shrugged, and took a sip of his own beer. "Or so I've heard."

Chloe angled the mouth of the bottle toward him as if pointing at him. "You, my friend, are a wealth of complexity, aren't you?"

Blue grinned. "Nah. I drink beer. I shoot guns. And, after tonight, apparently I can add terrorizing women to my list. It's pretty simple and basic. I'm just your normal, upstanding boy-next-door kind of guy. I'm exactly the type that mothers fantasize that their daughters will fall for."

Her gaze flicked to his cheek, and he suddenly remembered

the scar that bisected the side of his face. He never thought about it much. Who the hell cared about a scar? But Chloe was soft, gentle, and sensitive. What would she think about a six-inch scar that belied every claim he'd just made? The thought made him tense, and he didn't like that. He didn't like worrying about his scar, or what someone would think about it.

Scowling, he stood up and paced away from her. He leaned against the tiny kitchenette counter and folded his arms over his chest. "So, tell me, Chloe Dalton. Why were you barging into this cabin at ten o'clock at night in the first place?"

She raised her eyebrows. "I felt as though my life was too tame and predictable. I thought that getting the living daylights scared out of me would make my day more interesting."

He felt himself grin again, but he was learning not to be surprised by the fact she could coax a smile out of him. "Any other reasons?"

She took a drink of her beer, wrinkling her nose as the bitterness drifted across her tongue. "First of all, you're kind of nosy. Second of all, the beer is kind of horrible."

He grinned wider, amused by her inability to school her face into impassive, neutral expressions. "You know, the problem with trying to avoid questions with me, is that I'm an expert on not telling anyone anything that I don't want them to know, so I see right through that façade. So yeah, I'm nosy. Yeah, the beer sucks. But I still want to know what's going on that made you show up at this cabin and sprint into it without checking to see if anyone was here."

She cocked her head, studying him. "Why do you want to know so badly?"

He shrugged. "I don't know. I just do."

She smiled then, a gentle smile that made him want to

grin. "Fair enough." Her gaze flicked away from him, drifting over the bare walls of the rustic cabin, before coming back to rest on his face. "In addition to losing my job yesterday, I also got evicted from the place I've been living in for the last ten years."

Her voice was tight and calm, but he could instantly sense the depth of grief at her words, grief she was absolutely refusing to succumb to.

Respect flooded him, but also empathy. She was tough, refusing to be broken, but something really shitty had crashed down upon her. "Sorry about that."

"It's fine." She shrugged, tracing her fingers over the condensation on the bottle. "I was a little desperate, so Emma said I could stay here until I figure things out, because it was empty." She glanced at him, and cocked a sassy eyebrow at him. "She didn't realize, however, that Harlan had given you the keys. That phone call I just answered? That was Emma calling to warn me that you were already living here. Of course, being the intelligent woman that I am, I had already figured that out."

"You were planning to stay here?" Guilt shot through Blue. There was no chance in hell he was stealing her safe house. He stood up. "No problem. It'll take me five minutes to pack, and the place is all yours." He set his beer on the counter of the kitchenette, and strode across the room to where his duffel was stashed. "I've already been here two days, and I told Harlan I wasn't staying any longer than that—"

"Whoa." She stood up just as quickly, her hand going to his arm as he passed.

He froze, his senses flashing to awareness at the feel of her touch. Her fingers were gentle, barely there, and yet he couldn't move away from her. He took a breath, and turned his head to look at her. "It's okay," he said softly. "The place is yours—"

"No, I don't need it. Emma found another place, one that's in town, which I would prefer anyway." She rolled her eyes. "I was never a huge nature girl, but after tonight, I think I'd lie in bed all night waiting for the boogie man to get me if I stayed here. It's all good."

"But you'll have to pay for that one, right?" He didn't move away from her touch, and she didn't take her hand away either.

Her face softened. "It's very sweet of you to be concerned about that, but the answer is no, actually. You know how Harlan is a real estate agent in his spare time?" At his nod, she continued on. "He has a vacant listing that's for sale, but the owners said I could stay there for free while it's on the market. They figure it'll help sell if the windows are opened and the mustiness is aired out, so I'm good. That's where you're driving me tonight, unless you can work magic with my car."

He grimaced. "I don't want to complicate things for you—"

"It's not complicating anything," she interrupted. "Seriously, this works out better for me." She patted his arm. "But I appreciate your willingness to surrender the cabin to me." Her smile faded. "It's nice. Nice is good."

He still didn't move. "I'm not nice."

She raised her brows. "No?"

"No." Her face was so close to his. Only inches away. Her mouth...it was insanely tempting. He imagined brushing a kiss over her forehead. Across her cheeks. Against the corner of her mouth.

Her eyes widened, and she caught her breath. Suddenly, that same tension that had been strung so tight when they'd first walked in was back, only this time, it hummed with higher intensity, like the eerie silence when a night was too still, indicating that all hell was about to break loose.

He brushed his fingers along her jaw, and she froze, not even breathing. "Would it be inappropriate to kiss you right now?"

"Yes." She blurted out the answer before he'd finished asking the question. "Don't kiss me." But she didn't retreat, or even turn her head away from the brush of his fingers along her jaw. "Don't even think about it."

He shrugged. "Can't help thinking about it."

"Well, find a way." She swallowed hard.

"Can't." Silently, he moved his hands so his fingers were resting on her throat. The frantic fluttering of her pulse was like a butterfly beneath his touch, delicate, untamed, and beautiful. "You could stay here instead of going into town tonight."

Her eyes widened. "Stay here? With you?"

"Yeah." He ran his fingers along her collarbone, tracing the delicate curve of her body.

She closed her eyes, inhaling sharply at his touch, leaning into him ever so slightly. "Never."

"Why not?" He wanted to kiss that fluttering pulse in her throat. He wanted to trace it with his lips, and his tongue. He wanted to taste her lips.

"Because—" She stopped, her breath catching again as he bent his head and pressed a feather-light kiss to the delicate skin of her throat. "Oh, God. Really? You had to do that?"

"Yeah, I did. Your throat was calling to me. Didn't you hear it? It was whispering my name. *Blue, kiss me. Blue, kiss me now.*"

She made a strangled noise that sounded like a cross between laughter and disgusted, skeptical scorn. "My body would never beg for a man's kiss. Ever. You're delusional."

"Probably." He pressed another kiss to her collarbone, and

her fingers tightened on his arm, where they were still resting from her initial contact. "But as delusions go, it's an extremely pleasant one, so I'm just going to go with it." He pressed a kiss to her forehead. "Can you hear it? Now it's your cheek whispering to me. *Blue. Kiss me.*"

"My cheek is not saying that—" He brushed a kiss over her left cheekbone. "Damn you," she whispered.

He bent his head, so his lips were hovering over hers. "What about your lips? Can you hear them whispering?"

"They're telling you to stop bugging me." But her fingers continued to grip his arm, and she didn't pull away.

"What about the corner of your mouth? Right here?" He kissed the spot in question.

She tightened her grip on his arm. "Oh, yeah, maybe there. That might have been saying something to you."

"And this corner?" He tried the other.

She made a small noise of pleasure that made him grin. "It's a distinct possibility," she muttered. "But only because that particular corner of my mouth is stupid, irresponsible, and a glutton for situations that would leave it strewn across the highway in a thousand shattered pieces."

He slid his hand into her hair, tangling his fingers in the strands. "No need for shattered pieces," he said gently. "I can't have any of that when I'm around. I'm a sucker for picking up broken pieces and trying to glue them back together. I can't ever leave them scattered around. It's against my nature." His lips brushed hers, barely, just a whispered touch that made visceral longing course through him, tightening every muscle in his body. "I need to kiss you, Chloe. Like my life fucking depends on it."

Her eyes snapped open, and she searched his face. He knew he'd sounded too desperate, but he didn't pull back. He let her see the raw, brokenness of his soul. He let her see it, because she'd already ripped away his shields, leaving him with no defenses.

"Kiss me, Blue," she whispered. "Kiss me, now."

"*Chloe*." With a low groan, he closed the distance between them, and claimed her mouth with his own.

Like it? Get it now!

SNEAK PEEK: DARKNESS AWAKENED

Order of the Blade Series, Book 1

"What a mesmerizing story." ~*Voracious Reader (Amazon Review)*

When his blood brother goes missing, immortal warrior Quinn Masters will break every rule of his kind to save him, including teaming up with the sensuous, courageous woman destined to be his ultimate destruction.

~

Quinn Masters raced soundlessly through the thick woods, his injuries long forgotten, urgency coursing through him as he neared his house. He covered the last thirty yards, leapt over a fallen tree, then reached the edge of the clearing by his cabin.

There she was.

He stopped dead, fading back into the trees as he stared at the woman he'd scented when he was still two hours away, a lure that had eviscerated all weakness from his body and fueled him into a dead sprint back to his house.

His lungs heaving with the effort of pushing his severely damaged body so hard, Quinn stood rigidly as he studied the woman whose scent had called to him through the dark night. She'd yanked him out of his thoughts about Elijah and galvanized him with energy he hadn't been able to summon on his own.

And now he'd found her.

She'd wedged herself up against the back corner of his porch, barely protected from the cold rain and wet wind. Her knees were pulled up against her chest, her delicate arms wrapped tightly around them as if she could hold onto her body heat by sheer force of will. Her shoulders were hunched, her forehead pressed against her knees while damp tangles of dark brown hair tumbled over her arms.

Her chest moved once. Twice. A trembling, aching breath into lungs that were too cold and too exhausted to work as well as they should.

He took a step toward her, and another, then three more before he realized what he was doing. He froze, suddenly aware of his urgent need to get to her. To help her. To fill her with heat and breathe safety into her trembling body. To whisk her off his porch and into his cabin.

Into his bed.

Quinn stiffened at the thought. Into his bed? Since when? He didn't engage when it came to women. Not anymore. The risk was too high, for him, and for all Calydons. Any woman he met could be his mate, his fate, his doom. His sheva.

He was never tempted.

Until now.

Until this cold, vulnerable stranger had appeared inexplicably on his doorstep. He should be pulling out his sword, not thinking that the fastest way to get her warm would be to run his hands over her bare skin and infuse her whole body with the heat from his.

But his sword remained quiet. His instincts warned him of nothing.

What the hell was going on? She had to be a threat. Nothing else made sense. Women didn't stumble onto his home, and he didn't get a hard-on from simply catching a whiff of one from miles away.

His aching quads braced against the cold air, he inhaled her scent again, searching for answers to a thousand questions. She smelled delicate, with a hint of something sweet, and a flavoring of the bitterness of true desperation. He could practically taste her anguish, a cold, acrid weight in the air, and he knew she was in trouble.

His hands flexed with the need to close the distance between them, to crouch by her side, to give her his protection. But he didn't move. He didn't dare. He had to figure out why he was so compelled by her, why he was responding like this, especially at a time when he couldn't afford any distraction.

She moaned softly and curled into an even tighter ball. His muscles tightened, his entire soul burning with the need to help her. Quinn narrowed his eyes and pried his gaze off her to search the woods.

With the life of his blood brother in his hands, an Order posse soon to be after him, and his own body still half in the grave, he should be so focused on business that a woman could dance naked on his chest and he still wouldn't notice. It shouldn't be possible for a woman he didn't even know, hadn't met and barely even seen to rock him on his ass like this simply because he'd caught a whiff of her scent.

He was disciplined, dammit, and disciplined warriors didn't fall for that shit. It made no sense.

His intense need for her felt too similar to the compulsion that had sent him to the river three nights ago. Another trap? He'd suspected it from the moment he'd first reacted to her scent, but he'd been unable to resist the temptation, and he'd hauled ass to get back to his house. Yeah, true, he'd also needed to get back to his cabin to retrieve his supplies to go after Elijah. The fact she'd imbued him with new strength had been a bonus he wasn't going to deny.

But now he had to be sure. A trap or not? Quinn laughed softly. Shit. He hoped it was. If it wasn't, there was only one other reason he could think that could explain his reaction to her, and that would be if she was his mate. His sheva. His ticket to certain destruction.

No chance.

He wouldn't allow it.

He had no time for dealing with that destiny right now. It was time to get in, get out, and go after Elijah. His amusement faded as he took a final survey of the woods. There was no lurking threat he could detect. Maybe he'd made it back before he'd been expected, or maybe an ambush had been aborted.

Either way, he had to get into his house, get his stuff, and move on. His gaze returned to the woman, and he noticed a drop of water sliding down the side of her neck, trickling over her skin like the most seductive of caresses. He swore, realizing she wasn't going to leave. She'd freeze to death before she'd abandon her perch.

He cursed again and knew he had to go to her. He couldn't let her die on his front step. Not this woman. Not her.

He would make it fast, he would make it efficient, he would stay on target for his mission, but he would get her safe.

Keeping alert for any indication that this was a setup, Quinn stepped out of the woods and into the clearing. He'd made no sound, not even a whisper of his clothing, and yet she sensed him.

She sat up, her gaze finding him instantly in the dim light, despite his stealthy approach. They made eye contact, and the world seemed to stop for a split second. The moment he saw those silvery eyes, something thumped in his chest. Something visceral and male howled inside him, raging to be set free.

As he strode up, she unfolded herself from her cramped position and pulled herself to her feet, her gaze never leaving his. Her face was wary, her body tense, but she lifted her chin ever so slightly and set her hands on her hips, telling him that she wasn't leaving.

Her courage and determination, held together by that tiny, shivering frame, made satisfaction thud through him. There was a warrior in that slim, exhausted body.

She said nothing as he approached, and neither of them spoke as he came to a stop in front of her.

Up close, he was riveted. Her dark eyelashes were clumped from the rain. Her skin was pale, too pale. Her face was carrying the burden of a thousand weights. But beneath that pain, those nightmares, that hell, lay delicate femininity that called to him. The luminescent glow of her skin, the sensual curve of her mouth, the sheen of rain on her cheekbones, the simple silver hoops in her ears. It awoke in him something so male, so carnal, so primal he wanted to throw her up against the wall and consume her until their bodies were melted together in a single, scorching fire.

She searched his face with the same intensity raging through him, and he felt like she was tearing through his shields, cataloguing everything about him, all the way down to his soul.

He studied her carefully, and she let him, not flinching when his gaze traveled down her body. His blood pulsed as he noted the curve of her breasts under her rain-slicked jacket, the sensuous curve of her hips, and even the mud on her jeans and boots. He almost groaned at his need to palm her hips, drag her over to him, and mark her with his kiss. Loose strands of thick dark hair curled around her neck and shoulders like it was clinging to her for safety.

Protectiveness surged from deep inside him and he clenched his fists against the urge to sweep her into his arms and carry her inside, away from whatever hardships had brought her to his doorstep.

Double hell. He'd hoped his reaction would lessen when he got close to her, but it had intensified. He'd never felt like this before. Never had this response to a woman.

What the hell was going on? Sheva. The word was like a demon, whispering through his mind. He shut it out. He would never allow himself to bond with his mate. If that was what was going on, she was out of there immediately, before they were both destroyed forever.

Intent on sending her away, he looked again at her face, and then realized he was irrevocably ensnared. Her beautiful silver eyes were aching with a soul-deep pain that shattered what little defenses he had against her. He simply couldn't abandon her.

It didn't matter what she wanted. It didn't matter why she

was there. She was coming inside. He would make sure it didn't interfere with his mission. He would make dead sure it turned out right. No matter what.

Without a word, he grabbed her backpack off the floor, surprised at how heavy it was. Either she had tossed her free weights in it, or she had packed her life into it.

He had a bad feeling it wasn't a set of dumbbells.

Quinn walked past her and unlocked his front door. He shoved it open, then stood back. Letting her decide. Hoping she would walk away and spare them both.

She took a deep breath, glanced at his face one more time, then walked into the cabin.

Hell.

He paused to take one more survey of his woods, found nothing amiss, and then he followed her into his home and shut the door behind them.

Like it? Get it now!

A QUICK FAVOR

Hi! It's Stephanie.

Thank you so much for allowing me to tell this story that means so much to me. I appreciate you taking the time out of your life and offering a piece of yourself to these words and these pages.

Did you enjoy Ryder and Zoey's story?

People are often hesitant to try new books or new authors. A few reviews can encourage them to make that leap and give it a try. If you enjoyed *A Real Cowboy Always Trusts His Heart* and think others will as well, please consider taking a moment and writing one or two sentences on the *eTailer* and/or Goodreads to help this story find the readers who would enjoy it. Even the short reviews really make an impact!

Thank you a million times for reading my books! I love writing for you and sharing the journeys of these beautiful characters with you. I hope you find inspiration from their stories in your own life!

Love,
Stephanie

STAY IN THE KNOW!

It's me again! One more thing...

There will be more cowboys! The next book isn't ready for preorder, but it's coming! I think Brody's story is next, launching the Hart family series in the A Rogue Cowboy series, but as soon as I know for sure, I will announce it in my newsletter, so sign up here to be the first to know when it's coming!

I write my books from the soul, and live that way as well. I've received so much help over the years from amazing people to help me live my best life, and I am always looking to pay it forward, including to my readers.

One of the ways I love to do this is through my mailing list, where I often send out life tips I've picked up, post readers surveys, give away Advance Review Copies, and provide insider scoop on my books, my writing, and life in general. And, of course, I always make sure my readers on my list know when the next book is coming out!

If this sounds interesting to you, I would love to have you join us! You can always unsubscribe at any time! I'll never spam you or share your data. I just want to provide value!

Sign up at www.stephanierowe.com/join-newsletter/ to keep in touch!

Much love,

Stephanie

BOOKS BY STEPHANIE ROWE

CONTEMPORARY ROMANCE

WYOMING REBELS SERIES
(CONTEMPORARY WESTERN ROMANCE)
A Real Cowboy Never Says No
A Real Cowboy Knows How to Kiss
A Real Cowboy Rides a Motorcycle
A Real Cowboy Never Walks Away
A Real Cowboy Loves Forever
A Real Cowboy for Christmas
A Real Cowboy Always Trusts His Heart

A ROGUE COWBOY SERIES
(CONTEMPORARY WESTERN ROMANCE)
Her Rebel Cowboy (Prequel)
A Rogue Cowboy for Her, featuring Brody Hart
(Coming Soon!)

BIRCH CROSSING SERIES

(SMALL-TOWN CONTEMPORARY ROMANCE)
Unexpectedly Mine
Accidentally Mine
Unintentionally Mine
Irresistibly Mine

MYSTIC ISLAND SERIES
(SMALL-TOWN CONTEMPORARY ROMANCE)
Wrapped Up in You (A Christmas novella)

CANINE CUPIDS SERIES
(ROMANTIC COMEDY)
Paws for a Kiss
Pawfectly in Love
Paws Up for Love

PARANORMAL

ORDER OF THE BLADE SERIES
(DARK PARANORMAL ROMANCE)
Darkness Awakened
Darkness Seduced
Darkness Surrendered
Forever in Darkness
Darkness Reborn
Darkness Arisen
Darkness Unleashed
Inferno of Darkness
Darkness Possessed
Shadows of Darkness
Hunt the Darkness

HEART OF THE SHIFTER SERIES

ABOUT THE AUTHOR

NEW YORK TIMES AND *USA TODAY* bestselling author Stephanie Rowe is "contemporary romance at its best" (Bex 'N' Books). She's thrilled to be a 2018 winner and a five-time nominee for the RITA® award, the highest award in romance fiction. As the bestselling author of more than fifty books, Stephanie delights readers of all romance genres, with her always sigh-worthy contemporary romances, paranormal romances, and romantic suspense novels. She also writes funny paranormal romance and urban fantasy under S.A. Bayne. For the latest info on Stephanie and her books, visit her on the web at:

www.stephanierowe.com
www.sabayne.com

Made in United States
Orlando, FL
03 April 2022

16446011R00168